FOREVER THEIRS

ANNA STONE

CHAPTER 1

"Welcome to Blossom Flowers," Chloe said. "How can I help you?"

"I need some flowers," the customer replied brusquely. He was dressed in an expensive-looking suit, and he had a clean, sharp haircut. Was he some kind of executive? He had the haughty manner of one. Chloe's florist shop was in the middle of the city, right next to the business district, so customers like him came in often.

She mustered the warmest smile she could manage. "You've come to the right place. Who are the flowers for?"

"My wife," the man said. "It was her birthday yesterday."

Chloe gave him a sympathetic nod. She dealt with these kinds of problems daily. It was the third forgotten birthday today, along with two forgotten anniversaries, and the shop had only been open for an hour.

"Do you know what sort of flowers she likes?" Chloe asked.

The man looked at her blankly. "I don't know. Roses? Don't all women like roses?"

Chloe resisted the urge to roll her eyes, reminding herself just how badly she needed the customer's business. "Roses are popular, and for good reason. How about I make up a mixed arrangement with roses and some other flowers? If you tell me a little about your wife, I can put together something she'll love."

In her experience, when it came to flowers, people were happier to receive something more personal than the usual dozen red roses. And with a little information about someone, Chloe could create a tailor-made bouquet to suit their tastes. That was the part of her job she liked the most. And she was good at it.

Unfortunately, that wasn't enough to keep her little florist shop in business.

"Look," the man said. "I'm in a hurry. I don't have time for this."

"In that case, I have some ready-made bouquets." Chloe pointed to a shelf by the counter. "They're right beside you."

The man stared at the arrangements for a moment before pointing to a bouquet of white roses. "I'll take that."

"Are you sure?" Chloe said. "Those—"

The man huffed. "I told you, I'm in a hurry."

Chloe bit her tongue and grabbed the flowers, then began wrapping them up. What she'd tried to tell the customer was that it was a sympathy bouquet for illness or bereavement. Flowers had meanings. And although most people weren't aware of those meanings, the way flowers looked and smelled, the different combinations and arrangements, all evoked certain moods and feelings. The bouquet the customer had chosen said, *I'm sorry for your loss.* It wasn't going to do him any favors with his wife.

But Chloe needed all the business she could get. She couldn't afford to lose a single customer.

She finished wrapping up the flowers and handed them to the man. He paid for the bouquet and hurried out of the store without another word, leaving Chloe alone in her shop.

She leaned down on the counter on her elbows and looked around the empty store. It was small and sun-filled, every shelf overflowing with bouquets and bunches of flowers. She'd opened her shop after finishing floristry school five years ago, using what had been left of the windfall she'd received when she turned eighteen. It had been her dream to have her own florist shop for as long as she could remember.

But now, that dream was falling apart.

Her phone buzzed in the pocket of her apron. She pulled it out. The number on the screen belonged to one of her suppliers. She knew why they were calling her. She hadn't paid her latest bill.

But she couldn't afford to pay it right now, along with the bills of half her other suppliers. Her shop was in the red, and her personal financial situation was just as bad. She'd barely been able to scrape together rent for the month, and her cat, Mango, was due for a trip to the vet. Her truck, an ancient pickup that she mostly used to deliver flowers, was long overdue for servicing.

Plus, she had a certain personal debt to pay off. She was more afraid of missing those payments than the ones to her suppliers.

But she couldn't just ignore her problems. Slipping into the back room, she answered the phone call. Sure enough, it was about an overdue bill. The woman on the other end of the line wasn't happy when Chloe requested an extension, but after some groveling, she relented.

Chloe hung up the phone and let out a long breath. This would give her some wiggle room, but it wouldn't last long. She needed to figure something out, and soon.

Her stomach churned at the thought of losing her florist shop. She'd invested everything in it, and not only financially. Her shop had been a fresh start for her. It was a symbol of the fact that she'd finally overcome her past, that she'd become her own person for the first time in her life.

But sometimes, it felt like her past was always there, lurking just out of sight.

She sighed. She couldn't hide out in the back room forever. She had plenty of work to do. She brushed the dust from her apron and tucked a stray wisp of her hair back into her ponytail. It was curly, unlike the rest of her hair. For whatever reason, those little hairs that framed her face refused to straighten, no matter how hard she tried. Her curls were distinctive, as was their strawberry blonde coloring, which was why she'd dyed her hair a deep shade of brown. She didn't like how much her natural hair made her look like her past self. That girl no longer existed.

As Chloe left the back room, she spotted movement at the side of the store, behind a display. There was a customer in the shop? She hadn't heard anyone come in.

Suddenly, the customer stepped out from behind the display. Chloe's heart skipped a beat. It was a woman, and a breathtaking one at that. She had wavy brown hair that cascaded down her back, all the way to her tailbone. She wore an impeccably tailored emerald-green dress in an A-line cut that enhanced her hourglass curves, along with shiny black heels. She looked entirely out of place in Chloe's little florist shop, even more so than the usual suit-wearing businesspeople.

Chloe had seen the woman in the store before, a handful of times. Each time, the woman had bought one of the most expensive arrangements, making small talk with Chloe as she wrapped the bouquet up for her. And each time, Chloe had struggled to keep her cool.

The woman strode toward her, stopping in front of the counter. "I'd like to buy some flowers." Her voice was clear and composed, with a silken smoothness that sent a quiver down Chloe's neck.

"Sure," Chloe said. "I have a range of ready-made arrangements. Or I could make you something custom if you'd like." Clearly, the woman had money to burn, not to mention refined tastes. She didn't seem like the type to balk at the price of a custom bouquet.

"I like the sound of that," the woman said. "Make me something, then."

Finally, a chance for Chloe to put her talents to use. But more than that, she wanted the chance to impress the mysterious woman, to create something beautiful for her. And she wanted to keep the woman here, in her presence, for as long as she could.

"Do you have anything specific in mind?" Chloe asked.

"You're the expert," the woman replied. "What do you recommend?"

"It depends. What's the bouquet for? Is it a specific occasion? Are you giving it to someone special?"

The woman's lips curled up in a smile. "If you want to know if I'm single, all you have to do is ask."

Chloe's cheeks began to burn. "I mean, is it a gift for someone?"

The woman didn't answer immediately. Instead, she reached out to touch some flowers that Chloe had arranged in a vase on the counter, caressing a carnation with delicate fingers, taking care not to damage the petals. Her hands were slender, her skin pale and soft. But the woman seemed anything but soft.

Finally, she spoke. "Let's pretend, for a moment, that it is a gift for someone. Someone special. A woman." The suggestiveness in her voice implied that the woman in question wasn't just a friend. "What would you recommend?"

Chloe swallowed. "Well, that depends on what you want the flowers to say. When it comes to love, there are all different types. Romantic love? Affection? Eternal love?"

"'Love' is coming on a little too strong in this case. What if I want something that says less about love and more about attraction, desire?" Still stroking the flowers on the counter with her fingers, the woman locked her eyes on Chloe's. "Something that says, 'I want you.'"

Chloe's pulse sped up, a spark going off inside her. She tried her best to smother it. "There aren't any flowers that say exactly that, but purple roses could work. Roses symbolize love, but they have more nuanced meanings depending on the colors. Purple roses, they symbolize love at first sight, the allure of meeting someone and being completely enchanted by them, drawn to them in a way that defies all rational thought..." She trailed off. She was rambling. It was no wonder, given how enchanting the woman standing before her was.

"That's exactly what I had in mind," the woman said. "Make me an arrangement with purple roses, then."

"Coming right up," Chloe said.

After getting a few more details from the woman, Chloe made a loop around the store, gathering handfuls of flowers and greenery for the arrangement. She took her time, selecting only the most pristine of flowers. She didn't normally go through so much trouble for her customers, but something about this woman made Chloe want to impress her.

Was it the fact that her very presence seemed to take over the entire shop? Was it the insistent way the woman watched her, her red lips curving up slightly at the corners, her sultry brown eyes following Chloe's every move? Was it the fact that Chloe found her mesmerizing?

Finally, Chloe selected a dozen purple roses and a handful of orange blossoms. Orange blossoms were her favorite flower. Like so many other flowers, they repre-sented love. But more specifically, the small white blossoms symbolized eternal love, the kind that was everlasting and unconditional.

It wasn't what the customer had asked for, but Chloe had made a habit of including the sweetly scented blossoms in bouquets for lovers. It was a wish, a charm, that the love they shared would last for eternity. It was a silly tradition of hers, from back when she'd been a hopeless romantic. Nowadays, she knew better. Love was just like her flowers —beautiful at full bloom, but short-lived. In the end, love always withered and died.

As Chloe returned to her counter and began putting the arrangement together, the woman spoke up again.

"For the record, the flowers aren't actually a gift for someone."

"They're not?" Chloe asked.

"They're for me, for my office. They really brighten up a space."

"Oh." Why was Chloe so relieved that the woman wasn't planning to give the flowers to a lover? She was a complete stranger. A mysterious, commanding stranger who kept looking at Chloe in a way that made her feel hot all over.

"You seem pleasantly surprised to hear that."

Chloe dropped her gaze to the flowers before her. Was her attraction to the woman so obvious? "It's a little unusual, that's all." She continued assembling the bouquet, tying the bundle of flowers together with string. "I don't get many customers who buy flowers just because they like them. I wish more people appreciated flowers as much as you do."

"What do you mean?"

"Most customers just want a dozen cheap red roses or a generic get-well bouquet. It's nice to know that something I make will be appreciated."

"I'll certainly appreciate these," the woman said, her voice practically a purr.

Warmth rose to Chloe's skin. There it was again, that look.

"And I imagine it's hard to keep this shop running on cheap roses alone?" the woman asked.

Chloe nodded. That was exactly why her shop was

struggling. No one wanted to pay for lovingly handmade bouquets anymore.

But how could the woman possibly know that?

She winced as it hit her. "You heard me on the phone, didn't you?" The shop was small, and Chloe hadn't exactly been quiet when speaking to her supplier. She held back a curse. The last thing she wanted was for her customers to know the store had money problems, especially *this* customer. The woman was so sophisticated and put together that Chloe doubted she'd ever had money problems in her life.

"I didn't mean to eavesdrop, but it was hard not to hear you. It's a pity this lovely little shop is in trouble."

"It's not that bad, really." Chloe grabbed her shears and began snipping the flowers' stems down. "This shop is my entire life. I'm not going to let it get shut down."

"Good for you." The woman thought for a moment. "You know what? My company is hosting an event in a couple of weeks. We're going to need decorations. I'd like you to make some floral arrangements for it."

Chloe paused. The woman wanted to hire *her*? She'd take any work she could get right now. Plus, it would give her an excuse to see more of the woman.

But she resisted the urge to say yes immediately. She needed to find out what she was getting into first.

"What's the event?" she asked.

"It's a charity gala," the woman said. "It's just a few hundred people."

Chloe almost dropped her shears. *A few hundred?* She'd made flowers for events before, but they'd been much smaller. A gala with that many people would be a ton of work. It wasn't like Chloe was drowning in work, but she'd never taken on such a big project. "What kinds of arrangements do you need?"

"Just the basics. Centerpieces for the tables, some larger decorative pieces."

The woman rattled off a long list of requirements that were the opposite of basic. Chloe nodded along, trying her hardest not to let her rising panic show.

"Do you think you can handle that?" the woman asked.

"Sure, no problem." That was a lie. Given the short time frame and the number of flowers involved, Chloe would need to work around the clock for the next two weeks.

But she could pull it off.

"You'll be generously compensated for your time and materials," the woman said. "Do you require a deposit?"

Chloe nodded. "Fifty percent. I'll have to do the math on how much everything will cost."

"Why don't you work it out and call me when you're ready?" The woman reached into her purse and fished out a business card and a pen, then scribbled a number on the back of the card before handing it to Chloe. "That's my personal number. If you call the office, you'll just get my assistant."

Chloe stared at the handwritten number on the card, then turned it over to the printed side. It read *Gabrielle Hall, Co-Founder and Chief Marketing Officer, Mistress Media.*

Chloe's eyes widened. Mistress Media was an international female-led media empire. The building their offices were in was just a few blocks away. And this woman was the CMO? That explained her expensive clothes, her perfect hair, the unshakable air of confidence she possessed.

"Forgive me," the woman said. "I haven't properly introduced myself. Gabrielle Hall. And you are?"

"Er, Chloe. Chloe Campbell."

"Do we have a deal, *Chloe*?"

A shiver rolled through her. The way Gabrielle said her name, it was as though she were whispering it into Chloe's ear. "Yes."

"Wonderful." Gabrielle extended a hand for Chloe to shake. "I'm sure it's going to be a real pleasure doing business with you."

Chloe took Gabrielle's hand. Gabrielle's touch was gentle and unyielding at the same time. Even after she released Chloe's hand, her skin tingled where Gabrielle had touched her.

Seconds passed before Chloe remembered herself. Taking a length of silky white ribbon, she tied up the paper-wrapped bouquet. "All done."

Gabrielle paid for the flowers with a black credit card. Chloe handed the bouquet to her.

She admired them approvingly. "These are beautiful."

"Thanks." The rush of warmth that went through Chloe at the woman's words had little to do with pride. Why did she feel such an intense desire to earn Gabrielle's praise, her approval? There was something about her that made Chloe weak and pliant.

Chloe cleared her throat. "Is there anything else I can do for you?"

"There is one thing. You can take this."

Carefully, Gabrielle reached into the bouquet and plucked a flower from it—a single purple rose.

She held it out to Chloe. "This is for you. For all your help. Consider it a token of my appreciation."

Chloe stared at the flower. She opened her mouth, but no sound came out.

"Go on," Gabrielle said. "Take it."

Powerless to resist, Chloe took the flower from her. "Thank you," she stammered.

An alluring smile spread across Gabrielle's lips. "Believe me, the pleasure is all mine. I'd love to stay and chat, but I need to get to work. Call me later."

Chloe nodded. Giving her one last sweeping look, Gabrielle turned and strode out of the shop, the bell above the door chiming as it swung closed behind her.

Chloe stared down at the dark purple rose in her hand. She lifted it to her nose, the velvet petals tickling it, and breathed in its scent—sweet, rich, with a hint of spice. Her whole body flooded with heat.

I want you.

CHAPTER 2

I t was midmorning when Gabrielle arrived at the Mistress Media offices. They took up the entire top floor of the building and were packed with people, all working away busily behind glass walls.

She headed toward her office, the bouquet in her arms, the aroma of flowers hovering in the air around her. She breathed it in, savoring it. Her habit of buying flowers was recent. She'd discovered the quaint little florist shop tucked away in a side street a couple of blocks away from her office a few weeks ago while looking for a gift. Since then, she'd gone back to the shop whenever she'd had an excuse or an occasion that warranted buying flowers. And when she'd run out of occasions, she simply started buying flowers for herself.

In her defense, she did like the way flowers brightened up her office. But it was the florist—Chloe—who kept her going back to the store. There was something about her that Gabrielle found enticing. She was a tantalizing treat just begging to be unwrapped, unraveled, unwound.

Gabrielle wanted to be the one to unravel her. And the way Chloe looked at her said that she wanted that too.

Out of nowhere, Gabrielle's assistant appeared, falling into step beside her as she walked. The baby-faced, blond-haired man was irritatingly nervous, but he was very good at doing whatever she told him to do, no questions asked. That was exactly what Gabrielle wanted in an assistant. It was no coincidence that she wanted the same thing in certain areas of her personal life too.

"Good morning, Ms. Hall," he said. "Your coffee is on your desk. And Ms. Davenport called."

"Is she back from Paris?"

"Not yet. She said to remind you to send her the marketing budget reports."

Gabrielle held back a sigh. While she enjoyed her job, she found the finance side of it to be extremely dull. "I'll call her back later. And find me an intern to check all the numbers." Before her assistant could respond, she thrust the bouquet at him. "Put these in water and leave them on my desk."

The man nodded. "Yes, Ms. Hall."

"For the last time, Ms. Hall is my grandmother."

"Sorry. Gabrielle." He'd be back to calling her *Ms. Hall* within a week.

"Is Amber in today?"

"Ms. Pryce? I saw her earlier. She should be in her office."

Abandoning her assistant at her office door, Gabrielle strode inside, grabbed her coffee, and made her way to Amber's office. Amber was one of her oldest friends. The two of them had attended the same top prep school. Amber was also one of the four women who had founded Mistress Media together, along with Gabrielle. Amber's role was to run Mistress's non-profit wing. It was more of a hobby for her than anything. As the heiress to a wealthy family, Amber didn't need to work. Her job at Mistress consisted of soliciting donations and throwing elaborate galas to raise funds for various charities.

Gabrielle reached Amber's office to find the blonde woman sitting behind her desk with her usual regal demeanor, her back straight and her phone to her ear. Noticing Gabrielle, Amber waved her inside. Gabrielle took a seat and waited for Amber to finish her conversation. From what she could gather, Amber was speaking to a donor about Mistress's upcoming charity gala.

Finally, Amber said goodbye and hung up the phone. She folded her hands neatly on the desk in front of her. "Sorry for keeping you waiting. I've been trying to rustle up donations for the gala all morning."

"The gala is exactly what I want to talk to you about," Gabrielle said. "I need a favor."

"What kind of favor?"

"I have a… friend. She's a florist. I'd like her to do the flowers for the event."

Amber frowned. "I wasn't planning on hiring a florist. I wasn't planning to have flowers at the event at all. And the gala is less than two weeks away."

"I know, but this is important." Gabrielle leaned back in her chair, crossing her legs casually. "And I may have already told her it was a sure thing."

Amber regarded her with narrowed eyes. "Who exactly is this woman?"

"Like I said, she's a florist. I'm simply helping her out."

"And your motive for helping her out is entirely innocent?"

"I'm doing her a favor, that's all."

Amber shook her head. "If you say so. All right, this florist of yours can work the gala. Send me her details so I can coordinate with her."

"Actually, I'd prefer to handle communication with her myself."

Amber raised an eyebrow. "Fine. But if you insist on interfering with my meticulously planned event just to win over some woman, I expect a favor in return."

"Okay. What is it?"

Amber handed a sheet of paper to Gabrielle. "This is a list of all our major donors from our previous events. I need to call them to encourage them to make donations at the gala. I was planning to go through the rest of the list this evening, but we'll get through it more quickly if we split the job in two."

Gabrielle pursed her lips. Buttering up snobby old people to convince them to donate money wasn't her idea of a good time, but what choice did she have? "All right. I'll give you a hand with it after work."

"Then we have a deal," Amber said.

Gabrielle rose from her chair. "I have a meeting to get to. I'll come find you this evening."

"Let me know how everything goes with this florist." Amber gave her a sly look. "And I'm not just talking about the gala."

Ignoring Amber's insinuations, Gabrielle left the room and headed back to her own office. She hadn't been lying when she said she was doing this as a favor to Chloe. She sympathized with the woman. She'd hate to see that little shop of hers shut down.

But if helping her meant that Gabrielle would have an excuse to spend some quality time with her, and get to know her more intimately, that was a bonus.

What was it about Chloe that Gabrielle found so compelling? She was a mystery, one that Gabrielle was dying to delve deeper into. What was behind the woman she was on the surface, those pretty summery dresses she wore, those heart-shaped lips? There was something in Chloe's endless green eyes that seemed at odds with everything she appeared to be on the surface.

Was the charming florist really as sweet as she appeared?

It was unusual how drawn to Chloe she was. Chloe was nothing like the women Gabrielle usually attracted—the kind of women who were only interested in her for superficial reasons. As part owner of Mistress Media, she was one of the wealthiest women in the country, a claim that very few people in their 30s could make. But Chloe didn't seem the type to be impressed by expensive dinners and extravagant gifts.

Why, then, was Chloe interested in Gabrielle? Could she be what Gabrielle was looking for?

What *they* were looking for?

Gabrielle shook her head. It was absurd to think that way about a woman whose name she'd only just learned. But she was getting tired of women coming and going, nothing more than temporary playthings who were intrigued by her lavish lifestyle, her unconventional tastes in bed, her unique relationship. A part of her wished for something—someone—more lasting and real.

But if she took that chance, let someone into her life and her heart, could she ever really be sure that they were with her for her, and not for her money? After all, it wouldn't be the first time.

Gabrielle reached her office and shut the door behind her before taking a seat at her desk. She had too much work to do to waste time thinking about Chloe. She wanted Chloe. She had every intention of getting her. Why did it matter whether Chloe's interest in her was superficial or not? Gabrielle already had one woman in her life who she loved.

What more did she need?

CHAPTER 3

C hloe picked at the enormous floral arrangement at the side of the grand ballroom. The gala was due to start in an hour, and she'd spent the entire afternoon setting up. That was on top of all the time she'd spent putting the arrangements together over the past week.

She needed everything to be perfect. She took pride in her work, and the event was obviously an important one. There had to be a hundred staff members running around, making last-minute preparations. The food, the drinks, the decorations—they were all as extravagant as the ballroom itself. Chloe felt out of place, but she was planning to leave as soon as she was satisfied everything was in order.

"This looks magnificent."

Chloe turned to find Gabrielle striding toward her. She wore a low-cut backless blue gown with a slit up the side that showed a hint of leg. It bordered on salacious, but Gabrielle somehow made it look tasteful and sophisticated. Half of her long wavy hair was pinned up, with the rest tumbling loosely down her bare back.

Chloe tried her hardest not to stare. How did Gabrielle always manage to look so effortlessly enticing?

Gabrielle's eyes skimmed the flowers before them. "I'm thrilled with how these arrangements have turned out. Are you interested in working on future events? This is just one of our smaller galas. We throw a handful of these every year. We'd love your help with them."

If this was a 'smaller' event, what did a big one look like? This world of wealth that Gabrielle inhabited was so far removed from Chloe's own. She had always been wary of anyone with too much money. In her experience, money caused almost as many problems as it solved.

Why, then, had the wealthy, glamorous woman standing next to her taken over all of Chloe's thoughts?

Chloe blinked. Gabrielle was still waiting for an answer. "Sure. That would be great."

"Wonderful," Gabrielle said. "For now, is there anything else you need?"

Chloe shook her head. "I'm pretty much done. I was about to leave, actually."

"So soon? Why don't you stay? You know, in case we need you for some kind of emergency?"

"A floral emergency?" That happened occasionally with weddings, but at a gala, it was unlikely.

"You never know. At least stick around for a little while."

Chloe looked around the opulently decorated hall. "I'm not dressed for this." The few people milling about who weren't staff were all dressed as formally as Gabrielle, while Chloe had been wearing the same old creased sundress since the morning.

Gabrielle looked her up and down. "I think you look

lovely. But we have some time before the guests start arriving, so why don't you stay for a drink at least? We can talk, get to know each other a little."

It was then that Chloe noticed Gabrielle was holding two glasses of champagne. She held one of them out to Chloe, just like she had with the single purple rose in the florist shop that day.

Heat trickled down Chloe's back.

I want you.

"Just one drink," Gabrielle said.

Once again, Chloe found herself powerless to say no. With a nod, she took the champagne flute from Gabrielle and brought it up to her lips, sipping it slowly. She barely tasted it. It was like a haze had fallen over her. Why did Gabrielle have that effect on her?

"Now that I have you alone," Gabrielle began, "I have a confession to make."

Chloe's pulse sped up. What could Gabrielle possibly have to confess to her? Why was she so interested in Chloe in the first place?

But before Gabrielle could speak, someone called her name.

Chloe followed the voice to the other side of the hall where a blonde woman stood, frowning at a pair of decorators holding up a banner.

"Gabrielle," the woman called impatiently. "I need you."

Gabrielle gave Chloe an apologetic look. "That's Amber. She's coordinating all this. I should give her a hand."

"Go ahead," Chloe said.

"Don't go anywhere. This conversation isn't over."

Gabrielle's sultry but firm tone suggested it wasn't a request.

As Gabrielle disappeared to the other end of the ballroom, Chloe scanned the room idly, sipping her champagne while she waited. Out of the corner of her eye, she noticed that one of the floral arrangements near the stage was unbalanced. It was barely noticeable, but it bothered her enough that she needed to fix it.

She walked over to the arrangement and plucked a few flowers from the left side of it, reinserting them on the right side. She took a step back, inspecting her handiwork. There was still something slightly off about it, but it was an improvement.

"They're beautiful, aren't they?"

Chloe turned. Standing just a few feet from her was a woman, tall and striking, dressed in an off-white gown that contrasted with her rich brown skin. Her coily black hair was pulled back into a low, sleek bun, and the only jewelry she wore was a pair of gold teardrop earrings.

But the woman's outfit was the least interesting thing about her. Her brown eyes were so dark they were almost black, and her lips were an alluring crimson. Just the way she carried herself was captivating. Everything about her demanded Chloe's attention.

Yet, Chloe couldn't remember what the woman had just said to her.

"The flowers," she repeated. "They're beautiful." Although her demeanor was serious, her voice was just as mesmerizing as she was.

"Yes," Chloe stammered.

The woman stepped toward her, joining her in front of

the flowers. "Calla lilies. I've never seen them in this color." She reached a willowy hand out to touch one of the black-burgundy flowers. "I've always liked calla lilies. There's an elegance to them, don't you think?"

Chloe nodded. If this woman knew one thing, it was elegance. She radiated it.

She leaned in slightly, inhaling the scent of the flowers. "And roses. I'm told those represent love of different kinds, depending on the color."

Chloe nodded again. Here she was, standing before a goddess of a woman who was taking an interest in her flowers, and she'd forgotten how to speak.

The woman turned to Chloe, appraising her with probing eyes. "I saw you setting up. You're a florist, then? You made all these arrangements yourself?"

"Yes," Chloe managed to say.

"You have an excellent eye for your work. The color, the contrast, the combinations. It's all very arresting. It paints quite the picture."

"Thanks." Chloe wasn't used to getting compliments on her flowers. Most people didn't even notice them.

"I don't mean to make you uncomfortable," the woman said. "I get a little carried away when it comes to all things creative. I'm a designer."

"What kind of designer?" Chloe asked.

"Fashion," the woman said. "I should introduce myself. I'm Dana."

Dana. And she was a fashion designer? Why did her name seem familiar?

"And you are?" Dana asked.

For a moment, she forgot her own name. "I'm Chloe."

"Chloe." Dana rolled her name around on her tongue. "And what a pleasure it is to meet you."

She held her hand out to Chloe. Chloe took it. The woman's touch sent a spark of electricity up her arm, arcing through her entire body.

But Dana didn't let go of her hand. She held onto it for a moment that seemed to stretch on and on. Desire flickered inside her. Why was she suddenly getting all this attention from sophisticated, irresistibly commanding women?

"There you are, honey."

Chloe turned to see Gabrielle walking toward them. She pulled her hand from Dana's as Gabrielle's words registered in her mind.

Honey? Gabrielle obviously wasn't talking to her. Then, it clicked.

Gabrielle was talking to Dana.

Gabrielle slipped her hand around Dana's arm. "I see you've met Chloe."

Chloe looked from one woman to the other. Were the two of them a couple? Gabrielle had never mentioned having a girlfriend.

Dana nodded. "We were discussing her flowers. So you know each other?"

"I do," Gabrielle said. "She's a very talented woman."

"She certainly is," Dana said.

Chloe's heart began to pound. Dana was gazing back at her, her dark eyes piercing. And Gabrielle's red lips wore that tantalizing smile, the same smile she'd given Chloe in the florist shop that day.

Her breath caught. The way they were looking at her, like they wanted her, both of them…

This was all too much for her.

"I have to go," she blurted out.

Before either of them could speak, she set down her champagne glass and fled the ballroom without looking back.

Dana watched Chloe disappear out the door. "What was that about?"

She turned to Gabrielle, whose face wore a furtive expression, one Dana knew all too well.

Dana crossed her arms. "What's going on?"

Gabrielle held up her hands defensively. "I can explain."

Dana sighed. "You and Chloe. You knew each other before today, didn't you?"

"Guilty as charged. I've been going to her florist shop. I hired her for the gala personally."

It was obvious that Gabrielle hadn't been going to Chloe's shop just for the flowers. And it explained her sudden interest in flowers and their meanings.

"And why did she look so surprised to find out we're together?" Dana asked.

"Because I hadn't told her about you. Not yet. I was planning to tell her about you today, and you about her, but I never got the chance. When you found your way to Chloe yourself, by coincidence, I took that as a sign."

"You know you can't spring something like that on some woman."

"I know. I just couldn't help myself. And she isn't just 'some woman.' She's exactly your type." Gabrielle took a step closer to her, drawing her hand down the side of Dana's arm seductively. "*Our* type."

Dana shook her head. "Don't try to charm your way out of this. You know that doesn't work on me."

"That's what you think. And you know I'm right. I was watching the two of you together. There was chemistry there. You can't deny it."

Deep within Dana, desire swelled and flared. Her girlfriend was right. She'd been drawn to Chloe from the moment she first saw her standing by the stage.

"It doesn't matter," she said. "Chloe isn't interested. I've never seen anyone run away so fast."

"I wouldn't be so sure about that."

"Her response was clear. I don't like to play games."

"That's why you have me. The chase is half the fun."

Dana pursed her lips. While she herself didn't have the patience for games, Gabrielle seemed to enjoy the thrill and she was indifferent to any fallout.

"You can't go chasing after every pretty woman who looks our way," Dana said.

"Like I said, Chloe isn't just any woman," Gabrielle argued. "She's different."

"How do you know?"

"I just do. I have a feeling."

Gabrielle wasn't going to drop this. She and Dana were very different people, but in some ways, they were far too alike. They were both stubborn, strong-willed. And they both liked to be in charge in all areas of their lives, including their relationship.

While that should have made them incompatible, it didn't.

Instead, it simply meant that the two of them were on the same wavelength, connected on a deep, intimate level. They'd been together for almost five years, and they'd been close friends for ten years before that, ever since their freshman year of college. They'd always shared so much of their lives, and they approached their relationship the same way, seeking out a specific kind of woman, one who enjoyed being bossed around in bed, one they could be with, together.

But it wasn't that they wanted someone to serve as an outlet for them, a way to solve some kind of problem in their relationship. Sharing someone in that way was an intimate act, one that brought them closer, both to each other and to the other woman.

The problem was, the 'other woman' never stuck around. It was easy to find women who were happy to be theirs, happy to serve them in the bedroom and be spoiled shamelessly in return.

But once the shine wore off—and it always did—those women were out the door.

"Look," Dana said. "I just don't want you to end up hurt if things with Chloe don't work out."

"I'm not going to get hurt," Gabrielle said. "We've been doing this for long enough that I know not to get too attached."

Dana studied her face. Gabrielle was far more sensitive than she pretended to be. Her blasé attitude, the way she treated everything like a game—it sometimes seemed like a mask Gabrielle hid behind. It wasn't surprising, given what she had been through with her ex-fiancée. But Dana couldn't help but wonder if it was wearing on Gabrielle more than she admitted, the way that women always came and went, the way they always ended up leaving.

Was it starting to wear on Dana too?

But she had accepted long ago that any relationship they had with another woman would be temporary. People always left her in the end. That was the way it had always been. The only exception was Gabrielle.

Gabrielle draped her arms around Dana's waist and pulled her in close. "At the very least, I owe her an apology for being less than upfront with her. I'm sure I can find a way to smooth things over."

Dana sighed. "All right. Just don't do anything over the top." She doubted that Gabrielle's 'apology' would simply be comprised of words.

Gabrielle feigned offense. "Me, over the top?" She gave Dana a devilish smile. "Don't worry, I won't do anything too crazy. I already have the perfect plan for clearing the air with Chloe."

One thing was certain—Gabrielle was serious about making Chloe come around. And Dana found herself hoping that whatever Gabrielle had planned would work. Because Gabrielle was right.

Despite Dana's reservations, she wanted Chloe just as much as Gabrielle did.

CHAPTER 4

C hloe surveyed the selection of flowers before her, sketching out an arrangement in her mind. It was for a custom order, one that had come late in the afternoon, only an hour before closing time. A baby-faced, blond-haired man had walked into her shop, requesting the most expensive bouquet she could make to be anonymously delivered in the evening to a specific address. He hadn't given a name, and he'd paid in cash. When Chloe had asked him who or what the flowers were for, he had gotten nervous and claimed he was just the messenger.

It was an unusual request, but Chloe had gotten similar orders in the past. Flowers from a secret admirer to the object of their desire. A gift for a secret, forbidden love. More often than not, it was some rich businessman buying flowers for his mistress and trying to avoid a paper trail. Was the young man an intern or assistant to some wealthy CEO? He'd had that manner about him.

But Chloe wasn't going to question her good fortune. She needed the money. And she was going all out, determined to deliver the most extravagant bouquet she could come up with, for no reason other than for the fun of getting to create something without any limitations.

Her idea now solidified in her mind, she gathered all the flowers she needed. Roses, carnations, lilies, along with some extra greenery. Finally, she grabbed a handful of orange blossoms, her own little signature.

It didn't take her long to put the bouquet together. The arrangement complete, she tied a bow around it then stepped back to survey her masterpiece. It was a little over the top. She was going to have a hard time fitting it through the door. But other than that, it was perfect. She almost wished she could keep it for herself.

She checked the time. It was ten minutes past close. She shut up her shop, then grabbed the bouquet and headed out to her truck. After stashing the bouquet safely in the back, she got in and started the engine.

It sputtered to life reluctantly. She frowned. She didn't like the sound it was making. It was overdue for servicing, but she couldn't afford it. She'd been paid handsomely for working the Mistress Media gala, but most of that money had gone straight to her suppliers, as well as some vet bills for her cat, Mango, an old rescue with more health problems than whiskers. Then there was the personal debt she owed. She was already a month behind on her payments. She couldn't ignore that. She couldn't ignore *her*.

Chloe sighed. She was right back to where she'd been before the gala.

As she pulled out from the curb and started toward the address, her mind wandered back to the evening of the gala. She hadn't spoken to Gabrielle since then, and Gabrielle hadn't made any attempt to speak to her. The only contact she'd had from her was a check in the mail as payment for her services, including a generous tip.

Was it charity? Chloe hated the idea of Gabrielle giving her money out of pity. Maybe Gabrielle was simply thanking her in an extravagant way. Or was she trying to win Chloe's favor?

Chloe just didn't understand the woman, or the woman's interest in her. Especially given that Gabrielle was obviously in a relationship with Dana. But it had seemed like Dana wanted her too. They both did.

And Dana was even more of a mystery to her than Gabrielle. Chloe had looked her up after the gala, unable to shake the sense that she knew her, somehow. It turned out that there was a reason for that. Dana wasn't just any fashion designer. She was *the* Dana Obi, owner of the luxury fashion label Obi. While Dana herself was known for staying out of the spotlight, the brand was practically a household name. Dana's designs were stunning, and just as elegant as she herself.

Chloe couldn't get either woman out of her mind. They both had this manner about them that made her weak. She had a thing for women like them, commanding women who could make her melt with just a word.

For what had to be the hundredth time since the gala, she considered a scenario, a very kinky image of all three of them together flashing across her mind. An image of herself laid out before them, waiting eagerly...

Chloe pushed it aside, focusing her attention on navigating to the address she'd been given. She had to stop letting her imagination run wild. Even if there was the possibility of anything happening between the three of them, Chloe was still reeling from being ambushed by them at the gala. Had Gabrielle and Dana set her up, laid out a trap for her, waited for her to fall into it so that they could pounce?

The idea bothered her. But it excited her even more.

However, she had no interest in getting involved with the two of them, for plenty of reasons.

She reached the delivery address and parked her truck out front. She'd ended up in one of the more expensive parts of the city, only a short drive from her centrally located florist shop, but a long way away from her own apartment. She looked up at the house before her, an enormous mansion on an even bigger block of land, with tall wrought-iron gates across the driveway. It was rare to see actual houses in the middle of the city, let alone houses this big.

Who on earth was she delivering the flowers to?

She got out of her truck and grabbed the bouquet from the back of it, then started toward the house, heading for the intercom beside the gates. But as she approached them, she heard a click, and the gates creaked open mechanically. She glanced around. Was there a camera somewhere, with someone watching her on it?

Steeling herself, she walked through the gates and up the driveway, admiring the garden as she passed through it. The neat hedges and perfectly pruned rosebushes were a little too manicured for her tastes. She preferred something wilder. But she'd be thrilled just to have a garden, let alone one this big. She had a few window boxes in her apartment, but that was all.

Chloe reached the door and knocked on it. Five seconds passed, then ten, then thirty. Just as she was about to knock again, the doorhandle turned.

The door swung open. Chloe's heart stopped.

Standing in the doorway was a glamorous woman with wavy chestnut-brown hair. Gabrielle. And coming down the hall behind her, looking just as irresistible as she had at the night of the gala, was Dana.

CHAPTER 5

G abrielle looked Chloe up and down. "Hello again."
Dana sidled up behind her. "Good, you're here.
Why don't you come in so we can talk?"

Chloe opened her mouth to speak, but no words came
out. This was their house? Had they ordered the flowers?

Then, it hit her. They had ordered the flowers to lure her
here. If the gala hadn't been a trap, this definitely was one.

"Well?" Gabrielle said. "Are you coming in?"

If Chloe had any sense, she'd hand over the flowers and
run in the other direction. So why did she feel compelled to
walk through the door? And, more importantly, what did
these two women want with her?

There was only one way to find out.

Taking a deep breath, she stepped through the doorway
and into the house.

Smiling, Gabrielle shut the door behind her. "Come, let's
sit down and talk."

Chloe followed as they led her deeper into the house. It

was even more impressive on the inside than on the outside. She was half expecting to see servants walking around.

They reached a large lounge room. Dana gestured for Chloe to take a seat before she and Gabrielle sat down on the lounge across from her. Silence hovered between them. Chloe's pulse thrummed in her ears.

Remembering the bouquet in her hands, she thrust it toward the two women. "Your flowers."

"Keep them," Gabrielle said. "They're for you."

Frowning, Chloe placed the bouquet on the coffee table before her. So this was all an elaborate plot to bring her here. Why had they gone to such lengths when they could have just gone to Chloe's shop, or even called her? Had they simply wanted to make Chloe come to them, to meet her on their turf?

Dana gestured toward a small bar to the side. "Would you like a drink? Coffee? Tea? Something stronger?"

Chloe shook her head. "I shouldn't stay long."

"Do you have somewhere to be?" Gabrielle asked. "We wouldn't want to keep you."

Chloe didn't respond. She wasn't going anywhere, and the look in Gabrielle's eyes told her that she knew it. She had Chloe wrapped around her finger. They both did.

"Why am I here?" Chloe asked. "What is it that you want from me?"

Gabrielle crossed one smooth, toned leg over the other. "When a woman flirts with you and buys you flowers, it's usually obvious what she wants. What *we* want in this case."

"I…" Was Gabrielle saying what Chloe thought she was saying?

Dana held up her hands. "Let's take a step back. We owe you an apology."

"For what?" Chloe asked.

"The night at the gala. We try to be upfront about this kind of thing, but Gabrielle got a little carried away."

Gabrielle gave Chloe a seductive smile. "Can you blame me?"

Heat prickled at Chloe's skin. She averted her eyes from Gabrielle's piercing gaze. Between the way Gabrielle was looking at her and Dana's firm, velvety voice, she could barely keep herself together.

"What is it that you try to be upfront about?" she asked.

"Us," Dana said. "And what we want from you. Our relationship is one most people consider unconventional. We aren't quite monogamous, but that's not to say our relationship is completely open. We have a very specific arrangement."

Gabrielle spoke up beside her. "You see, we like to share."

Chloe's heart began to race. So she'd been right all along. They both wanted her.

She crossed her arms, willing her heart to slow down. They had ambushed her at the gala, then they had tricked her into coming here. She wasn't about to forget that.

"We should never have put you on the spot like that," Dana said. "We're sorry for placing you in an uncomfortable position."

Chloe pressed her lips together. *Uncomfortable* wasn't the word she'd have used to describe how the two of them made her feel that evening.

"We'd like the chance to make it up to you," Gabrielle said. "We want to take you out on a date."

Chloe blinked. "A date? With both of you?"

"Is that a problem?" Dana asked. "We're usually very good at reading signals."

"And the signals are all there," Gabrielle added.

Chloe hesitated. "No, it isn't a problem." Although dating two women was uncharted territory for her, that wasn't what gave her pause. She was still feeling blindsided by everything. First, by finding out that Gabrielle and Dana were a couple, and now by the fact that she was sitting in their living room.

"One date," Gabrielle said. "That's all."

Chloe chewed her lip, thinking. She couldn't deny that she found the idea tempting. Hadn't she just been fantasizing about both women on the drive over here?

But that fluttery feeling in her stomach, it wasn't just lust.

"I need to think about this," she said.

"Of course," Dana said. "Take your time. We'll be here."

Gabrielle folded her arms across her chest. "But don't keep us waiting too long."

A shiver spread down Chloe's back. At that moment, every inch of her body was urging her to say yes. She had to get out of there before she said or did anything rash.

She stood up from her seat. "I need to go."

"I'll walk you out," Dana said.

Chloe shook her head. "I remember the way."

As Chloe began to leave the room, Gabrielle called her name. She turned. Gabrielle was holding the bouquet in her hands.

"Don't forget your flowers," she said.

When Chloe arrived home, she was greeted by a scruffy orange cat. 'Greeted' wasn't quite the right word. Mango simply padded over to her, stared at her for a moment, then trotted off into the living room.

"Hello to you too," Chloe muttered.

She headed into her kitchen. At least Mango was acknowledging her presence now. She'd adopted the grumpy tabby cat several months ago after living alone for far too long. She spent most of her time and energy single-handedly running her shop, so she didn't have much of a social life, and she didn't have any family either. At least, not family that she wanted to talk to. Mango wasn't the most affectionate of cats, but she liked having him around for company.

She grabbed the largest vase she could find and filled it with water before arranging the flowers in it carefully. After refilling Mango's food and water bowls, she took the vase and carried it into the living room, placing it in the center of the coffee table. The enormous arrangement dominated the entire room.

She took a seat on the couch, stretching out along it. Mango was curled up in his usual place on the arm of a chair. He rose up and jumped onto the coffee table, then began circling the bouquet.

"What do you think?" Chloe had gotten into the habit of talking to Mango in an attempt to form some kind of bond with him. She couldn't tell if it was working. And right now, she wished she had someone to talk to who could talk back to her.

Mango gave the bouquet a tentative sniff, batting at a carnation with his paw before settling down beside it. Was that a sign of approval?

Chloe herself approved of the flowers. She could count on one hand the number of times anyone had given her flowers. No one ever thought to give flowers to a florist, but Chloe loved receiving them. After all, she understood the meaning they held. To her, the bouquet was the perfect gift, the perfect gesture.

But perhaps she was giving Gabrielle and Dana too much credit. After all, Chloe had made the bouquet herself. Plus, it had all just been a ruse to draw her into their trap.

She groaned. Why was she so conflicted over them? What was holding her back? She had too many reservations, too many doubts swimming around in her mind.

For starters, she was wary of getting involved with anyone who had as much money as they did. Chloe hated what money did to people, to relationships. Money made people feel entitled. And it always came with conditions, demands, attached.

Did Dana and Gabrielle view money that way? They seemed used to getting their way, used to everyone falling over their feet just to please them. They both had a commanding way about them that made Chloe want to do just that.

But what did they want from her? What did they want her to be to them? It was obvious just seeing Gabrielle and Dana together that they were committed to each other. Did they want a real relationship with Chloe, or did they want her to be nothing more than their plaything, their pet?

She didn't want to be the plaything of some woman, let alone two. She didn't want to be controlled.

At least, not outside the bedroom...

She banished the indecent thoughts forming in her mind. This was exactly what the problem was. There was something about Dana and Gabrielle that triggered the part of her that longed to belong to someone, to be possessed by them. If she let herself give in to those desires, let herself dive headfirst into them like she wanted to, she feared she would drown. And it wouldn't be the first time.

If she was going to do this, she needed to regain some control over the situation, to set boundaries, both for herself and for Dana and Gabrielle.

Chloe took her phone from her purse. "I can't believe I'm doing this."

Mango's response was his usual disinterested look.

Chloe drew in a deep breath and dialed Gabrielle's number. Gabrielle picked up after a few rings.

"Chloe," she said. "Good to hear from you so soon. I hope this means you have an answer for us."

"Not quite," Chloe replied. "I want to talk about everything first. Discuss... terms."

For a moment, Gabrielle was silent. Had Chloe caught her off guard? Was she weighing Chloe's words? Or had she just not expected Chloe to say anything other than *yes*?

"All right," Gabrielle finally said. "Let's meet in person so all three of us can talk. Tomorrow night. We'll have dinner."

Chloe frowned. "That sounds a lot like a date."

"We can have drinks instead, if you'd prefer."

"One drink," Chloe countered. "So we can talk. That's all."

"You drive a hard bargain, but it's a deal. We'll send a car to pick you up."

"I'd rather meet you there."

"Suit yourself. I'll text you the details." Gabrielle paused. "One last thing. Tomorrow night—wear something red."

Something red? That was an oddly specific instruction, but Chloe didn't question it. "All right."

"Then we'll see you tomorrow." With a brief farewell, Gabrielle hung up the phone.

Chloe exhaled slowly. There was no turning back now. And she didn't know why Gabrielle had told her to wear something red to have drinks, but she was beginning to suspect that dating Gabrielle and Dana meant being at the mercy of their every whim.

Why did the thought of being at their mercy make her heart race and her entire body burn?

Pushing the feeling aside, she got up from the couch, walked into her bedroom, and opened her wardrobe doors in search of something red to wear.

CHAPTER 6

The following night, Gabrielle and Dana waited for Chloe at The Lounge, a high-end club downtown.

Gabrielle looked around the club as she finished her drink. What would Chloe make of the place? Normally, the women they dated were impressed by the opulence of this kind of venue. But after Chloe's phone call the night before, it was becoming even more clear that Chloe wasn't the type to be seduced by the lavish lifestyle Gabrielle and Dana lived.

Was that a sign that Chloe wasn't interested in them for money? Of course, it could just be a façade. It wouldn't be the first time a gold-digging woman pretended she was indifferent about Gabrielle's money.

"Gabi?" Dana said, using her old nickname from college. "Are you all right?"

Gabrielle nodded. "I'm fine." She checked the time on her phone. "Chloe should be here any minute."

"Worried she won't show?"

"Of course not." From the moment Chloe had stepped

inside their house yesterday, they'd had her under their spell.

So why was Chloe so hesitant when it came to the two of them?

"And here she is," Dana said.

Gabrielle followed the path of Dana's eyes. Chloe was standing by the entrance of the club, dressed in a black blouse, heeled boots, and a red miniskirt that matched the color of her lips.

A smile pulled at Gabrielle's mouth. Chloe had done exactly as they'd told her to do.

Spotting Dana and Gabrielle, she strode purposefully over to them, greeting them as formally as she had on the phone the night before.

Gabrielle gave her a sweeping look. "I have to say, you look stunning in that shade of red."

Chloe kept a straight face, but the flush creeping up her cheeks was hard to miss. "I don't own much red clothing, so this had to do." She looked around at the room. "Why did you ask me to wear something red?"

"We'll get to that later," Dana said. "Take a seat."

Chloe sat down stiffly, choosing a chair across the table that maintained some distance between herself and them. This businesslike manner of hers was obviously forced, the desire hiding behind her eyes betraying her. It was immensely satisfying watching her try to fight it.

What would it feel like to make her come undone, to witness her truly letting go?

But Gabrielle was getting ahead of herself. "Let's get you a drink."

"Sure," Chloe said. "But remember, this isn't a date."

Dana nodded. "We know. One drink, that was the agreement."

They caught the eye of a nearby waitress. Gabrielle and Dana each ordered another cocktail. Chloe eyed their near-empty glasses before ordering a gin and tonic. It was a very austere choice. Was she that determined to keep their 'not a date' from getting too cozy?

Sure enough, as soon as the waitress disappeared, Chloe folded her hands on the table before her and spoke. "Let's talk about those terms."

Gabrielle raised an eyebrow. "Right down to business, I see."

"I just want to make sure we're on the same page," Chloe replied.

"Certainly," Dana said. "So what are these terms of yours?"

"There's only one." Chloe crossed her arms. "I don't want to go on a date with both of you, not yet. I want to go out with each of you separately first, get to know you one-on-one. Then, after that, I'll decide if I'm ready to date you both together."

Gabrielle frowned. This wasn't what she'd been expecting. None of the women they'd dated had ever proposed anything like this before, had never made any demands. Usually, women were more than willing to do whatever Gabrielle and Dana wanted. In exchange for being spoiled, of course.

But Dana didn't seem fazed at all. She leaned back and crossed her arms. "You're assertive. You know what you want. I like that."

Chloe shifted in her seat, her hand reaching up to twirl a

45

stray strand of hair at the nape of her neck around her finger. It was delightful, watching how hot and bothered Chloe got over Dana's firm, direct manner. While Gabrielle liked to tease, her girlfriend was far more straightforward.

Dana turned to Gabrielle, questioning her, a wordless conversation passing between them. Chloe's request wasn't unreasonable, but they'd never done anything like this before. They were a package deal. That was how they worked.

But Gabrielle didn't see a problem with them dating Chloe separately, as long as it was just temporary. And the small nod Dana gave her told her that she felt the same. Gabrielle knew her well enough to be able to read her.

Gabrielle turned back to Chloe. "That's fine with us. But just so you understand, in the long run, we're looking for someone we can be with together."

Chloe nodded. "I understand."

"Then we're all on the same page," Dana said.

Their drinks arrived. Chloe didn't touch hers. Instead, she waited for the waitress to disappear before addressing Dana and Gabrielle again.

"So, why did you want me to wear red tonight?" she asked.

Gabrielle stole a glance at Dana. "The real question is, why did *you* decide to wear red tonight?"

Chloe frowned. "Because you asked me to."

"And you didn't think to question why?"

"No. You told me to, so I did it."

Gabrielle folded her arms across her chest. "Do you always do what women tell you to do?"

"No," she stammered. "But-"

"That's a real pity."

Chloe took in a breath, obviously trying to regain her composure. "Look, just tell me why you asked me to wear red."

"It's simple," Dana said. "We wanted to see if you'd do it."

Chloe's brows drew together. "I don't understand."

"Perhaps *you* don't know why you did it, but we do," Dana said. "You walked through our front door yesterday because you wanted to know what we wanted from you. You came here tonight because you're intrigued by us. You wore that red skirt for no reason other than the fact that we told you to do it."

Gabrielle leaned forward, letting her eyes linger on Chloe's, drawing the woman's gaze to her. "You felt the need to do as you were told. You wanted to obey us, to *please* us. Isn't that right?"

Chloe didn't answer her. But Gabrielle didn't need Chloe's confirmation. The answer was written clearly on her face.

Dana spoke up beside her. "Let's cut to the chase. What we're looking for is someone who wants us to take charge. Someone who will be ours in every way imaginable. And we think you're exactly who we're looking for."

Chloe averted her eyes, looking down into her drink instead, but that didn't hide the flush rising up her face. "What makes you think that?"

"Call it a feeling," Gabrielle replied. "Between the two of us, we've developed a sixth sense for spotting women like you."

"Women like me?"

"Women with…" Gabrielle chose her words carefully. "Submissive desires."

"Of course, being ours goes beyond just what happens in the bedroom." Dana's voice took on a sultry tone that made even Gabrielle shiver. "You'll have your every need taken care of, your every desire fulfilled, all for the simple price of your unwavering submission."

Gabrielle watched Chloe's face as she took in their words. Her lips parted just a fraction, her eyes shimmering with lust.

This was how she reacted to the mere suggestion of submission? Oh, how Gabrielle was looking forward to the chance to make her melt into a puddle of submissive bliss. She was just dying to see that side of Chloe.

"Is that what you want?" Gabrielle asked.

"I…" The blush on Chloe's cheeks deepened. "Maybe. I mean, I've… dabbled in that kind of thing before."

Dana examined Chloe's face. "So you're experienced then?"

"Experienced enough to know what I like," Chloe said.

"Oh?" Gabrielle raised her cocktail to her lips and sipped, gazing at Chloe over the top of the glass. "And what is it that you like?"

Chloe shrugged. "The usual. Bondage, impact play, power play." She crossed her arms. "I'm open to other activities, but only with prior discussion. And I have limits. No edgeplay of any kind. That's a hard limit. And no power exchange outside of the bedroom. That's… a soft limit."

"That's all very specific," Dana said. "So you do understand what we're about."

Chloe nodded. "I do."

Gabrielle smiled. Chloe was proving to be full of surprises. This was the first of them that was good. This development certainly made things easier. As much as the two of them enjoyed inducting curious women into their deliciously twisted lifestyle, so few of those women truly enjoyed it—no, *needed* it—the way that Dana and Gabrielle did.

But Chloe? She didn't need to be introduced to their world. She was already a part of it.

"Then we have an understanding," Dana said. "But we have some terms of our own. I'm sure you already understand this, as experienced as you are, but for this kind of relationship to work, we need to be open with each other. That's even more important when there are three of us involved. Gabrielle and I don't keep anything from each other, and we expect the same from you."

Chloe nodded. "Sure."

"So," Gabrielle said. "Which of us do you want to take you out first?"

Chloe paused. "I haven't thought about that yet." She studied them both for a moment. "You know what? I'll let you two decide."

Gabrielle raised an eyebrow. Was she imagining it, or was Chloe toying with them? Had she finally realized just how much Gabrielle and Dana wanted her, and how much power came with that?

It only made Gabrielle more desperate to bring Chloe to her knees.

"All right," Dana said. "We'll figure it out and get back to you."

"That's settled then." Chloe took her glass and downed

her gin and tonic in one long swig. "And I've finished my drink. I should go."

"So soon?" Gabrielle said. "Why don't you stay for another?"

"Because then we'd be getting into date territory. I wouldn't want to ruin our first dates." Chloe stood up, grabbed her purse from the seat next to her, and straightened out her red miniskirt with a shimmy of her hips. "You have my number. Let me know when you've decided who's taking me out first."

With the briefest of goodbyes, Chloe turned and walked away.

Gabrielle watched with narrowed eyes as Chloe disappeared out the door. "Is it just me, or was she playing with us just now?"

Dana chuckled. "You just don't like that she didn't immediately roll over and give in to what you wanted like everyone else does." She patted Gabrielle's leg affectionately. "This is a good thing. Chloe is setting boundaries. That means she knows what she wants, and she knows how to handle herself. We might have just met our match."

Gabrielle hated to admit it, but her girlfriend was right. "Just as long as she understands who's in charge where it really matters." Either way, Gabrielle had every intention of showing Chloe just that. "So, which of us is taking her out first?"

CHAPTER 7

C hloe tapped her fingers on the steering wheel of her truck, waiting for the red light to turn green. The cab and back seat were overflowing with bunches of uncut flowers from the market. She always went to the flower market herself when she had the time. That way she got to handpick the most perfect, pristine flowers to use in her arrangements. And it was more affordable than having them delivered to her florist shop.

She checked the time. She needed to get to her store so she could open it up in time for the morning rush. Customers often came in before work to buy flowers or order them to be delivered later in the day. She couldn't afford to miss out on those sales. Her money problems were getting worse every day.

It didn't help that her landlord had just informed her that he was raising the rent on her store. It was extortionate, how much he was charging her. While rents in this part of the city were expensive, her shop wasn't exactly prime real estate. It was tiny, tucked away in a side street that got hardly any foot traffic. Her sales would be far better if her shop was bigger, and on a main road, but she couldn't afford the cost of a better location.

Finally, the light turned green. Not half a mile later, she found herself stopped again, this time by the thick city traffic. As she waited for the cars in front of her to start moving again, her mind wandered to the flowers that were sitting on her coffee table, the flowers that Dana and Gabrielle had given her. They were in full bloom now. Every time she saw them, they made her heart skitter.

It was unusual, the effect Dana and Gabrielle were having on her. Chloe wasn't the romantic type, but she was spellbound by the two women, especially after meeting with them the other night. No small part of that was because of what they'd told her they were looking for.

Desire stirred deep inside her. That was why she'd been so drawn to them both all along, why she'd found herself weak at the knees in their presence. Gabrielle and Dana, two seductive, dominant women, were everything she'd ever wanted.

But that was only in the bedroom. When it came to all other parts of a relationship, Chloe refused to give up her power, to be someone's possession.

Although, she couldn't deny that a part of her craved that, to find someone she trusted enough to let those lines blur, to hand over control, to let herself be just as vulnerable outside of the bedroom as she was inside of it. But she would never again put herself in that position. After a lifetime of living under someone else's control, she'd vowed to never let that happen again.

It was why she'd ended her last relationship. Her ex-girlfriend had been controlling too, just in a more subtle way than her mother had been. It had taken Chloe far too long to figure that out. For most of their relationship, she'd been too broken, too preoccupied with dealing with the aftermath of the past she'd run away from to notice.

But that was all behind her now. She needed to focus on the present.

The traffic before her started to move. She shifted gears and took off. She was almost at her shop. She glanced at her phone, which she'd left sitting on the passenger seat. She was still waiting to hear back from Gabrielle and Dana. It had only been a few days, but still, she was nervous. It was obvious that her proposal had taken them off guard. What if they'd changed their minds, decided that they didn't want to jump through all these hoops for her?

But it was important to her to get to know them each separately before jumping into anything with them both. It was her way of taking things slow, at least emotionally. What they wanted of her—what they wanted her to be—it was what she wanted too. But truly giving oneself to someone, body and mind, required a certain degree of trust. Learning to trust two people, building that connection with them, was more difficult than learning to trust one.

Plus, she was still a little nervous about the prospect of dating both of them. Although her excitement, the desire they both invoked in her, was greater than her nerves, she couldn't silence them.

Plus, Dana and Gabrielle's assertion that they didn't keep any secrets from each other gave Chloe pause. She understood why it was important in their relationship. But Chloe had her fair share of secrets. Her entire life was one big secret, a lie so big that it had become true for her. So it wasn't like she was lying to them, not really. The identity she'd constructed for herself was real. There were very few people who knew about her old self, and she intended to keep it that way.

She turned onto a side street, escaping the flow of traffic. As she did, she noticed a faint rattle coming from under the hood of her truck. Her ancient pickup was constantly making unsettling noises, but this was the first time it had made this particular sound. The truck was overdue for servicing, but she hadn't been able to afford it.

Suddenly, the rattling under the hood turned into a grinding sound.

Chloe groaned. "Not now. Please, not now."

As if on cue, smoke began rising from her truck's hood. She cursed and pulled onto the side of the road, then turned off the engine.

Chloe got out of her truck and opened the hood. Instantly, a plume of smoke rose from it. She fanned it away in an attempt to get a closer look at the engine. She didn't know what she was looking for, but it didn't take a mechanic to know that something was seriously wrong.

She cursed again. This couldn't be happening at a worse time. She didn't have any money to spare for repairs.

With a defeated sigh, she got out her phone and dialed her mechanic's number.

Dana entered Blossom Flowers, the bell above the door chiming as it swung open. It was a quaint little shop, every shelf and surface bursting with flowers. While Dana rarely bought flowers herself, she could see their appeal.

However, she was here for something far more appealing than the flowers. At the back of the shop, Chloe stood behind the counter, a scattering of flowers and string strewn before her. Her long, dark hair was tied back in a ponytail, and the sunlight streaming through the nearby window illuminated her in a way that made her skin look radiant.

As Dana watched her, she was struck with the urge to dress Chloe up in one of her designs, perhaps even something custom-made for her. Chloe was an undeniably attractive woman. But she wasn't attractive in the generic sense that the high-fashion models Dana usually worked with were. Chloe was far more unique. The practical apron she wore over her dress couldn't hide her full curves. Those green eyes of hers were two dark, bottomless pools. Her pinkish-red lips formed a perfect heart shape.

But right now, those lips were screwed up in thought, and those eyes were staring vacantly out a nearby window.

As Dana strode up to the counter, Chloe finally seemed to notice her.

"Dana," she said. "What are you doing here?"

"I was in the neighborhood, so I thought I'd drop by." That was stretching the truth. While the shop was within walking distance of Dana's studio, it was tucked away on a little street she'd never noticed before. "I can't stay long, but I wanted to see your shop. It's lovely. This is all yours?"

Chloe nodded half-heartedly.

Dana frowned. This wasn't the reception she was expecting. "Is something bothering you?"

"I had a rough morning, that's all," Chloe said.

"What happened?"

"My truck broke down. I use it for deliveries, so I really need it."

"Do you know what the problem with the truck is?" Although Dana wasn't an expert on cars, she knew a thing or two about them.

"Something about the engine, maybe? I don't know." Chloe's shoulders slumped. "I don't know where I'm going to find the money to fix it, but if I can't do deliveries, I'll lose even more money."

Dana pursed her lips. She didn't make a habit of getting involved in the problems of the women she and Gabrielle dated. That was a great way to get taken advantage of. And why would she waste time getting involved with women who would inevitably leave?

But Chloe was different. She didn't seem like the type of woman who would use them. Her interest in Dana and Gabrielle seemed genuine. She wanted to get to know them properly, and she'd made her boundaries and expectations clear. Were those signs that she might be in it for the long haul?

Against her better judgment, Dana reached into her purse and began digging around in it. "Do you know how much it will cost to fix the truck?"

Chloe shrugged. "No idea. I'm still waiting on a quote from the mechanic, but he warned me that since my truck is so old, if anything needs to be replaced, it's going to cost a lot."

Locating her checkbook, Dana pulled it out of her purse along with a pen. "I'm sure we can work something out."

Chloe blinked. "Wait, what are you doing?"

"You need your truck repaired, don't you?"

"Yes, but—"

"I'll cover the cost for you."

Chloe's eyes widened. "What? No. You can't do that."

Dana crossed her arms. "Why not?"

"Because," Chloe stammered. "I don't even know how much it will cost. It could be thousands of dollars. I don't know how I'd ever pay you back."

"That's not a problem. And you don't have to pay me back."

Chloe took a deep breath. "Look, I appreciate the offer, but I don't want this. I don't want to owe you anything."

"You wouldn't owe me. I'm giving it to you. Consider it a gift."

Chloe shook her head. "I can't accept it. It's nothing personal, I just don't like taking things from people. And really, the situation with my truck isn't a big deal. I can handle it myself."

"Are you sure?" Chloe didn't sound at all convincing.

"I'm sure. This shop of mine has survived for years. I always figure out how to make things work. I'll figure this out too."

Dana slipped her checkbook back into her purse. "If you say so. But if you change your mind, let me know. The offer still stands."

Chloe nodded. Dana had to respect Chloe's need to be self-reliant. After all, Dana herself was the same way. But at the same time, she wished Chloe would let her help.

"So, you wanted to see my shop?" Chloe asked.

"That's right," Dana said. "But I have an ulterior motive

for coming here. I wanted to speak to you. I'm sure you've been waiting to hear from Gabrielle and me."

Chloe nodded, a little too casually. Had she been sitting by her phone waiting for them to call her?

She didn't have to wait any longer.

"After some discussion, Gabrielle and I decided that she'll be the one to take you on a date first," Dana said. "I'm going to Berlin for a fashion show in a couple of days, and we didn't want to make you wait until I come back. I didn't need to see you to tell you that, but since Gabrielle has a head start from all the times she's come in here to see you, I thought it was only fair that I get to catch up. Gabrielle has been a little too smug about getting to take you out first."

Chloe glanced away bashfully. "Sorry. I didn't mean to make the two of you fight over me."

"Let me be clear. Any competition between me and Gabrielle is entirely friendly. There's no jealousy between us. When it comes to you, we're both on the same page."

Chloe's gaze flicked back up to meet Dana's. "And what does that page say?"

Dana rested her elbows on the counter, leaning close to Chloe. "It says that we both can't wait to make you ours, together."

Chloe exhaled softly. Gabrielle had been so right when she'd pegged Chloe as their type. As self-assured and assertive as Chloe was, it only took a few words to make her come apart.

What Dana wouldn't give to get her behind closed doors. Then she could really make Chloe come apart.

Suddenly, Chloe's phone began to ring.

She took it out of her apron pocket and looked down at the screen. "It's Gabrielle."

Of course. Dana had told Gabrielle she was going to visit Chloe's shop but she hadn't told her when, and somehow, Gabrielle had managed to interrupt them.

She straightened up. "I'm sure she just wants to set up your date. I should get back to work anyway."

Chloe smiled. "It was good seeing you."

"Likewise."

Dana said goodbye and headed for the door. As she left the shop, she heard Chloe greeting Gabrielle over the phone. Gabrielle hadn't told Dana what she had planned for her date with Chloe, but Dana was sure it would be something extravagant. That was Gabrielle's style.

But Dana would get her chance with Chloe too, soon enough.

CHAPTER 8

Gabrielle waited by the pier for Chloe to arrive. She'd just checked in with the captain of *The Queen Bee*. Everything was good to go.

She spotted a car pulling up nearby. The back passenger door opened and Chloe slipped out from the back seat, not bothering to wait for the driver to open the door for her. She didn't seem to be deliberately flouting etiquette. It was becoming more and more clear that Chloe felt the need to be independent. Gabrielle had been surprised that Chloe had allowed her to send a car to pick her up in the first place.

She strode over to Chloe and greeted her, letting her eyes drift down Chloe's body, taking in the figure-hugging black dress she wore. Gabrielle had gotten used to seeing Chloe in sundresses and aprons, and as appealing as she looked in them, this was something else entirely. There had always been a hint of suggestion behind Chloe's sweet exterior, a tease of something a little more sinful. And with her hair down, wearing a pair of high-heels, and a hint of red on her lips, that side of her was impossible to ignore.

"Don't you look delectable tonight?" Gabrielle said.

Chloe tucked a stray strand of hair behind her ear and murmured a thank you. "What are we doing here? You said we're having dinner."

"We are. You don't get seasick, do you?"

Chloe shook her head.

"Good. Follow me."

As they started down the pier, Chloe looked around, taking in the luxury yachts lined up in rows on either side of them. The private marina attracted only the most elite clientele, the kind that both had enough money for vessels like these and were crazy enough to spend that money on such a notoriously expensive hobby.

"Are we getting on one of these?" Chloe asked.

Gabrielle nodded. "I have a yacht down at the end."

"You have your own boat?"

"I have a few. I've been sailing since I was a girl. Sailing was always such a boys' club, so naturally, that made me even more determined to try it. I learned plenty of useful skills along the way. How to tie knots, for example." She gave Chloe a sideways glance. "I'm quite adept at ropework."

The blush her comment elicited from Chloe was entirely predictable. Gabrielle smiled. She was going to enjoy this.

"But we won't be going on a sailboat tonight," she continued. "Tonight is about getting to know each other without any distractions." She stopped. They were right at the end of the pier. "This is it. *The Queen Bee.*"

Chloe looked up at it, gaping. *The Queen Bee* usually elicited that reaction. The luxury yacht had multiple decks and enough room for several people to live on it. It was well equipped enough for that, too.

Gabrielle found herself admiring it alongside Chloe. *The Queen Bee* was her pride and joy, one of the first things she'd bought when she started making money of her own. She'd come from a wealthy family, but she'd always been determined not to ride on their coattails, wanting to make something of herself in her own right. Of course, growing up with money and all the opportunities that came with it had helped, but the life she had now was one she'd spent the last decade building.

She had everything that anyone could ever want. But there were some things money couldn't buy.

She turned to Chloe. "Shall we?"

She offered Chloe her hand to help her up the ramp onto the boat. Chloe hesitated, then took it.

Gabrielle led her onto the deck where the captain stood by, waiting for them. They greeted him and headed upstairs.

"Dinner will be served on the upper deck," Gabrielle said. "The view from there is magnificent."

They reached the upper deck, where a table set for two was waiting for them. But Chloe swept right past it, making a beeline for the railing. She leaned over it to look out at the water stretching before them. The sea was calm, and the sun had fallen just below the horizon, the sunset painting the ocean's surface in streaks of orange and pink.

"What did I tell you?" Gabrielle said. "The view up here is superb."

Chloe nodded, her eyes fixed on the ocean. "It really is."

So Gabrielle had read Chloe right. While she wasn't interested in anything material, like the gifts of dresses or jewelry coveted by most of the women Gabrielle and Dana had dated, there were still things that impressed her. Simpler things, like watching the sun set over the ocean.

Why was Gabrielle going to such lengths to impress her, to figure out what she desired, just so she could be the one to provide her with them? It would have been much simpler to find one of the many women who were perfectly content with expensive gifts and long nights of uninhibited pleasure.

But those women weren't Chloe. And there was something about her that made Gabrielle want—no, *need*—to win her over, to capture her, to possess her.

The familiar hum of the engine joined the symphony of ocean sounds as the boat roared to life. Soon, the yacht was streaking out into the open ocean, the marina and the city beyond it receding behind them.

Gabrielle placed her hand on the small of Chloe's back. "Come. Let's sit."

Chloe pried herself away from the railing. They took a seat at the table.

"Dinner is being prepared," Gabrielle said. "I managed to poach the chef from La Petite Maison for the night. It took some legwork, but I'm sure it will be worth it. They don't give out Michelin stars to just anyone."

"I hope you didn't go to too much trouble," Chloe said.

Gabrielle waved a hand dismissively. "It was nothing."

A waiter appeared, pouring them each a glass of wine, a light white as a prelude to their meal. The dinner ran six courses, each paired with a different wine. As Gabrielle told Chloe this, Chloe eyed her wine glass hesitantly.

"I'm really not used to all this," she said.

"Well, get used to it," Gabrielle said. "There's nothing I enjoy more than the chance to spoil a woman. And I don't mean with gifts. I prefer to spoil her with more sensual pleasures."

Chloe glanced around, her cheeks flushing pink. What kinds of naughty thoughts had Gabrielle's words planted in her mind?

She lifted her wine glass. "Of course, I'm referring to epicurean pleasures. Good wine, fine food, experiences that stimulate the senses."

She swirled her wine around in her glass before taking a sip, savoring the taste of it along with Chloe's obvious desire. But as much as Gabrielle wanted to spend the entire evening toying with her, tonight was about the two of them getting to know each other.

"So," she began. "You said you want to spend some time with me and Dana separately. To get to know us each a little more... intimately?"

Chloe nodded. "I guess I don't know that much about you. You're just this mysterious woman who kept coming into my florist shop."

"Oh? I'm mysterious, am I?"

Chloe grimaced. "I didn't mean to say that out loud. It's how I used to think of you."

"I'm sure tonight will dispel some of the mystery surrounding me. Besides, I'm just as curious about you. To me, you're the mysterious one."

Chloe's eyes darted away furtively. "I'm not mysterious. I'm not even interesting."

Gabrielle examined Chloe's face. She didn't seem like the modest type, so why the sudden self-consciousness?

"I'm sure that's not true. Why don't you tell me about yourself?"

"There isn't much to tell."

"Let's start with where you're from. Have you always lived here in the city?"

"I grew up in the Midwest. Minnesota. I moved here when I finished high school."

"Really? You don't have the accent."

"I know. It faded when I moved away."

"Where in Minnesota did you live? I have relatives there."

Chloe shrugged. "Nowhere interesting. Just a small town down south."

"What was it called? I spent a lot of time downstate growing up, so I know the area well. My aunt has a cabin on Fountain Lake."

Chloe shifted uncomfortably in her seat. "It was just some little town. You've probably never heard of it."

Why was Chloe being so evasive? It was almost like she was hiding something.

Gabrielle pushed her suspicions aside. Even if Chloe was hiding something, this was their first date. She could hardly fault Chloe for keeping some parts of herself close to her chest.

But Gabrielle had a good reason to be wary of secrets.

Chloe shook her head. "I'm sorry. I just don't like talking about my past, that's all."

"It's all right," Gabrielle said. "I understand. And I'm happy to talk about mine. I grew up right here in the city. My family has lived here for generations. We even have a ranch upstate, a couple of hours north. How about you, do you have family back in Minnesota?"

"I used to," Chloe said. "But now, it's just me. I'm an only child, and my parents, they... aren't around anymore."

"Oh, I'm sorry." So her parents were dead? Was that why Chloe didn't want to talk about her past? "I didn't mean to bring up something painful."

"No, it's fine," Chloe said. "It's not a big deal. Honestly, I'm just a little nervous."

"There's no need to be. Let's just start over. Talk about something else. Like your florist shop." That was a topic Chloe always seemed more than happy to talk about. "How long have you had your store?"

Just as Gabrielle expected, Chloe perked up. "Five years or so. I've always wanted to be a florist, ever since I was a kid. A few years after finishing high school, I decided to take the leap and follow my dreams. I enrolled in a floristry course, and then I set up my shop. I've been running it ever since."

"I have to say, I'm impressed. It's hard to succeed in small business, especially in a city this big and expensive. And you started your business so young, without any experience."

Chloe shrugged. "It isn't as impressive as it sounds. I came into some money when I turned eighteen, so I had most of the funds I needed to cover the startup costs. That gave me a real head start. And I wouldn't call myself a success. Business isn't exactly booming."

"The fact that you've kept the shop running this long is impressive on its own," Gabrielle said. "So why did you choose floristry? You say you dreamed of becoming a florist as a girl?"

"I've always loved flowers. And what I love the most about them is the meanings they carry, all the different things that each type of flower symbolizes. It's like a language in itself. Every arrangement, every single flower, is a message. And I love that I get to compose that message."

Gabrielle studied Chloe's face. "Interesting. So you're the romantic type? I've been trying to figure you out."

"Not really. Maybe I was back when I opened my shop, but I'm older and wiser now."

"What are you, 25? You're far too young to be that jaded."

Chloe crossed her arms. "I'm 26. And I've been through enough to know how the world works."

"So, you're a lapsed romantic."

"I guess you could say that." For a moment, Chloe's gaze grew distant. "I don't know. Maybe there's still a part of me that believes in all that. Or wants to, anyway."

"I understand." Gabrielle had been the same way before everything with her ex-fiancée. In the aftermath, she'd found it hard to believe in love.

So what had happened to Chloe that made her feel that way?

"What about you?" Chloe said. "Your job. Mistress Media. Have you always wanted to do what you do?"

Gabrielle nodded. "I'm a bit like you in that I dreamed of doing this as a girl. Not founding a media company specifically, but getting to run the show. I'm told I was a very bossy child." She took a sip of her wine. "But my job isn't at all interesting. I'm sure there are plenty of other things you'd like to know about me. I'm an open book."

Chloe thought for a moment. "I am a little curious about

you and Dana. How long have you been together?"

"Almost five years now. We've known each other since we were eighteen, but our romantic relationship was a more recent development."

"How did you meet?"

Gabrielle raised an eyebrow. "I thought you wanted to get to know each of us separately."

"I do. But I'm curious about the two of you, from your perspective."

"All right. We met in college. We were roommates in our freshman year. We did *not* get along at first."

"Really?" Chloe said.

"Really. Dana, she's always been very serious, and that was even more true when I first met her. There I was, in my freshman year, living away from home for the first time, ready to go wild, and I got stuck rooming with a stick in the mud engineering student whose idea of a good time was reading textbooks."

"Are you talking about Dana?"

"That's right."

"That doesn't sound like her. She was an engineering student?"

"Not for long. You'll have to ask her for the details, but all I can say is, plenty changed over the course of our freshman year. At first, we fought constantly. Our lifestyles clashed. Dana was always studying, while I spent most of my spare time partying and chasing girls. Eventually, we had this huge fight and words were said that made us realize we'd misjudged each other. We became friends, and over the years that friendship evolved into something more. We went through a lot together. Dana helped me through some difficult times. But it took us a while to realize we had feelings for each other."

"How did you finally figure it out?" Chloe asked.

"It's… complicated." It wasn't, not really, but the topic of Gabrielle's failed engagement and her ex-fiancée's betrayal was a mood killer. "And it isn't just my story to tell. It's Dana's, too. We're happy to share it when the time comes that all three of us are together."

"Right." Chloe fell silent. Was she thinking about just that, about all three of them together?

"Is that really what you want to ask about me and Dana, our relationship? I'm sure there's plenty you'd like to know. I'm well aware that most people find our relationship unusual. I take it you've never dated two women before?"

Chloe shook her head.

"So you must have questions. Don't be shy. Like I said, I'm an open book." Gabrielle folded her arms on the table before her. "So, what else are you curious about when it comes to the two of us?"

"Well… there is something I've been wondering," Chloe said. "Have the two of you always done this? Dated another woman?"

"On and off, for the past few years. When we first got together, we tried to make things work between just the two of us, but it never quite felt right."

"Because you're both Dommes?"

"That's right." It was close enough to the truth. The reality was more complicated.

"And that's why you involve other women?" Chloe asked. "Submissive women?"

"Yes."

"Have there been many of them?"

"Would it bother you if there have been?"

Chloe shook her head. "No, of course not."

"There have been quite a few. But I'm guessing what you're really wondering is if it was serious with those women? Whether the women we date are long-term girlfriends or just temporary playthings?"

Chloe nodded. So which of those two did she want to be?

"The truth is, we'd prefer someone more permanent, but it's hard to find the right person. It's easy to find women interested in dating us casually, but very few of them want a genuine relationship. So while we search for someone who does, there's no harm in having a little fun."

Chloe mulled over Gabrielle's words silently for a moment. "I guess I'm just trying to figure out what to expect. This is new to me, dating a couple." She paused. "Do you have any boundaries, any rules about what you're allowed to do with the other woman when you're alone with her?"

A smile pulled at Gabrielle's lips. "Like right now, for example?" She didn't give Chloe a chance to respond. "While Dana and I are a package deal, we're still two separate people. It's only natural that we have individual relationships with the woman we're dating. As long as we're open with each other, we can do anything and everything. Tonight, there are no limits."

Chloe bit her bottom lip. Was she thinking about where the night would take them, thinking about all the delicious possibilities? It certainly seemed that way. Her dark, expressive eyes always hinted at what was going on in her mind, and the lust flickering behind them was hard to miss.

Gabrielle leaned toward her slightly, letting her voice drop an octave. "I'm sure you'll find that dating Dana and me is just like dating anyone else. The only difference is, you're in the lucky position of having two Mistresses to serve. We can't wait to find out if you're up for the challenge."

A pink flush spread up Chloe's neck and face. There was little doubt now what was going through her mind. Was she picturing herself at their feet, imagining herself serving two Mistresses? Because Gabrielle was imagining just that.

She picked up her wine glass, swirling it around. "One thing you should know about the two of us is that we're very different in that department. Dana, she's strict, far too strict for my liking. Me? I like to have a little fun with our submissive." She took a sip of her wine before setting the glass down again. "So, which kind of Mistress do you prefer?"

She locked her gaze on Chloe, pinning her in place. She could almost feel the heat radiating from her across the table, could taste the attraction hanging in the air between them, could hear the desire in her every breath.

But as Chloe opened her mouth to speak, the waiter reappeared.

He set appetizers on the table before each of them. "Smoked salmon and caviar on cumin-roasted Dutch baby potatoes," he announced before producing a fresh bottle of white wine. "And a sauvignon blanc from the Marlborough region of New Zealand."

The waiter poured them each a glass while describing

the character of the wine in detail. By the time he left, Chloe was staring at her plate with ravenous eyes, and Gabrielle's stomach was rumbling.

She stifled a sigh and picked up her fork, making a mental note to hire a new waiter, one who could read a room. The moment was gone.

But they still had the rest of the night ahead of them.

Chloe leaned over the railing, looking out at the sparkling city lights in the distance. They were miles out to sea now. The boat was drifting gently in the waves, the cool ocean air breezing around them. She and Gabrielle had finished dinner, and now they lingered on the upper deck, alone.

She glanced at Gabrielle. The woman stood beside her, her eyes fixed on the horizon, the wind whipping her long, wavy hair around. It almost looked like it was floating.

Sensing Chloe's eyes on her, Gabrielle turned to face her. "It's breathtaking, isn't it?"

Chloe nodded, her grip on the railing tightening. She felt dizzy, the combination of the swaying boat and her overindulgence in food and wine making her head spin. Or perhaps that was just Gabrielle's presence.

"This is why I love to sail, why I love the sea. There's nothing more satisfying than being out on the open ocean, just the waves and the stars for company. Of course, the company of a beautiful woman makes it even better."

Chloe averted her gaze. It was always hard for her to see compliments and praise as anything but hollow. In her past life, all the praise she'd been showered with had been nothing more than false, empty words used to manipulate her. They had only come when she did what others wanted, when she played the part that those around her wanted her to play. She'd left that life behind, but she still carried the ghosts of it with her.

"Hey." Gabrielle reached out to her, touching her arm gently. "Look at me."

Chloe's stomach fluttered. She turned to face her, skin tingling from Gabrielle's touch.

"Why do I get the feeling you don't believe me when I say I find you beautiful?" Gabrielle asked.

Chloe gave a small shrug. "I'm just bad at taking compliments."

Gabrielle shook her head. "You don't believe me. And here I thought this coy, seductive way of yours was intentional. All those teasing looks, those smiles." She tilted her head to the side, studying Chloe with probing eyes. "You have no idea how much you've been on my mind, do you? How completely and utterly convinced I've been that I *need* to have you?"

Chloe's pulse began to pound. The way Gabrielle was looking at her told her that she meant every word she said. Why did Gabrielle want her so badly? She was just a florist with as much debt as she had problems. It didn't make sense. Yet here she was, alone with Gabrielle on her boat, Gabrielle looking into her eyes as if captivated by her.

Gabrielle took a step toward her, closing the already small space between them. Chloe's breath caught in her chest, her body seized by desire.

"I asked you a question earlier," Gabrielle said. "You didn't answer it."

It took Chloe a moment to find her voice. "What question?"

Gabrielle ran her hand along the railing beside them, sliding it up Chloe's forearm, all the way to her shoulder. "What kind of Mistress do you prefer? A strict Mistress, or a playful Mistress?"

A shiver spread down Chloe's back. "I don't know," she whispered.

"But I do," Gabrielle purred. "I know what you want. You just want a Mistress, any Mistress, to fulfill that insatiable need to belong to another." She skimmed the backs of her fingers up Chloe's cheek, letting them graze the side of Chloe's mouth. "Isn't that right? Is that what you want?"

Chloe trembled, the feel of Gabrielle's hand on her cheek flooding her with heat. She let out a soft breath, unable to move or speak. But Gabrielle gazed back at her, her smoldering eyes demanding an answer.

Chloe wanted her. She *needed* her. But no words could capture the depth of that desire.

So, heart racing, she closed her eyes and pressed her lips to Gabrielle's in a desperate, needy, kiss.

CHAPTER 9

G abrielle seized Chloe by the waist, pulling her close as she deepened the kiss. Chloe's whole body turned to liquid, desire rippling and swirling within her. She grabbed onto Gabrielle's shoulders, bracing herself. Gabrielle's lips were soft but unyielding, tender but demanding, the hunger in them undeniable.

Gabrielle slid her hand down to Chloe's hips, grasping onto them firmly. Chloe murmured into Gabrielle's lips, the press of the woman's body against hers sending heat rushing into her core. She wrapped one arm around Gabrielle's neck, letting her other hand skate down her side, sweeping it over the curve of her breast, the dip of her waist, the swell of her hip.

Gabrielle placed a hand on Chloe's chest, pulling away slightly. "Before we get too carried away, why don't I show you the master bedroom?"

Chloe nodded, glancing around them. They were alone on the deck, but they were out in the open, exposed.

Gabrielle led her inside and down a hall, passing a dozen

different rooms as they went deeper into the boat. The large yacht was like a floating apartment. But Gabrielle didn't give her a chance to gawk. She dragged Chloe along, past a flustered member of the crew who ducked to the side, trying her best to pretend she had no idea that Gabrielle was about to rip Chloe's clothes off.

They reached a door at the end of the hall. Gabrielle pushed it open. Inside was a large, luxurious bedroom decorated in a subtly nautical theme. The windows overlooked the deck, giving a view of the night sky and the ocean beyond.

Chloe's eyes fell on the plush bed in the middle of the room. Beside it was a table, a bottle of champagne in a bucket of ice sitting on top of it, waiting for them.

But Gabrielle didn't seem interested in the champagne at all. She drew Chloe into the room, shutting the door behind her. "Where were we?"

Slowly, she backed Chloe against the wall by the door and slid her hands down the insides of Chloe's wrists, pinning them to the wall at either side of her.

She leaned in close, speaking into Chloe's ear. "When you showed up in this little black dress, I knew I had to have you out of it by the end of the night."

Chloe let out a trembling breath, overcome by the sheer need in Gabrielle's voice.

Releasing her wrists, Gabrielle reached down to the hem of Chloe's dress, gliding her hands up the front of her thighs, drawing the dress up her hips and past her stomach and waist. Chloe lifted her arms, allowing Gabrielle to yank the dress up over her head. She was desperate to feel Gabrielle's touch on her skin, her lips on hers again.

Gabrielle took a step back, her eyes flicking down Chloe's body, taking in the red bra and panties she wore. "Wearing red again? This can't be a coincidence. You know exactly how to make me want you." She ran her palm down the center of Chloe's chest. "I always suspected that the sweet, charming florist who sold me those roses was more wicked than she appeared."

Chloe's pulse quickened. Gabrielle leaned in close and pressed her lips to Chloe's in a scorching kiss even hotter than the last. Chloe melted against her, her whole body quivering with lust. Without breaking the kiss, Gabrielle pulled her over to the bed, then reached around to unclip Chloe's bra. She slid it from Chloe's shoulders and tossed it aside before pushing her down onto the bed.

Chloe shifted back toward the pillows, waiting eagerly for Gabrielle to join her.

"Before we begin," Gabrielle said. "What's your safeword?"

"Parachute," Chloe replied.

"And without a hint of hesitation. Then I'm sure I don't need to tell you how and when to use it."

Chloe nodded.

"Good pet." Gabrielle reached down, drawing her fingers down the side of Chloe's face. "Now that that's out of the way, what shall I do with you?"

Devour me, Chloe wanted to say. *Ravish me.*

But she kept her mouth closed, pleading with Gabrielle with her eyes. Still, Gabrielle didn't join her on the bed. Instead, her eyes wandered around the room, searching for something.

What was she looking for? Chloe followed the path of

Gabrielle's eyes to some coils of hemp rope hanging from hooks on the wall beside the bed. She'd glimpsed them earlier, but the rope had blended in with the rest of the nautical decor.

It *was* just decor, wasn't it?

A devilish smile crossed Gabrielle's lips. She walked over to the wall, lifted a coil of rope from its hook and began unwinding it slowly. "I did tell you that I learned all about knots when I learned to sail. You'd be surprised how often that skill comes in handy."

Chloe's heart began to pound. Was she going to let Gabrielle tie her up, half-naked on a boat in the middle of the ocean?

Yes, she was. She wanted this. And that thirst, that craving, was overpowering all rational thought.

Gabrielle stretched the rope between her hands. "Lift up your arms."

Chloe raised her arms, looking up at her wrists as Gabrielle bound them together. For a moment, Gabrielle glanced at the headboard, seemingly debating whether to tie Chloe to it. But then, she simply secured the ends of the rope around Chloe's wrists, tucking them in.

The rational part of Chloe's brain felt a flicker of relief at that. While she was no stranger to bondage, it took some time for her to trust someone enough to allow them to put her in a position of such vulnerability.

Could Gabrielle sense that in her? Given the way she liked to push Chloe's buttons, it was easy to view Gabrielle and her games as careless, reckless. But maybe there was more to her than what appeared on the surface.

Gabrielle sat on the edge of the bed and snaked a finger

down Chloe's up-stretched arms. "I'm going to need you to be a good pet and keep those hands up. And stay very still. I want to have some fun with you."

Chloe obeyed, lying still on the bed with her arms raised, in nothing but her red panties, inviting Gabrielle to finally do what her searing brown eyes told Chloe she wanted to do.

But Gabrielle just reached across to the table beside the bed and grabbed the bottle of champagne from the ice bucket.

Chloe frowned. What was Gabrielle doing? Chloe watched as she popped the champagne bottle open, taking care not to spill any of the foaming liquid on her dress, then grabbed a crystal flute, pouring herself some champagne before returning the bottle to the bucket.

Glass in hand, she turned back to Chloe. "Now, let me look at you."

She raised her flute to her lips, sipping slowly, surveying Chloe's body from head to toe as if it were a sumptuous banquet she was about to feast on. Chloe's face grew hot, matching the heat swelling at the peak of her thighs. Lying on her back, with her arms stretched up above her, she was unable to shield herself from Gabrielle's eyes. But she liked the way they felt on her, lustful and approving.

"This champagne is just divine," Gabrielle said, lifting the champagne flute into the air. "But I think it would taste even better with you as the vessel."

She leaned forward, holding the glass over Chloe's prone form, and tilted it over her stomach. Chloe sucked in a breath as the cold, fizzing liquid hit her, dribbling down her skin. A second later, Gabrielle drew her finger up the trail of golden liquid on Chloe's stomach and brought it to her lips, licking the champagne from it.

She purred with approval. "I was right. You taste as good as you look."

Without giving Chloe a chance to react, Gabrielle poured a trickle of champagne onto Chloe's stomach again. But this time, she dipped down and licked it from Chloe's skin in one long stroke of her tongue.

Chloe let out a pleased murmur, her fingers curling into her palms above her head.

Gabrielle smiled. "And you sound as good as you taste."

Without breaking Chloe's gaze, Gabrielle tipped the champagne glass once again, pouring it over the peaks of Chloe's breasts, letting it dribble down them. She dipped down again, licking the champagne up, her tongue flicking against Chloe's nipples. A moan slid from Chloe's lips, her nipples tightening. The champagne was cold, but Gabrielle's lips and tongue scorched her skin.

Emboldened by her cries, Gabrielle placed the champagne flute aside and picked up the whole bottle. She poured it generously over Chloe's breasts, her neck, her shoulders, letting it trickle all over her chest before licking it up. She poured a trail of champagne down the center of Chloe's stomach, down to her bellybutton, her tongue and lips following in the wake of the stream to lap it up.

Chloe gasped and bucked, silently begging Gabrielle to strip off her red panties, to keep going lower and lower...

Instead, Gabrielle set the champagne aside and slid back up her body, bringing her lips up beside Chloe's cheek.

"I like the way your body tastes," she whispered. "Let me show you."

Gabrielle kissed her greedily. Chloe's head spun, the scent and taste of Gabrielle's champagne-tinged lips intoxicating her. Gabrielle snaked her hands down Chloe's sides, roaming over her curves, until finally she reached her panties. Chloe lifted her hips, allowing Gabrielle to strip the panties down her legs and tear them from her ankles. Deep inside her, desire throbbed and pulsed.

Dropping the panties to the floor, Gabrielle got up from the bed, pulled her dress over her head, and kicked it aside with a foot. She did the same with her bra, leaving her in her panties and heels, her long dark hair flowing all the way down to her tailbone.

Chloe drank Gabrielle in with her eyes, marveling at the fullness of her curves and the golden sheen of her skin. She had the figure of a goddess from a painting, full-hipped and pink-lipped. Why was such a goddess so determined to take Chloe as a prize?

And why had Chloe ever attempted to resist the idea?

Gabrielle crawled back onto the bed, staring down at Chloe with ravenous eyes. "Now, where was I?"

Chloe bit the inside of her cheek, anticipation building down between her thighs.

But Gabrielle wasn't done playing with her yet. She reached over to the table and slipped her hand into the champagne bucket, digging around in it. After a moment, she withdrew it. In her hand was a cube of ice.

Chloe's eyes widened. What was Gabrielle going to do with that?

Her pulse sped up, the rush of adrenaline thrumming in her ears. Gabrielle watched her for a moment, a question in her eyes.

Did she trust Gabrielle not to burn her?

Chloe took a deep breath and closed her eyes. *Yes.*

A moment later, she felt the cold shock of the ice on her stomach, just below her bellybutton. She hissed and squirmed, a chill spreading over her skin. Her bound hands jerked down to shield herself before she forced them to return to the pillow above her head.

Gabrielle pulled away. "Hold still," she ordered. "I can't have you wriggling everywhere, or I just might slip."

Chloe froze in place. She was sure that Gabrielle wouldn't be so careless, but there were places on her body where Chloe definitely didn't want that ice cube to go.

Satisfied, Gabrielle took the ice cube and slid it up Chloe's stomach. Chloe sucked a sharp breath through her teeth. This time, once the shock passed, it gave way to a tingling burn that made her heart race and sent shivers through her.

She cleared her mind and let her body relax, leaning into the sensation, keeping her bound wrists raised above her head as Gabrielle had instructed her. When she stopped thinking, let her body take over, obedience came naturally. And soon, the sharp sting of the ice was like a chilly kiss.

Gabrielle drew the ice cube up between Chloe's breasts, circling one nipple with it, then the other. Chloe's chest bucked, tiny rivulets of icy water streaming down breasts, melted by her body heat. Slowly, carefully, Gabrielle skated the ice cube over a pebbled bud. Chloe gasped, pleasure darting deeply into her. It wasn't just her ice-numbed skin that burned now. Every part of her did.

A whimper fell from her lips. She needed Gabrielle. *Now.*

Gabrielle pressed a finger to Chloe's lips. "Don't rush me," she said. "I'm not done having my fun with you yet."

Chloe fell silent. The ice cube now melted down to nothing, Gabrielle took another from the bucket and trailed it along Chloe's stomach, painting a meandering line down it, skating it around her belly button and over her hip bones. From there, she drew it down Chloe's thighs, letting the cold water trickle in between them.

Chloe's legs parted of their own accord. Gabrielle took that as an invitation to skim the ice cube along her inner thighs. Chloe whimpered and shook. The skin on the insides of her thighs was sensitive, but Gabrielle didn't let the ice linger long enough for it to burn her, just long enough to tease her with its icy kiss.

She trembled. How was Gabrielle able to read Chloe's body so well? Was it the same way she'd been able to sense Chloe's submissive desires, the same way she knew how much this torment was driving Chloe wild?

Finally, Gabrielle drew back. "Let's find out what you really taste like."

Chloe bit her lip, the ache in her core deepening. Gabrielle retrieved another ice cube from the bucket and positioned herself between Chloe's knees.

Then, her eyes fixed on Chloe's, she slipped the ice cube between her lips and buried her head between Chloe's thighs.

"Oh!"

Chloe jolted, her head tipping back as Gabrielle's ice-cold tongue met her searing hot folds. A tremor went through her. The sensation was so deliciously unexpected that she almost came there and then.

She closed her eyes. Gabrielle grabbed hold of Chloe's thighs, her fingers digging into her skin. The ice cube held in her mouth, she dragged her tongue up and down Chloe's slit, darting it inside her entrance and swirling it around her clit. Chloe shuddered. Although the ice never touched her, she could feel its chill on Gabrielle's tongue, intensifying the pleasure of her touch.

"That feels... so... good..." Chloe's eyes rolled into the back of her head. She could feel her climax looming, but she was torn between wanting release and wanting to stay suspended in this state of bliss longer, reveling in Gabrielle's sweet torture.

But she didn't have any choice in the matter. Gabrielle had complete control over her. And with every sweep of her tongue, Chloe came more and more undone until she was nothing but a helpless mess of arousal.

"Please," Chloe begged. "Please!"

That one little word set off a spark in Gabrielle. Her grip on Chloe's thighs tightened, her tongue and lips working more frantically. Within seconds, Chloe's pleasure skyrocketed, finally reaching a peak.

A cry flew from her, her back arching and her hips bucking as an orgasm surged through her unrelentingly, rocking her entire body. She clutched onto the pillow above her head with bound hands, riding out her pleasure, until finally it faded and she sank into oblivion.

Chloe stretched out beside Gabrielle on the bed. Her muscles had started working again now, but she still felt like she was off on another plane. The gentle rolling of the boat was heavenly, the silk sheets cool and soft on her sensitized skin.

She couldn't deny that there were advantages to dating someone like Gabrielle. The woman didn't skimp on luxuries. And she didn't skimp on spoiling Chloe in bed either.

Chloe rolled onto her side to face Gabrielle. In her orgasm-addled state, she hadn't considered the other woman's pleasure at all.

She traced her fingers up Gabrielle's arm. "So, can I return the favor?"

"Not tonight." Gabrielle reached up to cradle Chloe's cheek, letting her thumb graze Chloe's lips. "Believe me, you'll get your chance. I'm dying to see what this mouth of yours can do. But I have to give you something to look forward to for next time."

Next time. Was Gabrielle stringing Chloe along, giving her a reason to want to see her again? Because she didn't need to give her a reason. Chloe already wanted so much more of her.

But before that could happen, she had to go on her date with Dana.

Her stomach fluttered. Dana was even more of a mystery to her than Gabrielle had been. And tonight had only increased Chloe's curiosity about her. So Dana was a much stricter Mistress than Gabrielle? That thought alone made Chloe's heart race.

Gabrielle looked at her curiously. "What's going on in that head of yours?"

"Nothing," Chloe said quickly.

"You're a very bad liar, you know that?"

Chloe hesitated. "I was thinking about Dana, actually."

"Were you? And you thought it would bother me, you thinking about her while you're in bed with me?"

Chloe nodded sheepishly.

Gabrielle chuckled. "As much as I enjoy commanding your undivided attention, both in person and in your head, it doesn't bother me when you think about her. In fact, I like it that you're thinking about her. I like it that you're fantasizing about her. I want you to be ours, not just mine. And Dana feels the same way. You have no idea how much we're looking forward to having you, together. When you're ready, that is."

Butterflies flitted in Chloe's stomach. Gabrielle alone was almost too much for her to handle, and that was even before she'd dragged Chloe into bed. But both Gabrielle and Dana, together? Chloe would be entirely helpless.

And she was growing more and more excited about the idea.

Gabrielle seemed to read her mind. "You know, what? Dana is coming back from Berlin early. She'll be home by morning. How about, when I get home, I tell Dana all about tonight, in intimate detail?"

"I…" Chloe found herself getting even hotter at the thought. "I'd like that."

A smile spread across Gabrielle's lips. "I'm going to enjoy making her jealous."

She stretched out her arms, wrapping them around Chloe's shoulders and drawing her in. Silence fell between them. Chloe closed her eyes and rested her head on Gabrielle's chest, relishing her softness and the sweet, floral aroma of her hair.

"Chloe?" Gabrielle said.

"Hm?"

"I know I keep telling you how strict and serious she is, but really, she's soft at heart. So be patient with her."

It took Chloe a moment to realize that Gabrielle was talking about Dana. "I will."

"And whatever you do, don't tell her I said that."

Chloe nodded. Did this break their 'no secrets' rule? She didn't question it. There was something sweet about Gabrielle worrying about her strict Mistress of a girlfriend.

"Speaking of Dana," Gabrielle began, "she told me you're having problems with your truck."

"Right." Chloe had forgotten all about her broken-down truck. In fact, she hadn't thought about any of her problems the entire night. She couldn't remember the last time she'd felt this unburdened.

"Dana said she offered to pay the repair costs, but you turned her down. Why?"

Chloe shrugged. "I don't like owing anyone anything, that's all." It was bad enough that she was letting Dana and Gabrielle take her out on fancy dates. Accepting money from them was a line she wouldn't cross.

"You wouldn't owe us. It would be a gift. I'm with Dana on this one, we're happy to help you."

"I know, but I'd rather sort it out myself." Money, gifts, they always came with strings. Chloe had learned that lesson in her last relationship.

"If you say so."

Chloe studied Gabrielle's face, trying to decipher the strange expression on it. Was she disappointed with Chloe's reaction, or the opposite?

"This is just something I need to solve by myself," she said. "But I appreciate the offer, really. And I appreciate tonight. The boat, dinner, everything."

"Don't forget the mind-blowing sex."

"That too. Thanks for showing me a great time." Chloe let out a contented sigh. It was already past midnight, but she didn't want the night to end. She peered out the window. She couldn't see anything other than a stretch of darkness. "We don't have to go back yet, do we? I have to open my shop in the morning, but not until late since it's a weekend."

"We can stay out here as long as you want. The boat doesn't go back until I say so."

"Maybe a little longer, then."

As Chloe settled back into Gabrielle's warm embrace, she glanced over her shoulder at the empty stretch of bed beside them.

What would it feel like to lie here with Dana beside her too?

CHAPTER 10

Gabrielle returned home early the next morning, two cups of takeaway coffee in hand. She found Dana in the sun-filled sitting room in the back of the house, reading a newspaper. She looked fresh and alert, and not at all as if she'd just stepped off a ten-hour flight.

As Gabrielle entered the room, Dana looked up and placed her newspaper on the coffee table. "You're home."

"Good morning to you too." Gabrielle greeted her with a kiss before handing her a cup of coffee. "How was your trip?"

"Chaotic. The show was one crisis after another, but I managed to keep everything contained behind the scenes. After all that, I decided I'd rather come home and relax than stick around all weekend for the social events. They're always so boring."

Gabrielle took a seat on the couch, stretching out next to her. "I'm sure your absence will only add to the air of mystery surrounding the famous Dana Obi." But something told her that wasn't Dana's real reason for coming home from her trip early.

"Well?" Dana said.

"Well, what?"

"Oh, please. You know exactly what."

Gabrielle shrugged innocently. "I have no idea what you're talking about."

Dana crossed her arms. "Aren't you going to tell me how your date with Chloe went last night?"

"Oh, that? It went well. I took her out on *The Queen Bee*."

Dana's lips curled up in a slight smile. "Let me guess, you gave her a firsthand demonstration of your sailing knots?"

Gabrielle frowned. "Am I really that predictable?"

"Only to me, darling."

"It seems I need some new material. Next time, I suppose. Fun and games aside, we had a wonderful time. We had dinner, got to know each other." Gabrielle paused. "Although, Chloe was a little cagey about certain things. Like her past. She grew up in Minnesota, but when I asked her for more details, she clammed up completely and refused to talk about it."

Dana gave her a concerned look. "Are you worried she's hiding something?"

She of all people understood why Gabrielle might be wary of Chloe keeping secrets. After all, she'd been there throughout Gabrielle's failed engagement. Since then, Dana was the only person Gabrielle had been able to trust. She knew that Dana was with her for her and didn't have any ulterior motives.

But could Chloe's motivations be so pure?

Gabrielle shook her head. She was being paranoid. "I'm sure it's nothing."

Dana frowned. It was obvious that she didn't believe her. Gabrielle wasn't sure she even believed herself.

She changed the subject. "We spoke about her florist shop too. I broached the topic of her truck, extended our offer to help her pay for repairs again, but she turned it down."

"I'm not surprised. She's made it clear that she wants to deal with things herself. At least we know she isn't after our money."

That was true. While Gabrielle was generous in spoiling the women they dated, she was always wary of letting them take advantage of her. Was this proof that she wouldn't have to worry about that with Chloe?

"Still, it's slightly infuriating that she won't let us help her," she said.

"Yes, but we need to respect her decision."

"I know." Gabrielle crossed her arms. "What can I say, I'm not used to being told *no*."

"That's certainly true," Dana murmured.

"What are you implying? I'm not that spoiled brat you met in college anymore, you know."

Dana took a deliberate sip of her coffee. "I'm not implying anything."

Gabrielle plucked the coffee cup from Dana's hand and placed it aside, then leaned in close to her, drawing a hand up Dana's thigh. "Have I ever told you you're a terrible liar?"

Dana shivered slightly in response to her touch, desire sparking behind her eyes.

Nevertheless, Dana kept a straight face. "Have I ever told you you're a terrible tease?" she said.

"More than once. But that's why you love me."

"While that's true, I prefer it when it's someone else you're teasing."

"Someone like Chloe, perhaps?" Gabrielle slid her hand further up Dana's leg. "I know you're looking forward to watching me tease her. It's so easy to make her blush. And I know you're just dying to get a taste of our sweet little florist."

Dana's breath deepened ever so slightly. Over time, Gabrielle had learned how to read all the subtle signs her girlfriend gave off. And the meaning of this sign was very obvious.

Gabrielle slipped her hand inward, her fingertips grazing Dana's inner thigh. "Do you know what I told Chloe last night? I told her that when I got home, I was going to describe every single intimate detail of our night. Do you want to hear about it?"

That was all it took for Dana to crack. She took Gabrielle's wrist and pinned it to the couch beside her, looking back at her with simmering eyes.

"Tell me *everything*."

Gabrielle let out a satisfied murmur. "Yes, *Mistress*." Although Dana would never admit it, it was just as easy to pull her strings as it was to pull Chloe's.

As she whispered her recount of her night with Chloe in the master bedroom of *The Queen Bee*, everything she'd felt for Chloe came flooding back. Gabrielle wanted her far more than she'd ever wanted any of the other women they'd invited into their bed, their life. Could Chloe be who they were looking for?

And more importantly, could they trust her?

The bell above the door of Chloe's shop jingled. Abandoning the flowers she was trimming, she left the back room, taking her place behind the counter as a customer approached. She was a young woman, probably still in her teens, dressed in jeans and sneakers. She wasn't Chloe's usual kind of customer.

"What can I do for you?" Chloe asked.

The girl shoved her hands in her pockets, her eyes darting around the shop. "I want to buy some flowers."

"I can help with that. What are the flowers for?"

"A birthday." The young woman hesitated. "My girl-friend's birthday."

Chloe gave her a warm smile. "That's great. Do you know what kind of flowers she likes?"

The girl looked visibly relieved for a moment, but then her shoulders slumped. "I don't know. I don't know what I'm doing. We've only been dating for a couple of months, and she's my first girlfriend, and I've never bought a girl flowers before. I'm not good at this stuff."

"Lucky for you, I'm very good at this stuff. I can help you out. Why don't you tell me a little about your girlfriend? What kind of person she is, what she likes? Then I'll help you pick out something she'll really love."

The young woman gave her a nervous smile and began telling Chloe all about her girlfriend. She seemed grateful for the help. Chloe was just happy to have any customers at all. With her truck broken down, she'd had to temporarily halt deliveries, which meant she was losing money. She'd need to come up with a solution soon. She was almost considering accepting Dana and Gabrielle's offer of help.

Almost.

When the young woman was finished, Chloe gave her a reassuring nod. "I know just the thing for her."

Armed with knowledge about the young woman's girl-friend, she made a loop around her shop, grabbing handfuls of flowers. Roses, but not red ones. Pink and white. Some lilies, disbuds, a sprinkling of foliage and greenery. And, as always, orange blossoms, a wish for everlasting love.

As Chloe put the bouquet together, she couldn't help but wonder what the young woman's relationship was like. She always did when customers bought flowers for partners and lovers. Was their relationship a strong one? Were they happy together?

And, like always, she wondered—would it last?

Finally, Chloe finished assembling the bouquet. She wrapped it in paper and tied it up with a red ribbon.

"Here you go." Chloe handed the bouquet to the young woman. "Your girlfriend is going to love these, I promise."

The girl murmured a thank you, then paid for the bouquet, which Chloe gave her a heavy discount for. Considering how badly her shop was doing, it wasn't the smartest move, but she couldn't help herself. For some reason, she'd found herself rooting for the young woman and her girlfriend.

What was happening to her? It was true what she'd said to Gabrielle about being a lapsed romantic. She wanted to believe in love, but life had taught her that love of all kinds came with strings attached. She'd learned that as a child. And she'd learned it again as an adult.

So why did she still cling to the hope that she would one day find the love she'd always yearned for? True love, unconditional and eternal. Someone she belonged with, someone she could call family, someone who loved her for her.

Or maybe, not just some*one*.

She leaned down on the counter and sighed. Was it crazy to fantasize about that, about the idea of something real with Dana and Gabrielle? This infatuation was so unlike her. She still had the flowers they'd given her, sitting on the coffee table in her apartment. It had been more than a week now, and they were beginning to wilt and die. She'd need to throw them out soon, but a part of her was reluctant to let them go.

She needed to get a hold of herself. She'd only been on one date, and that had just been with Gabrielle.

But what an amazing date it had been.

She felt a pang of guilt. She'd lied to Gabrielle that night when she'd asked Chloe about her past, her family. She wasn't really from Minnesota, although she'd gone there often as a child, visiting relatives. It was why she'd chosen to pretend she'd grown up there. But she hadn't expected Gabrielle to be familiar with the area, to ask her for details.

And it was true that her father was dead, but as far as Chloe knew, her mother was still alive back in Los Angeles. At least, she had been when Chloe walked out of their home for the last time all those years ago. Chloe's mother was no longer a part of her life. Chloe had left her in the past, along with her old identity.

She wasn't really lying to Gabrielle. The lies she'd told her were the same lies she told everyone else, including herself.

Her phone vibrated in her apron pocket. She took it out. Her heart sped up. It was a text message from Dana.

It's my turn. Saturday night, 7 p.m. I'll pick you up. Dress for a night out.

As Chloe reread the message, she felt a stirring deep inside. Unlike Gabrielle, Dana hadn't called her to set up their date. She'd simply sent Chloe instructions. Was she so deep under Dana's spell that such a simple command left her just as weak at the knees as Gabrielle tying her up had?

As she composed a reply to Dana's message, her phone began to ring. Chloe didn't recognize the number flashing on the screen. Was it one of her suppliers reminding her of an overdue bill?

She took the call. "Hello?"

"Hello, Chloe."

Chloe's stomach dropped. She knew that voice. It wasn't one of Chloe's suppliers, but it *was* someone Chloe owed a debt to.

Tracy. Her ex-girlfriend.

Chloe swallowed. "Tracy. Hi."

"Let's skip the small talk," Tracy said coldly. "You've missed your last two payments."

"I know. I'm a little short on money right now." Chloe had managed to keep up with her payments since the day they'd ended their relationship, so they'd rarely had to speak to each other. However, she'd fallen behind in recent months, so Tracy had started sending her messages and calling her constantly, then Chloe had started ignoring her. It explained why Tracy was calling her from an unfamiliar number.

"I'll pay you when I can, I swear," Chloe said. "But right now, I just don't have the money. My florist shop isn't doing great."

"If it wasn't for me, that florist shop of yours wouldn't even be standing."

Chloe cursed internally. She hated that Tracy was right. The money Chloe had gained access to when she'd turned eighteen had been enough for her to support herself after she'd left home, enough to eventually put her through floristry school. What was left at that point had covered most of her florist shop's startup costs, but some unexpected expenses meant she'd come up short in the end. Tracy had given her the funds she'd needed to get her shop up and running.

"I said that I'd pay you, and I will," Chloe said. "Just as soon as I get the money. Things are really tight right now. I've been having problems with my truck and I need to get it fixed, but I can't even afford that."

"I don't want to hear excuses," Tracy said. "We had an agreement. You lost the right to leniency when you decided you were done using me."

Chloe scowled, irritation boiling inside her. "That's not fair and you know it. I never used you. The money you gave me, that was supposed to be a gift."

"I'm not talking about the money. Who was it that found you when you were all alone? Who took you in, took care of you, provided you with a home? Who gave you a shoulder to cry on whenever you needed it?"

"I—"

"Who promised to keep your secrets, to play along with this silly fake identity of yours?"

Chloe felt a sharp stabbing in her chest. She ignored it. This was what Tracy did. She manipulated her, belittled her into compliance.

She wasn't putting up with it any longer.

"Look," she said. "I don't have your money, but as soon as I do, I'll pay you what I owe. Right now, I need to go. I have work to do."

Before Tracy could respond, Chloe hung up the phone.

She let out a long, slow breath. Her pulse was racing. Thankfully, there weren't any customers in the store, because she needed a moment to pull herself together.

She took a few more deep breaths. Why did this always happen? Why was it that whenever she started to feel like things weren't so bad, like something good was within her grasp, something else would always come up to remind her that life wasn't a fairy tale?

She glanced at her phone. She hadn't replied to Dana's message yet. She finished typing out her confirmation for Saturday night and pressed send.

But her excitement about the date was muted now. With her truck broken down, her ex-girlfriend dogging her, and the threat of losing her florist shop looming, it was hard to not be wary of getting sucked into Dana and Gabrielle's world of money and power games. Because inevitably, the two would intertwine.

CHAPTER 11

D ana pulled up in front of Chloe's apartment just in time to see her emerge from the building. She got out of the convertible, opening the passenger side door as she greeted her.

Chloe slid gracefully into the seat. Dana shut the door and rounded the car, taking her place in the driver's seat.

"This is a gorgeous car," Chloe said. "Is it vintage?"

Dana nodded. "There are very few of them left in the world. It usually sits in my garage collecting dust, but I thought I'd take it for a spin tonight." The convertible, a classic BMW 507 roadster, was the jewel of her collection. It was far too valuable to drive regularly, but tonight warranted something exceptional.

Chloe reached out, running a hand gingerly along the leather dash. Dana found her eyes drawn to her, to Chloe's delicate fingers, up her bare arm, all the way back to her body. She was dressed in a black sleeveless blouse and a knee-length floral print skirt that emphasized her waist and full hips. She always wore outfits that subtly showed off her best features, but her carefree manner made Dana wonder if it was intentional or not.

"You look lovely tonight," Dana said.

Chloe pulled her arm back, blushing self-consciously. "So do you." Her eyes flicked down to take in Dana's outfit, a casual, feminine-cut pantsuit she'd paired with heels and a lace blouse. "Is that outfit from your label?"

"I designed it, but not for my label. I made it for myself. Now, are you ready to go?"

Chloe nodded.

"Seatbelt on," Dana said.

They fastened their seatbelts. As Dana pulled out from the curb, Chloe spoke again.

"So, you're into cars?"

Dana nodded. "They're not as impressive as Gabrielle's boats, but they're much more practical. I have quite a few, some for everyday, and some as collector's items. This is the latter, but I decided tonight was a special enough occasion."

"It's definitely impressive," Chloe said. "So, what is the occasion? Where are we going, all dressed up like this?"

"Have you ever been to the ballet?"

Chloe shook her head. "I took lessons as a kid for a while, but that's all. I was terrible at it, but I liked it."

"Then you'll enjoy yourself tonight. There's a certain artistry in ballet, which I'm sure you'll appreciate, being artistic yourself."

"I wouldn't consider myself artistic."

"Floristry is an art, is it not? It's all about color, pattern, movement, composition?"

"Well, yeah." Chloe paused in thought. "I've just never looked at it that way."

They stopped at a stoplight, the car drawing stares from nearby pedestrians. Dana was used to it. Chloe didn't even seem to notice.

"Floristry is an art when *you* do it, at least," Dana said, speeding off as the light turned green. "When I said to you at the gala that you have an excellent eye, it wasn't just flattery. Your arrangements, there's a real beauty in them, equal to any painting or sculpture. Anyone can see that if they take the time to look." She stole a glance at Chloe. "There's art all around us, beauty everywhere. Sometimes it's right before our eyes."

"Well, the same can be said of the clothes you design," Chloe said. "They're beautiful."

"You're familiar with my label?"

"Of course. I looked you up after the gala. When you told me your name and said you were a fashion designer, I wasn't expecting you to be *that* Dana. I had no idea who I was talking to."

"That was intentional," Dana said. "When people know who I am, they treat me differently. I don't want fame. I don't want the spotlight. I want my designs to speak for themselves. And I'm a very private person. I prefer to live a normal, unremarkable life."

"I understand that. I've had a brush with fame before. It isn't something I'd like to experience again."

There was an unexpected heaviness in Chloe's voice. Just what kind of 'brush with fame' had she had?

But before Dana could ask, Chloe changed the subject. "Why did you decide to become a fashion designer? Gabrielle said you were an engineering student in college."

"I was, briefly. I dropped out at the end of freshman year

so I could go to fashion school. I've always been drawn to creative pursuits. I've always longed to express the beauty I see in the world as art." Dana had felt that way ever since she was a child, but her upbringing had discouraged her from pursuing her creative side, so her road to following her passion had been a long one. "I suppose what attracted me to fashion was the opportunity to design something beautiful that's living, breathing. Something people can wear to express their inner selves."

"I understand that," Chloe said. "It's kind of why I like my job too."

Dana questioned her further about her work, leading to Chloe chattering away about her flowers. It was easy to see why Gabrielle had been drawn to her after meeting her in her florist shop, why she'd been so determined to chase after her despite everything. There was something magnetic about her. That carefree radiance. Those coy looks. Those delectably sexy smiles. And she somehow seemed oblivious to the fact that her every word, her every action, was irresistible.

Chloe looked at Dana, trailing off mid-sentence. "I'm talking too much, aren't I? I get carried away sometimes when it comes to my job."

"You're not. I like hearing you talk about your passions." Dana slowed the car as they approached their destination. "But the rest of our conversation will have to wait. We're here."

Dana gestured into the opera box. "This is us. After you."

Chloe slipped past Dana and into the box, taking a seat. She peered down over the railing. They were high up at the back of the theater, giving the perfect view of the stage along with the rest of the seats below.

Dana sat down beside her. "I chose a box so we could have some privacy. We don't have to worry about anyone overhearing us up here."

Overhearing them? What was Dana suggesting? While she was far more reserved about her desire for Chloe than Gabrielle was, those dark eyes of hers, the way she looked at her, spoke far more than words ever could.

Dana raised an eyebrow. "What I mean is this way I can talk you through everything without disturbing anyone else. You said you've never watched a ballet before. They can be difficult to follow, especially a production as unusual as this one. What did you think I was talking about?"

"Nothing," Chloe said quickly.

A faint smile crossed Dana's lips. "Gabrielle was right. It *is* easy to make you blush."

That only made Chloe's cheeks burn even more.

"As I was saying, we're witnessing something very special tonight," Dana continued. "The principal dancer is a guest from London. She came out of retirement just for this production."

Before Dana could explain further, they were interrupted by the arrival of a waiter offering them a choice of refreshments.

"How about some champagne?" Dana said. "Don't worry, I intend to drink it out of a glass."

Chloe grew hot all over. How much had Gabrielle told

Dana about that night on the boat? "Sure," she stammered. "That would be great."

The waiter poured them each a glass of champagne. Dana sampled hers before thanking the waiter and giving him a generous tip.

As soon as he was out of earshot, Dana leaned in closer to Chloe, the sweet scent of her perfume filling Chloe's head.

"Oh yes," she said, her voice low. "Gabrielle told me all about that night you spent together. She told me every naughty little detail."

Chloe shifted in her seat, glancing around them. While she'd given Gabrielle permission to tell Dana everything, she hadn't expected that Dana would bring it up so casually. There was something erotic about how Dana spoke the most suggestive of statements as if they were simple facts.

"It sounds like the two of you had quite the night," Dana continued. "But you should know, Gabrielle and I are very different. I have no patience for games. And I expect any submissive of mine to be unquestionably obedient and disciplined."

Dana's words alone were enough to send Chloe's imagination racing, along with her pulse. And when the lights around them dimmed, her heart sped up even faster.

"Hold that thought," Dana said quietly. "The show is about to begin. I want to give you a rundown on the story before the first act starts."

Dana whispered into Chloe's ear, describing the story of the ballet to her. At the same time, the music rose and the prologue began, and a lone dancer, a woman, appeared on the stage. Chloe listened and watched, entranced by the sensuality in Dana's voice and the hypnotic movements of the dancer on stage. From Dana's words, she managed to gather that the ballet was a romance, a tragic story of forbidden love between a young man and a princess.

"That's the traditional version of the story," Dana said. "But this production is… different."

She didn't elaborate. As the show moved on to the first act, the woman was joined on stage by her lover as they met for the very first time. But her lover wasn't a man, like in the story Dana had described.

The dancer, the lover, was undeniably female.

Chloe peered at Dana out of the corner of her eye, but she hadn't reacted at all to the turn of events.

"I told you it was different." She cocked her head toward the stage. "Pay close attention. You don't want to miss anything."

Chloe turned back to the stage obediently. Dana's bossiness should have bothered her, but it didn't.

Dana leaned in close to her, speaking softly into her ear once again. "Watch them. See how they move, both individually and together. Watch the push and pull between them, the way their bodies react to each other."

Chloe exhaled slowly, her eyes fixed in front of her. She and Dana hadn't so much as touched the whole night. But Dana's voice, the whisper of her breath on Chloe's neck, the heat of her body and her very presence—it made Chloe's skin shiver and tingle as if Dana were touching her, caressing her with her soft, slender fingers.

"It's almost erotic, isn't it?" Dana said softly. "The way they move as one?"

"Yes," Chloe whispered. She stole a glance at Dana.

Didn't she feel the tension lingering in the air between them, like a thick fog? Didn't she feel the need to dispel it?

But Dana kept her gaze locked on the dancers on the stage. "Watch," she said. "Listen. Feel."

Chloe obeyed, immersing herself in the story playing out on stage. The sensuality of it all, of the dancers' movements, the way they touched each other, did little to stem the desire within her.

The next hour passed like this, with Chloe suspended in a state of awe, her every sense aroused. The intermission came and went, and the show moved on to the second half.

Finally, the story reached a climax, ending in a bitter-sweet goodbye. But the tragic ending did nothing to dull the impact of the performance. Even as the curtain fell, Chloe found herself as spellbound by it as she was by Dana herself.

As the lights turned back on, they remained in their seats, waiting for the crowds to disperse. Chloe fanned herself with the program. She was unseasonably warm. She needed some air.

"Let's get out of here," Dana said. "Go somewhere quiet. There's an excellent wine bar nearby."

Chloe nodded. "Sure."

They joined the last of the stragglers filing out of the hall, making their way to the foyer.

"What did you think of the performance?" Dana asked.

"I loved it," Chloe said. "I don't know much about ballet, but there was something enchanting about it. It was beautiful."

"It truly was. It isn't easy to adapt a classical ballet with two female leads. It's very complex technically, and the principals pulled it off wonderfully. And the choreography, there was a sensuality to it not usually found in classical ballets. I found it refreshing, honest. Humans are passionate beings. Lust is as much a part of a new romance as love is, don't you think?"

Chloe nodded. For Chloe, when it came to romance, love didn't come easily. Lust, on the other hand, that instant, immediate, irresistible attraction? She already felt that. She'd felt it the moment she first laid eyes on Dana.

"You know what?" Dana said. "Let's skip the bar and go somewhere… quieter."

"Do you have somewhere in mind?" Chloe asked.

"I do. And there's something I want to show you. Something I've been working on."

Working on? "What do you—"

"Cassidy?"

Chloe's stomach sank. She froze in place, resisting the reflex to turn toward the sound. Who was calling to her, and by that name? It wasn't a voice she recognized.

"Cassidy? Is that you?"

This time, the voice was right beside her. She couldn't ignore it. And Dana was looking at her curiously. She had to do something.

She turned to see a woman around her age, dressed in the uniform of the theater's ushers. Her face was familiar, but Chloe couldn't place it. If the woman was calling her by her old name, she had to be someone from her past.

And Chloe wanted nothing to do with that past.

The woman smiled. "I knew it was you. Don't you remember me?"

Chloe pushed down the panic rising within her. "I'm sorry, do I know you?"

"It's Rachel, from high school. LA Arts, remember?"

Chloe stifled a curse. That was why the woman seemed familiar.

Chloe gave her a confused look. "I think you've mistaken me for someone else. My name isn't Cassidy. I've never even been to LA."

The woman frowned. "But I was sure you were her. You look just like her..." She scrutinized Chloe's face for a second, then shook her head. "You're right. I must be mistaken. Sorry for bothering you."

Chloe pressed her lips together, saying nothing. The woman gave her one last up-and-down look before walking away.

Chloe let out a breath. That was a close call.

"That was strange," Dana said beside her.

"Yeah." Chloe shrugged, trying to look nonchalant. "Maybe I have a lookalike out there." She couldn't tell if Dana was suspicious or not. She needed to change the subject. "What was it you were saying before?"

"Ah, yes. As I was saying, how about we go somewhere more private?"

"Sure." Chloe's hand wandered up to her head to twist a stray lock of hair. "What did you have in mind?"

Dana smiled. "How would you like to see my studio?"

CHAPTER 12

I t was only a short drive to Dana's studio, but for Chloe, time seemed to stretch on and on. She was a mess of nerves, her anxiety over running into someone from her past mixing with the butterflies forming in her stomach at the prospect of being alone with Dana.

They reached the building and rode the elevator up to the top floor. As soon as they stepped out of it, it was obvious why Dana had chosen this space for her studio. It was wide open and spacious, full of desks littered with patterns and sketches, fabric and sewing machines. Dozens of dressmaker's mannequins were lined up next to the floor-to-ceiling windows at the side of the room.

"This place must look amazing during the daytime," Chloe said. This high up, with no other buildings around to block the sun, the entire room would be filled with light.

"It does," Dana said. "When it comes to working with color and texture, nothing compares to natural lighting."

As Chloe wandered further into the room, her eyes were drawn to the large sign on the wall. It had a single word

ANNA STONE

written on it in bold script—*Obi*. Chloe knew the story of Dana's label from when she'd looked her up after the gala. Dana had started Obi before she'd even finished fashion school. Her luxury designs had been a runaway hit and her label had taken off, growing into an internationally renowned brand. If there was anyone whose success and wealth could rival Gabrielle's, it was Dana.

Chloe walked over to the windows, examining the half-dressed mannequins arranged before them. She could see Dana's signature in all the garments, a kind of minimalistic richness with subtle elements that were surprising and unexpected. A touch of color on an otherwise monochrome coat. An asymmetrically cut skirt. A sleek black and white dress made of intricately patterned fabric. Everything was somehow bold and understated at the same time, and undeniably elegant, just like Dana herself.

"What do you think?" Dana asked.

"They're stunning," Chloe said. "Not that I know anything about fashion."

"You don't need to know anything about fashion to appreciate it. It's all about how it makes you feel."

Chloe peered at Dana out of the corner of her eye. It was interesting how whenever Dana talked about art, or her work, her serious, restrained countenance seemed to slip, her passion revealed in her eyes and words.

"Are all these going to end up on a runway in Paris?" Chloe asked.

"Perhaps. Only a selection of the pieces I design end up in my final collections." Dana brushed the sleeve of the patterned dress, smoothing out a crease before turning back to Chloe. "There's something I want to show you. Come."

Dana put her hand on Chloe's arm, sending goosebumps tingling along her skin. Dana drew her away from the mannequins, leading her to an open door at the far end of the room.

"This is my office," Dana said. "I rarely use it unless I feel the need for some privacy."

They stepped through the doorway. As Dana shut the door behind her, Chloe suddenly realized how alone she and Dana were. They'd been alone the entire time, but here in Dana's office, it was even more apparent. While the room was large and the floor-to-ceiling windows gave a view of the city beyond, Dana's commanding presence made Chloe feel like they were crammed in a closet together.

Dana took her hand, sending electricity shooting through her, and drew her further into the room. "I've been working on something different. Something less... restrained than my usual pieces. I started it the day I went to see you in your shop, which makes it fitting that you're the first to lay eyes on it."

She gestured toward a mannequin in the corner. It was dressed in a bell-shaped skirt made from layers of overlapping fabric in various shades of purples and blues. It didn't look anything like Dana's usual designs, but it was just as exquisite.

As Chloe examined the skirt, it came together in her mind. "It looks like it's made of petals. Flower petals." It was subtle, but the resemblance was there.

Dana ran her hand down the side of the skirt adoringly. "So you can see where my inspiration came from. *Who* my inspiration came from." She turned to Chloe, her eyes alight with passion. "I haven't had a chance to see it on anyone other than the mannequin. Would you like to do the honors?"

Chloe nodded slowly. "I'd love that." How could she say no to the chance to try on something so beautiful? How could she say no to Dana, even if she wanted to?

Dana unzipped the skirt, stripped it from the mannequin and held it out to her. "Here. Try it on."

Chloe took the skirt from her reverently. Dana turned around, her eyes fixed ahead of her. Why was she being proper right now, when she had Chloe all alone in her office, under her spell?

She slipped out of her skirt, then stepped into the one Dana had given her, zipping it up at the side. It fit perfectly, like it was made for her. It was cut to fit snugly around her waist before flaring out over her hips and thighs, flowing down her legs and ending just below her knees.

Stealing a glance at Dana to make sure she was still facing away, Chloe twirled around, watching as the skirt flowed and rippled like petals in the wind. Every time she moved, its color seemed to shift.

"Are you done?" Dana asked.

Chloe stopped. "Yes. I'm ready."

Dana turned to face her. Her eyes fell to the skirt, inspecting it intently. She took a step closer and reached out for it before stopping herself. "May I?"

Chloe nodded. Dana took the waistband of the skirt, adjusting it so it fell more neatly, then ran her hands down Chloe's hips, smoothing out the creases in the fabric. Heat rose to Chloe's skin. Could Dana feel how warm she was? Could she feel the tremors going through Chloe as she touched her? Could she hear Chloe's pulse pounding?

Could she feel how much Chloe wanted her?

Finally, Dana straightened out and took a step back, inspecting her again. But this time, it wasn't the skirt she was looking at.

"Just as I thought," she said. "A perfect fit. And you're the perfect model."

Her gaze locked with Chloe's. Her eyes, they simmered, on the verge of boiling over. Chloe's heart skipped a beat, the flame of lust growing inside her with every moment that passed.

"Do you like it?" Dana asked.

Chloe nodded. "It's beautiful. It's like a work of art."

Dana stepped in close. "*You* are beautiful. You're the inspiration for this piece of art."

Chloe's breath caught. She stared up at the taller woman, mesmerized. Her dark eyes, her scarlet lips, her flawless brown skin—every part of her was tantalizing, inviting Chloe's admiration.

Dana reached out to her again, this time drawing her fingers up the side of Chloe's neck ever so slowly.

Chloe quivered.

Dana tipped Chloe's chin up toward her. "I've spent the entire night waiting to do this."

Not a heartbeat later, Dana's lips crashed against hers, a blistering kiss that sent need surging through her body. Chloe closed her eyes, dizzied by the other woman's heady scent, overcome by the taste of her lips, overpowered by her desire.

A murmur spilled from her as she fought to keep herself from crumbling under the intensity of Dana's kiss. This only seemed to invigorate her. She backed Chloe toward the desk in the center of the room, pinning her against it, and slid her hand up the nape of Chloe's neck, pulling her closer, kissing her harder. Chloe grabbed onto the edge of the desktop, holding on as shock waves rolled through her. With her other hand, she clung to the front of Dana's blazer, trying to urge her on with what little control of her body she still had.

Dana trailed her hand down the front of Chloe's chest, skimming it over her breasts. Chloe arched into her touch, her nipples hardening inside the cups of her bra. Dana pulled at the top of Chloe's blouse, tugging it down—

Dana drew back. She was looking down at Chloe's bra. "You wore red again."

Chloe's cheeks grew warm under Dana's gaze. After Gabrielle's reaction the other night, she hadn't been able to help herself.

"While I appreciate the attempt to please me, you should know that I'm not as easily seduced as Gabrielle is. Like I said, I don't play games. And I have far higher expectations of my submissive." Dana traced her fingers over the lace cup of Chloe's bra. "I expect her to obey without the need for restraints, for discipline. I expect her to give over control willingly."

Chloe trembled, her knees threatening to give out from under her. At that moment, she would have given Dana whatever she asked of her, whatever she wanted.

Dana leaned in, her lips brushing Chloe's ear. "I expect her to be the perfect pet, deferring to me in every manner possible, willingly submitting every part of herself to me." She swept her hands down Chloe's front, down past her waist, caressing her hips and thighs through the skirt. "And that includes her body."

Chloe's breath deepened. Was Dana relishing having her adorned in something of hers, having Chloe as her model? Because Chloe was. She longed to be the perfect pet that Dana wanted.

"Tell me," Dana said. "Are you that kind of woman, the kind who craves that sweet surrender?"

"Yes, Mistress," Chloe whispered.

A smile spread across Dana's lips. "Oh, I'm so looking forward to having a woman like you as mine. And I see now why Gabrielle was so convinced I'd like this sweet florist of hers." Dana pressed her body harder against Chloe's, her thigh pushing between Chloe's legs. "You're not really sweet at all, are you?"

Chloe's mouth fell open in a silent moan. She rocked back against her, stoking the fire raging deep in her core. Her skin felt flushed, and the desktop dug into the back of her thighs, but she was too overcome with need to care.

Still pressing her leg between Chloe's thighs, Dana kissed down the side of her neck, sending shivers down her shoulders and back. Chloe glanced out the floor-to-ceiling windows beside them. They were dozens of floors up, but she couldn't help but feel like they were exposed, like any minute someone could walk by and see them. Why did the thought only make her even hotter?

She reached for Dana, drawing her hands down the woman's shoulders, letting them wander down to her chest. As her hand lingered on Dana's breast, Dana took hold of Chloe's wrist and pulled it away.

"No touching," she said firmly. "Not *that* kind of touching. Not unless I give you permission."

Chloe nodded. Dana didn't have to explain herself further. Considering Chloe's inclination toward women who liked to take control, this wasn't the first time she'd encountered someone with touch-me-not leanings. But she couldn't help but wonder if there was a reason why Dana didn't like to be touched in that way. Was it just the way she was? Was it about control for her? Something deeper?

And more importantly, was it a hard limit, or a soft one?

"Is this going to be a problem?" Dana asked.

Chloe shook her head. "No."

Dana hesitated, her stony façade dropping for just a moment. "Perhaps if you prove you can be a good submissive, you'll one day earn the right to touch your Mistress."

Relief swelled inside Chloe. Although she'd told Dana that not touching her wasn't a problem, the thought of never, ever being able to touch her was almost unbearable.

So what did it take to 'earn' the right to touch her?

"Until then, it's hands off," Dana said. "Do you understand?"

Chloe nodded. If that was what Dana wanted, that was what she would get. Chloe's desire was to serve, to satisfy her Mistress. And Dana seemed like the kind of woman who found satisfaction in the simple act of having Chloe on her knees.

"Now, where were we?" Gazing down into Chloe's eyes, Dana dragged her hand up the front of Chloe's thigh. "Here's another difference between me and Gabrielle. While she likes to play with her food, I do not. I prefer to get straight to the point."

She took the hem of Chloe's skirt and drew it up around her waist. Chloe's lips parted, a soft breath of air escaping from them. She closed her eyes, trying her hardest not to dissolve into the desk behind her.

Then, Dana slipped her hand inside Chloe's panties.

Chloe's mouth fell open, her head tipping back. A short, sharp gasp rose from her chest as Dana's fingertips grazed her swollen clit. She was already dripping wet. And when Dana began sliding her fingers up and down Chloe's slit in long, slow strokes, she fell apart completely.

Dana rolled a fingertip over Chloe's entrance. Chloe let out a begging groan. She needed Dana inside her.

"Apparently, you prefer me to get straight to the point too," Dana said. "Is that what you want? Me to fuck you, right here and now?"

Chloe nodded frantically. "Yes, Mistress."

Dana withdrew her hand from Chloe's panties. A moment later, they were at Chloe's hips, ripping her panties down. Chloe disentangled them from her ankles and nudged them aside. They disappeared somewhere under the desk, but retrieving them was the last thing Chloe was thinking about.

Dana reached up and brushed Chloe's hair back over her shoulders, letting her hand trail down her neck and chest. Chloe exhaled slowly, her skin sizzling where Dana had touched her.

"One more thing," Dana said. "You will ask me before you come. If you come without my permission, I'll be very disappointed."

"Yes, Mistress," Chloe replied, breathless. How quickly she had fallen into the mindset of thinking of Dana as her

Mistress to please. While Gabrielle had her panting and begging, with Dana, Chloe longed to be on her knees.

What would it feel like to experience both at the same time?

The thought only made the throbbing between her legs even stronger. She let out a murmur of desperation. It had only been minutes since they'd entered the room, but it felt like so much longer. Every moment Dana wasn't touching her was infinite, every second that passed excruciating.

Mercifully, Dana didn't make her wait any longer. She snaked her hand down to where Chloe's thighs met and slipped her fingers inside her, unhesitating. Chloe grabbed hold of the edge of the desk, gasping for air as Dana plunged her fingers deeper.

She leaned in close, speaking into Chloe's ear. "Gabrielle told me how sweet you sound when you come. I've been dying to hear it for myself."

A moan fell from Chloe's lips. Dana cut it off with a firm, insistent kiss. At the same time, she began pumping her fingers slowly, the heel of her palm rolling against Chloe's swollen bud. Chloe quivered. Dana's touch was so exquisite. She was already close to coming.

Abruptly, Dana withdrew. She seized Chloe's chin, gripping it firmly between her thumb and forefinger, looking hard into her eyes.

"You weren't about to come, were you?"

Chloe's heart thumped. She shook her head, her fingers clenching the desktop harder, trying to suppress her growing arousal.

"You know the rules. You only get to come when I say so."

Chloe nodded.

Dana pressed her harder against the desk, pushing her back to sit on the edge of it, then eased her fingers into her again. This time, she didn't start slow. She thrust inside her, unrelenting, stroking so fast and deep that Chloe feared she was going to combust.

She screwed her eyes shut and grabbed onto Dana's shoulders, her arms hooked behind them, burying her face in Dana's neck. Her knees clenched at Dana's hips, her body beginning to tremble as the flame in her core swelled and flared.

She whimpered. She was so close!

"Go on," Dana whispered, her lips brushing the side of Chloe's cheek. "Come for me."

At once, an eruption went off deep within her. She threw her head back, her arms and knees locking around Dana's waist, ecstasy flooding her body. It was almost too much for her to handle—too much pleasure, too much of Dana. But Dana didn't stop. She didn't stop moving her fingers inside her, didn't stop kissing her.

She didn't stop until she'd coaxed every last drop of pleasure from Chloe's body.

CHAPTER 13

As Chloe got dressed, Dana returned the skirt to the mannequin in the corner. It looked a little worse for wear, but it was only a sample. Like always, Dana would remake it again and again until it was perfect.

Once she was done, she found Chloe sitting on the side of the desk, trying to fix her mussed-up hair. As she noticed Dana watching her, she got up from it, self-conscious.

"Don't get up." Dana joined Chloe at her desk and sat on the edge of it, patting the space beside her. "Sit."

Chloe did as she was told. Dana wrapped an arm around her, drawing her close. Chloe sank into her and let out a long, slow sigh. Dana found herself relaxing too, her body loosening. Sex always had that effect on her.

"I was wondering," Chloe murmured. "Are you going to tell Gabrielle all about tonight?"

"That depends," Dana said. "Do you want me to?"

"I think so. I think... I'm warming up to the idea of trying this. All three of us. Together."

She lowered her gaze before stealing a glance at Dana.

Dana couldn't help but smile. Considering Chloe had just had a room-shaking orgasm on Dana's desk, her sudden shyness was as unexpected as it was endearing.

Dana gave her a reassuring kiss on the forehead. "I'm glad to hear that. And I know Gabrielle will be glad to hear it too. We're looking forward to having you all to ourselves, together. When you're ready."

Chloe nodded, seemingly ruminating on Dana's words.

"Remember, there's no rush," Dana added. "Just take your time. We'll be here." She paused. "And when that time comes, there's something I want you to keep in mind. It's about Gabrielle."

"What is it?" Chloe asked.

"Just be gentle with her. She acts as if nothing fazes her, like she doesn't care about anything or anyone, but she has a sensitive heart. Do not tell her I said that."

Chloe smiled. "Okay. I won't."

Dana narrowed her eyes. "Why are you smiling?"

"No reason. It's just that you two are far more alike than I thought." Chloe snuggled closer, resting her head on Dana's shoulder. "About you and Gabrielle... how did you end up together?"

"Gabrielle didn't tell you already?"

"She did. But I want to hear it from you too."

"It isn't particularly interesting. We met in college. We were roommates in our freshman year. I'm sure she told you we didn't get along at first?"

Chloe nodded.

"It was mutual. I was overly studious in my younger days, and I wasn't happy about getting stuck with a spoiled party girl as a roommate. But I'm sure I was more insufferable than her. I used to get angry at her every time she came back to the dorm late at night, even on weekends. And thank god we had separate bedrooms because she used to bring a different girl home every night, which I found entirely scandalous at the time." Dana couldn't help but laugh to herself when she thought about that now. "But eventually, we became good friends, became family, even before we started a relationship."

"So the two of you have been close for a long time."

"We have. We went through a lot together over the years. At one point she was all I had. My relationship with my own family was rocky, and when they turned their backs on me, Gabrielle was there."

"I'm sorry. About your family, that is."

"It's all in the past now," Dana said dismissively. "Besides, we reconnected recently. Things are still shaky between us, but that's to be expected, given everything that happened."

"What happened with them?"

"That's a long story," Dana said.

Chloe glanced up at her. "Sorry, I'm being nosy. I shouldn't have asked."

Dana said nothing. She'd already shared far more than she'd meant to. She wasn't the type to pour her heart out to anyone, let alone the women she and Gabrielle dated. There was no point in forming any kind of personal attachment to someone who would inevitably leave.

And yet, she felt compelled to open up to Chloe.

"Where to begin?" Dana leaned back, resting her hands on the desk behind her. "Growing up, my parents had high expectations of me. My mother is a doctor, and my father is a lawyer. They're Nigerian immigrants, and very strict and stereotypical at that. To my parents, the only acceptable career choices for their children were lawyer, doctor, or engineer. Pursuing a career in a creative field was never an option for me growing up.

"I reluctantly chose engineering, but my desire to be creative wasn't something I could suppress. College made me miserable, and so did the idea of spending my life doing something I hated. It was Gabrielle who made me realize that. Once we stopped fighting long enough to properly get to know each other, we quickly came to understand one another. She saw how unhappy I was, and she encouraged me to follow my passion."

That side of Gabrielle, the kind-hearted, thoughtful side, was one that few people ever got to see. It was exactly why Dana had fallen in love with her in the first place. "But when I told my parents about my plan to drop out of college and enroll in fashion school, they threatened to disown me. That didn't stop me. I did it anyway. So they cut me out of their lives."

"That must have been awful," Chloe said.

"Perhaps it would have been if I didn't have Gabrielle. She supported me, and so did her family. She's always stood by me, unconditionally." Dana took a moment to compose herself. Why was she feeling so sentimental? "Since then, my parents and I have mended our relationship. They reached out to me, apologized for what they did."

Her parents had since admitted that their threat to disown her had only been intended to deter her from dropping out of college, but when it didn't, they'd been too proud to go back on their word. If Dana had inherited anything from her parents, it was her stubbornness.

"It took me some time, but I've forgiven them, moved on." At least, she had on the surface.

"Well, even if everything is good between you now, it must have been hard going through all that," Chloe said. "I understand it, a little. I don't talk to my family at all. Well, my mom is my only family, but we don't talk anymore. She was a lot like your parents. She had this idea in her head of what she wanted me to be, and she forced me to be it. She only ever showed me love when I played the part of her perfect little doll. She was motivated by money in a way, but it went deeper than that. Her obsession with turning me into what she wanted consumed our entire lives."

Dana studied Chloe's face. She had a distant look in her eyes, as if she were both trying to remember something and trying not to remember it at the same time.

But a moment later, Chloe's usual liveliness returned.

"Anyway, that's in the past now too," she said. "All I care about now is the present, and the future. Maybe one day I'll have a family of my own, one built on love instead of just blood."

"I'm sure you'll find that," Dana said. "I'm sure you'll find everything you're looking for and more."

Chloe smiled. "Thanks. For tonight, for everything. I had a really good time."

"I'm glad I could make the night special for you. And I hate to ruin the moment, but there's something I want to speak with you about."

"What is it?"

"I've been doing some thinking, and I've come up with a solution for your car troubles." Dana held up her hands defensively. "Don't worry, I'm not going to try to pay for repairs again. This is a compromise that doesn't involve giving you money."

"Okay…"

"I have a truck sitting in my garage, unused. I bought it years ago so I'd have a practical vehicle at hand in case I ever need to move something, but I've barely used it. It's yours if you want it."

Chloe shook her head. "I couldn't possibly accept that."

"I suspected you'd say that, which is why I'm offering to *lend* it to you for the foreseeable future instead. No strings attached."

"Oh." Chloe hesitated. "That's a kind offer."

"Again, I'm not using it, so it's no trouble."

Chloe was silent for a moment. Finally, she nodded. "Sure. I'd really like that. It'll be a big help. And I'll get it back to you soon, I promise."

"I'm in no rush to get it back. You can keep it for as long as you want."

"Okay. Thank you."

Chloe leaned over and kissed her briefly, the softness of her lips filling Dana with unexpected warmth. But Dana couldn't help but feel like Chloe didn't really believe her when she said this favor didn't come with any strings.

Why was it that Chloe felt that way?

CHAPTER 14

Gabrielle poured herself a glass of whiskey at the bar by the kitchen, then made her way to the living room at the front of the house, looking out the window as she sipped on her drink. It was late on Monday evening, and Dana was still at her studio. She occasionally stayed back after hours when she found herself consumed by creative impulses. Gabrielle encouraged these late nights. Dana's work was one of the few areas of her life in which she allowed herself to freely express her passion.

However, tonight Gabrielle wanted Dana home. There was something on her mind that she needed to discuss with her. No, someone.

Chloe.

All three of them had now had more than enough time to think about their next steps, and those were steps Gabrielle was eager to take. She was certain that Dana felt the same way.

So why did the idea of doing so make her hesitate?

They'd invited women into their relationship before, but this was different.

Was it because of how strongly Gabrielle was drawn to Chloe? Was it because Chloe seemed interested in getting to know them for them, rather than simply wanting to enjoy the benefits of being their spoiled, temporary pet?

Of course, that could all be a ruse, a way to get closer to the both of them.

Gabrielle took a seat on the lounge and set her drink aside, attempting to dismiss her paranoia. Her suspicions weren't rational, and she knew it. But after everything that had happened with her ex-fiancée, she found it difficult to let her guard down. Her ex had been dishonest with Gabrielle from the very beginning. Their entire relationship had been a lie.

But to Gabrielle, the relationship had been real. Finding out the truth had hurt her more deeply than she'd ever thought was possible. If it hadn't been for Dana, she didn't know how she would have gotten through it all.

That was the one good thing that had come out of her failed engagement, the one silver lining. She and Dana had realized their feelings for each other.

It's always been you. Those had been the words she'd said to Dana that fateful night. Dana had always been there for her. Dana loved her for her. Dana was the one person she was sure would never lie to her, never use her, never break her trust.

Could she ever say the same about anyone else?

Gabrielle was so deep in thought that she didn't notice Dana had come home until she strolled into the room.

"Sorry I'm so late," she said. "I lost track of time at work."

"It's all right," Gabrielle replied. "Did you get much done?"

"Not as much as I'd like." Dana pulled her hair out of its usual sleek, neat bun, running her fingers through her tight coils as she took a seat next to Gabrielle. "I had other things on my mind. I was thinking about us. About Chloe."

"It seems we're on the same wavelength tonight." It no longer surprised Gabrielle how often that happened.

"Then what do you think about taking things to the next level?"

"You read my mind." But those doubts still lingered in Gabrielle's mind, just beneath the surface.

"Why do I get the feeling there's a 'but' coming?"

Gabrielle sighed. "Is it that obvious? I'm sure I'm just being paranoid, but I can't shake the feeling that Chloe is hiding something."

"Perhaps she is. But we can't expect her to open up to us about everything this early on. There's plenty we haven't told her."

"I know, but can we really trust her?"

Dana was silent for a moment. "You're worried that what happened with your ex will happen with her." Both of them had gotten into the habit of never mentioning Gabrielle's ex-fiancée by name. Hearing her ex's name didn't bother Gabrielle anymore, but once upon a time, it had been enough to send her spiraling into despair.

"Not exactly. I know Chloe isn't like that. If anything, she's the opposite. But she's so tight-lipped about certain things, especially when it comes to her past. Maybe it's to do with her family, her parents being dead and all."

Dana's brows drew together.

"What is it?" Gabrielle asked.

"Did she tell you that? That her parents are dead?"

Gabrielle nodded. "Yes, why?"

"I don't know about her father, but she told me a little about her mother. It sounded to me like her mother is still alive, they just don't talk anymore. They're estranged."

"Hm." Gabrielle recalled her conversation with Chloe before dinner on *The Queen Bee*. Had she explicitly said her parents were dead? Gabrielle couldn't recall. "Perhaps I misunderstood her."

"Perhaps. Now that you mention it, there is something else," Dana said. "There was a minor incident on our date. One of the ushers at the theater approached Chloe claiming to be an old friend from high school in LA, but Chloe denied knowing her."

"Well, she's from Minnesota."

"Then I'm sure it was a case of mistaken identity, some kind of coincidence. And the woman called Chloe the wrong name." Dana paused. "But Chloe did seem overly flustered by it. It was very odd."

Gabrielle frowned. Had Chloe lied about where she was from? After all, she'd refused to tell Gabrielle the details of where in Minnesota she'd lived.

"I'm sure it's nothing," Dana said. "Even if Chloe did know the woman, there's probably a perfectly innocent explanation for her behavior, along with everything else."

"You're right," Gabrielle said. Dana had always been the voice of reason for both of them. "You're always right."

"I think that's the first time I've heard you admit that. I should record it for posterity."

"Very funny." Gabrielle picked up her drink and took a

sip. It had grown warm. She set it down again. "So what's next? If we're taking the next step with Chloe, the three-day weekend coming up is the perfect opportunity to do it. We could take her to the ranch with us."

"You want to invite Chloe to the ranch? Are you sure?"

"Why not?"

"We've never taken a woman there before. I'm not opposed to it, but I know how special the ranch is to you."

The ranch *was* special to Gabrielle. It had belonged to her parents, and she'd spent much of her childhood there. When her parents had decided that managing the upkeep and all the staff was too much work, Gabrielle had offered to take over, so her parents had gifted it to her and Dana. Over time, it had become their personal sanctuary. The women they dated never stuck around long enough to earn the right to get so much as a glimpse of the place.

Chloe hadn't been around for long either, but she was different from all the other women. And perhaps, the two of them letting her into their sanctuary was just what Chloe needed to feel more at ease with them.

"Don't get me wrong," Dana said. "I think it's a good idea. I just want to make sure you've thought this through."

"I have." Gabrielle paused. "Are *you* okay with this?" It was just as big a step for Dana as it was for Gabrielle. Dana was always slower to open up to the women they dated. It wasn't surprising, given her history with her family. Gabrielle sometimes wondered if Dana wasn't really over her family's past actions.

"I am," Dana said. "Let's give her a call?"

Gabrielle picked her phone up from the table and dialed Chloe's number, putting the call on speakerphone. It took several rings before Chloe answered. When she greeted them, she sounded out of breath.

"Did we catch you at a bad time?" Dana asked.

"No, I just got out of the shower," Chloe replied.

"Really?" Gabrielle let the image settle in her mind. "Tell us more."

She could almost hear Chloe blush through the phone. "So, what's up?" Chloe asked.

"Just checking in. Dana told me about how much fun the two of you had on your date, but she was sparing with the details." Gabrielle shot Dana a sly glance. "Did she make you call her Mistress? I know how much she likes that."

Chloe mumbled something inaudible, which Gabrielle took as confirmation.

"Gabrielle, stop torturing the poor thing," Dana said.

"I suppose she had enough torture the other night with you. I know firsthand how much you like to keep your submissive on edge."

Dana gave her a sharp look. "Let's get to the point, shall we?"

Gabrielle rolled her eyes. "Fine. Here's the deal. Dana and I have been talking, and we feel it's time you got to experience the benefits of having both of us spoil you at once. If you're up for it, that is," she added.

"And what benefits are those?" Chloe asked sweetly.

Gabrielle smiled. There was no hesitation in Chloe's voice. It seemed she was finally on board with the idea of dating the two of them together. "We'd like you to join us for a weekend away at our ranch. It isn't just any old ranch. It's furnished with every luxury you could ever want. You'll be waited on hand and foot, all the staff at your beck and call to bring you whatever your heart desires. And we'll have the whole manor and miles and miles of countryside to ourselves. Who knows what kind of naughty things we could get up to?"

It took Chloe a moment to respond. "All right. I'll come to your ranch with you. But I have some terms."

Gabrielle raised an eyebrow. "It isn't often that we allow our pet to dictate terms, but we're open to negotiation. What is it that you want?"

"I want my own room."

"Consider it done," Dana said.

"Okay then." Chloe hesitated, uncertainty showing in her voice for the first time. "But I don't want to give you the wrong impression. I'm excited about this. It's just, I don't know if I'm ready yet. To be with you that way. Both of you. Together." Her worlds ran into each other. "But I'll tell you when I am."

"We understand," Dana said.

"You have nothing to worry about," Gabrielle said. "We'll keep everything G-rated until you say otherwise. Either way, we're going to give you a weekend you'll never forget."

"Great." Chloe's confidence quickly returned. "Then it's a deal."

They took a few minutes to work out the details. Chloe had already planned to close her shop over the long weekend since her usual office-working customers wouldn't be around. That would give them three entire days together.

The possibilities were endless.

After a brief goodnight, Gabrielle hung up the phone

and turned to Dana. "So, how long do you think it will take before she ends up in bed with us?"

Dana gave her a look of warning. "Don't get carried away. We need to respect Chloe's boundaries."

"I have every intention of doing that. And like you said, Chloe can handle herself. She isn't going to end up in our bed unless she's 150 percent certain that's what she wants." Gabrielle leaned in close to her, running her hand up Dana's arm. "Until then, what's the harm in having a little fun, hm?"

Dana crossed her arms. "You know I don't like games."

"How could I forget?" Gabrielle feigned irritation. "You don't have to be such a wet blanket."

"You don't have to be such a tease."

Gabrielle smiled seductively. "What are you going to do? Spank me?"

Desire flashed behind Dana's eyes, her voice dropping low. "Don't challenge me, darling. Not unless you mean it. We both know I won't hesitate to do exactly that."

Gabrielle couldn't deny how tempting she found the idea. It had been a long time since they'd played that particular game.

But she wasn't in the right mood. She was too distracted, her thoughts still on Chloe. She couldn't just let Chloe's secrets go.

Gabrielle needed to be sure she could trust her.

A few hours later, while Dana was getting ready for bed, Gabrielle slipped into the study and shut the door behind her. Dana was at the other end of the house, but Gabrielle was being cautious.

She dug through the bottom drawer in her desk, looking for a business card she had stashed there years ago. She didn't think she'd ever need it again, but she'd kept it just in case.

Locating the business card, Gabrielle retrieved it from the drawer and set it on the desk before her. It read *Robert Clarke, Private Investigator*. Gabrielle had hired him when she'd first caught wind of her ex-fiancée's lies. Unwilling to accept her excuses, Gabrielle had taken matters into her own hands, determined to find out the truth once and for all.

And the truth had crushed her.

But when it came to Chloe, Gabrielle wasn't expecting to discover anything harrowing. She didn't seem like the type who would deceive them. No, this was simply a precaution, a way for Gabrielle to put her mind at ease. After all, she had plenty to protect. Her assets, her reputation, her relationship. It was sensible, given what was at stake.

She knew Dana wouldn't approve, which was why she hadn't told her. But if they were going to take the extraordinary step of truly letting someone into their relationship, it was worth making sure that someone was who they said they were, and that they had no skeletons in their closet. That was all this was. Confirmation.

That didn't ease the guilt Gabrielle felt as she composed her email to the investigator. Her request was nothing extreme, just a thorough background check. She attached a photo of Chloe from one of her social media pages—all of which were suspiciously sparse—along with everything she knew about her. Her name. Her age. No living parents, or possibly a living mother. Grew up in Minnesota, or Los Angeles. The name of her flower shop, and all the other details Gabrielle could find on her.

She read over the email a final time, then added a line at the end.

Let's keep this between the two of us.

It didn't need to be said, but she couldn't risk Dana finding out that Gabrielle had hired him. If all went well and the investigator didn't find anything, she would tell Dana about it and beg for forgiveness. And if he did find something?

Then they'd have a bigger problem on their hands.

CHAPTER 15

Chloe stared out the window of her shop as she pruned the leaves from a long-stemmed rose. Dana's truck was parked just outside. Chloe had borrowed it from her more than a week ago, but she still wasn't used to driving around in such an expensive vehicle.

She should have known that when Dana said she owned a truck, it wouldn't be some beat-up pickup like Chloe's. Dana's truck could only be described as luxurious. Chloe had almost expected to find a bottle of champagne in the glove compartment, but all she'd found was a pair of leather gloves that smelled faintly of Dana's perfume.

Chloe sighed. First, she'd borrowed the truck from Dana and Gabrielle, and now she was letting them take her away for a weekend getaway to their ranch. They were leaving in just a few hours. Chloe suspected that their 'ranch' was as much a ranch as the truck parked out front was a 'truck.'

Why was she letting them spoil her like this, letting them treat her to nice things? It was the opposite of what she wanted, wasn't it? So why did she get butterflies in her stomach when she thought about spending the entire weekend being doted on by them in every way imaginable?

She looked down at the rose in her hand. She'd absent-mindedly stripped every single leaf from the stem. She hadn't meant to do that.

She placed it aside and leaned down on the counter, taking the weight off her tired feet. Apparently, she was so infatuated with Gabrielle and Dana that she was losing her focus. But maybe that wasn't such a bad thing. Was there any harm in letting herself enjoy that feeling? How many times in her life had she ever felt this way about anyone, let alone two people?

It was true what she'd said to Gabrielle and Dana, about not feeling ready to dive in headfirst with the both of them yet. However, the idea excited her. Her date with Dana had only confirmed what she'd known from the moment she met them. Both of them were more than enough to satisfy Chloe's submissive desires on their own, in completely different ways. While Gabrielle liked to tease her, toy with her while she was helpless, pleading, powerless to resist, Dana wanted nothing less than Chloe's unflinching obedi-ence. No, she demanded it.

Both of them were irresistible. Together, they were everything Chloe wanted and more. She'd always longed for someone she could give up control to, surrender to. She longed to let go of the reins.

Could she trust Dana and Gabrielle to take them for her?

The bell above the front door chimed. Chloe straight-ened up eagerly. She'd barely had any customers all day, and it was almost closing time. She needed all the sales she could get. Now that she had Dana's truck, she'd been able to resume her deliveries, which was already helping. However, business was still slow.

But as the customer approached, Chloe realized that they weren't a customer at all. Striding toward her was someone Chloe was intimately familiar with.

Tracy.

Chloe's stomach lurched. Tracy had never come into her store before, not since they'd broken up. Chloe already knew why she was here. Chloe still hadn't made the payments she owed her.

And it was clear that Tracy wasn't happy.

She stopped in front of the counter. "Hello, Chloe."

Chloe swallowed. "Tracy."

It had been a long time since she'd seen her ex-girlfriend in person. The older woman still looked the same, her short blonde hair brushed back, the trademark crimson lipstick that Chloe had once found so attractive now looking garish. Chloe had been eighteen when they met, and Tracy had been almost twice her age. At the time, Tracy had seemed like her savior. Chloe had been all alone, having fled from her controlling, money-grubbing mother.

And then she'd run straight into the arms of someone who was just as controlling, but in a different way.

"You look well," Tracy said, a sharp edge to her voice.

Chloe replied in the exact same tone. "So do you." Tracy had always hated it when she showed any sign of having a spine.

"I'm sure you know why I'm here. You missed last month's payment. And this month's."

Tracy was cutting to the chase. That had to be a sign that

she knew Chloe couldn't be intimidated by her anymore. The debt was the only weapon Tracy had left.

Unfortunately, it was an effective one.

"I just need a little more time," Chloe said.

"That's what you said last week. And the week before. And the week before." Tracy crossed her arms. "I'm done waiting."

"I'm sorry, but I don't have the money. I spent the last of it on Mango's vet bills."

"Mango?"

"He's my cat."

"How sweet," Tracy said dryly. "I don't care."

Chloe huffed. "Look, I don't have the money right now, but I'll get it to you as soon as I do."

"Are you sure about that? Because it looks to me like you've found some money." Tracy turned and looked over her shoulder and out the front of the shop. "Enough to get yourself a fancy new truck."

Chloe scowled. "It's not mine. I'm borrowing it from... a friend."

Tracy raised an eyebrow. "Got yourself another sugar mama, have you?"

Chloe held back a snort. Tracy had *not* been her sugar mama. The money Tracy had given her had been a one-off. But she'd been dependent on Tracy in other ways, the ways Tracy had wanted her to be. It had been entirely toxic. But innocent eighteen-year-old Chloe had just been enough of a fool that Tracy had convinced her she was this perfect woman who had it all. She'd seemed so much older, wiser, more experienced.

But it had all been a façade. Chloe had seen through it,

eventually. She'd left. And this was Tracy's way of punishing Chloe for leaving her.

Did she even care about the money, or did she simply gain satisfaction from the fact that it kept Chloe tied to her?

"Maybe you can ask your 'friend' for money," Tracy said. "If she can afford that truck, she can afford to pay your debts."

Chloe crossed her arms. "My debts are my own. There's no need to bring anyone else into this."

But Tracy didn't stop there. "Does this new woman of yours know who you really are? Does anyone? Or am I the only one who knows your secret?" A wry smile crossed Tracy's face. "I've kept it all this time, you know. It would be a pity if it got out. I wonder, what would this 'friend' of yours think of you if she knew the truth, *Cassidy*?"

Chloe's stomach sank. Would Dana and Gabrielle care about her past? Or, more importantly, would they care about her lying to them all this time? She wasn't ready to tell them the truth yet. And the last thing she wanted was for them to get involved in anything to do with Tracy.

Chloe gritted her teeth. "Fine. If you want money so badly, here."

She opened up her cash register and reached underneath the tray, grabbing the handful of bills she'd stashed there. She counted them out. It was only a few hundred dollars, but it was money Chloe sorely needed.

Nevertheless, she threw the bills onto the counter before Tracy. "This is everything I have. It's yours. Are you happy?"

Tracy squinted at the pile of bills scornfully, then picked them up. "That will have to do, for now. But I expect the rest by the end of the month."

"What? But that's impossible." The month was already halfway gone.

Tracy glanced through the window at Dana's truck. "I'm sure you'll figure something out." She slipped the bills into her purse. "The end of the month. I'll be waiting."

With that, she turned and strode out of the shop.

Chloe let out a hard breath, her heart thumping hard. She wasn't eighteen anymore. She was smarter, stronger. She wasn't going to let Tracy's games unnerve her like they used to.

But this was the first time Tracy had threatened to expose her. And just thinking about her past—about her childhood spent as her mother's puppet, about what had happened when Chloe finally decided she'd had enough—it sent her anxiety skyrocketing. She'd left her past behind, gone through such drastic measures to keep it from ever catching up with her, for good reasons. She'd moved cities, changed her entire identity.

It wasn't just so she could hide from her mom, and so her teenage headshots wouldn't come up when people searched her name online, although those were advantages. The real reason she'd given herself a new identity was so that she could start fresh as the person she wanted to be. Her mother had never let her have an identity of her own. So as soon as she'd left Los Angeles, she'd reinvented herself, and Chloe Campbell had been born.

At first, Chloe had just been a character she was playing, one who was confident and strong instead of lost and alone like Cassidy had been. But over time, Chloe had become more and more real, until she wasn't Cassidy any longer.

But if Tracy decided to expose her, that lost girl that

Chloe kept hidden inside her would be forced up to the surface.

She took a few deep breaths. She wasn't going to fall apart. She wasn't going to let Tracy get to her.

She wasn't going to let her ex ruin the one good thing she had going for her.

Well, the two good things.

Chloe looked at the clock. It was just past closing time. She began packing up her shop. She didn't have long until Dana and Gabrielle were due to pick her up from her apartment. Her bags were already packed, and she'd enlisted her neighbor to look after Mango and water her plants while she was gone.

In just a matter of hours, she'd be far away from all of this.

CHAPTER 16

By the time they reached the ranch, it was late. They'd been on the road for hours. Dana had insisted on driving them in one of her cars, a flashy Mercedes that Chloe was sure she'd have been even more impressed with if she knew anything about cars. It was a convertible, but the rain meant they'd had to keep the top up.

As they drove through the gates to the ranch. Chloe stretched out in the front seat. The car was spacious enough, but she was tense. She'd spent the whole drive trying not to think about Tracy. Plus, the humidity meant that her hair was attempting to revert to its curly state.

She glanced at her reflection in the sun visor mirror. Her roots were starting to show too. She'd have to deal with that soon.

Beside her, Dana looked at Gabrielle through the rearview mirror. She sat in the back seat, dozing off silently.

"Gabrielle," Dana said. "We're here."

Gabrielle yawned, her eyes blinking open as she peered out the window. "Home sweet home." She leaned forward, draping her arm over the side of Chloe's seat. "What do you think of the place?"

Chloe had been so distracted that she'd barely noticed their surroundings. They were traveling down a long, winding drive, lit by rows of lamps at either side, illuminating the trees and land surrounding them. And up a hill, at the end of the road, was a mansion.

"This place is gorgeous," Chloe said.

"It's our second home," Gabrielle said. "I used to spend my summers here as a girl. It's been in my family for generations, and I took it over from my parents a few years ago. Now, it's our little getaway."

When they reached the house at the top of the hill, Dana parked the car in the driveway in front of it. Despite the late hour, a handful of people waited for them, all dressed in crisp, tailored uniforms. Were they the staff?

Chloe tried not to gape at everything. The mansion was huge, and the staff looked like they worked at a high-end hotel. This wasn't like any ranch Chloe had ever been to. Given that it belonged to Gabrielle, a woman who thought nothing of hiring a Michelin star chef for a night, Chloe hadn't expected cows and farmland. But she hadn't expected this either.

Dana got out of the car and opened Chloe's door. As she slid out of the seat, she noticed that the rain had stopped and the clouds were clearing, making way for the full moon. She stared up at the sky. Out here, she could see the stars clearly.

The staff greeted them all politely, rushing to grab their bags from the trunk to take inside the house. Dana handed over the keys before turning to Chloe.

"Shall we go inside?" Dana asked.

Chloe snapped out of her trance. "Sure."

Together with Gabrielle, they headed up to the house and stepped through the doors. The mansion was even bigger than Gabrielle and Dana's house in the city. It was older too, but well kept, and there were touches of luxury everywhere. Marble floors. Chandeliers. Fireplaces. A grand staircase that split off into two.

"It's so good to be back here," Gabrielle said. "It's been too long."

She introduced Chloe to the head housekeeper, who greeted her warmly. What did the staff all think of Chloe's presence at the ranch? They were probably used to Dana and Gabrielle bringing women here.

"If you need something, just ring the bell," Gabrielle said. "The staff will bring you whatever you want. Food, something to drink, spare towels or pillows. Anything."

Chloe nodded, but she couldn't imagine feeling comfortable ordering people to do things for her.

Dana put her hand on Chloe's shoulder. "I know this is all a bit much. Gabrielle likes to live a lavish lifestyle. But you'll get used to it in time."

Chloe wasn't surprised that all the luxury surrounding them was Gabrielle's doing. While Dana obviously had expensive tastes too, she seemed to favor simplicity and minimalism.

"Come," Dana said. "Let's show you to your room."

Chloe followed the two of them up the grand staircase and down a hall where several photos of Gabrielle, her parents, and Dana hung from the walls. They passed several bedrooms before reaching one near the end of a hall.

"This is yours," Gabrielle said.

She gestured into the bedroom where Chloe's bags were already waiting. The room was spacious and luxuriously furnished, but all Chloe cared about was the large bed in the center. It was getting late, and she was suddenly aware of how tired and achy her muscles felt. All she wanted was to curl up in the bed and sleep all her troubles away.

"Our room is at the end of the hall," Dana said. "If you need anything, come find us."

"That's right," Gabrielle said. "And if you change your mind about joining us, you know where we'll be."

Dana gave Gabrielle a chastising look, one Chloe suspected she wasn't supposed to see.

"What I mean is, in case you want some company," Gabrielle added. "It's a big house. It can get lonely at night."

Chloe nodded. "I'll keep that in mind."

She couldn't deny that she was tempted to spend the night with them. She was still feeling overwhelmed by her money troubles, by everything with Tracy. A part of her wished she could share what was going on with them, but she didn't want to drag them into her problems. And she especially didn't want them to offer her help.

Maybe she didn't even need to tell them anything. Maybe simply sleeping next to them would make her feel a little less alone.

But Chloe didn't want to rely on them for anything. She didn't want to rely on anyone other than herself. And this was a problem of her own making. She needed to deal with it herself.

"Is everything all right?" Dana asked.

Chloe nodded. "I'm a little tired, that's all. It's been a long day."

Gabrielle reached out and cupped Chloe's cheek. "Then get some rest. You have a long weekend ahead of you. We're going to spend the entire time spoiling you senseless."

A smile tugged at Chloe's lips. Before she could stop it, a yawn emerged from her.

"We'll let you get some sleep," Dana said. "Remember, we're just down the hall if you need us."

Gabrielle smiled. "Sweet dreams."

The two of them left Chloe in her bedroom, longing lingering deep within her. That firm but sweet side of Gabrielle warmed her heart. And there was something reassuring about the way Dana could make her feel like she had someone looking out for her.

Would letting them in a little be such a bad idea?

CHAPTER 17

G abrielle set down her knife and fork and leaned back in her chair, letting out a satisfied sigh. "Now that breakfast is out of the way, what should we do?"

Chloe looked around, taking in the scenery. They were outside at a table on the deck, finishing off an extravagant brunch after sleeping in late. Chloe had needed the extra rest. When she'd woken up, all her problems had seemed a world away. And it was hard to feel down on a day like this. The rain had stopped, the sun was shining, and she had a whole weekend ahead of her to do nothing but relax.

"We could take a dip in the pool," Gabrielle said. "Spend some time in the sauna. Get a massage. Although we'd have to take turns since there's only one masseuse on staff. If you're in the mood for something active, there are tennis and squash courts, or we could play croquet."

Chloe frowned. The number of choices was paralyzing. She didn't even know what croquet was.

"How about something more low-key?" Dana said. "I

could use a long walk on the grounds, out in nature. It's been so long since we've gotten away from the city."

Gabrielle nodded. "I have a better idea." She turned to Chloe. "Do you know how to ride?"

"A bike?" Chloe asked.

"A horse."

"Er, kind of. I took lessons when I was a kid." Well, *Cassidy* had taken lessons.

"Wonderful," Gabrielle said. "We'll go for a ride to the lake."

Before Chloe could warn her that she hadn't been on a horse in years, Dana came to her rescue.

"Don't worry, I'll give you a hand if you need it," she said. "I'll look after you."

Gabrielle looked her up and down, eying the sundress and sweater she wore. "We'll find some riding gear for you. I should have some spare things in your size."

Half an hour later, dressed in borrowed jodhpurs, a polo shirt, and boots, Chloe joined Gabrielle and Dana at the stables. The two of them were immaculately dressed in riding clothes of their own, wearing them as confidently as they wore everything else.

Chloe tried not to stare at them both. Somehow, Gabrielle's jodhpurs and tailored jacket seemed impossibly tight, emphasizing her curves in the most enticing way. And Dana's ink-black knee-high boots fit her slender calves like they were made of latex, not leather. Just seeing Dana in them was enough to fill Chloe's mind with all kinds of kinky scenarios.

She tugged at the collar of her borrowed shirt. It had the initials *G.H.* embroidered on the left breast. Her pants were marked with Gabrielle's initials too. Was it a coincidence that Gabrielle had given Chloe clothing to wear that had her name on it?

The look of approval Gabrielle gave her suggested it wasn't an accident. "Don't you look fetching?"

Chloe glanced down at her boots, her skin growing hot. Dana was looking at her the same way Gabrielle was. She took a deep breath. The reason she'd wanted to date the two of them separately first was because she'd been worried about how she'd handle being at the mercy of two irresistibly commanding women at the same time.

And now that she was faced with that exact situation, she was finding it hard to keep herself together.

Two grooms emerged from the stables, each leading a tacked-up horse. These horses weren't anything like the animals Chloe had learned to ride on. They were majestic beasts, meticulously groomed, with shining coats and voluminous manes.

Gabrielle and Dana each took a horse, claiming them with a level of familiarity and care that suggested a personal connection. Dana's horse was a deep chestnut color, somewhere between black and brown. The muscular horse looked powerful and intimidating, but it was clear from the way Dana led it along that she could handle it. Gabrielle's horse looked much friendlier. It was a tan, almost golden color, with a long, silky mane.

Another groom appeared, carrying an armful of helmets and other gear. He politely informed Chloe that her horse was being prepared before handing each of them helmets and gloves. As Chloe fiddled with the buckle on her helmet, she found herself staring at Gabrielle, distracted by the way she shook out her long, voluminous hair before putting her helmet on, the way she slid her fitted leather gloves onto her slender hands. At once, Chloe was transported back to that night on Gabrielle's yacht, when she'd lain on the bed, her wrists bound, Gabrielle's smooth, soft fingers exploring her body.

The groom cleared his throat. He'd returned, this time presenting them with a selection of riding crops.

Dana waved him away immediately. "We won't be needing those. Riding crops have always struck me as cruel." She glanced sideways at Chloe. "At least, when it comes to using them on horses."

Chloe's cheeks began to burn, a vivid image forming in her mind. Dana had already proved she had command of Chloe's body, but now she was commanding Chloe's thoughts too?

How was Chloe going to survive the entire weekend with Dana and Gabrielle without disintegrating into a help-less heap of lust?

"Put your helmet on," Dana instructed her. "We need to protect that pretty head of yours."

Chloe did as she was told, donning the borrowed helmet. A moment later, another groom emerged from the stables with a third horse.

It was the most magnificent horse she'd ever seen. It had a dappled gray coat, its white spots evoking the stars in a night sky.

"Is that mine?" she asked hesitantly. The beast seemed friendly enough, but it had been a long time since she'd ridden a horse.

"He's all yours," Dana said. "Don't worry, you're in good hands. Silver is the most placid horse we have."

Dana passed the reins of her own horse to the groom, then took Silver's reins. "Here, I'll give you a hand."

Dana proceeded to do just that, helping Chloe up onto Silver and leading her around the small paddock at a glacial pace. After a couple of minutes, Dana released her to trot around the paddock. It didn't take long before everything Chloe had learned in her lessons all those years ago came back to her.

Gabrielle trotted up beside her. "Looks like we're good to go. Shall we?"

Once Dana was sure Chloe felt confident in the saddle, they set off down a trail leading away from the mansion. Gabrielle led the way, followed by Chloe, with Dana at the rear.

They took it slow, walking along at a speed that allowed them to enjoy their surroundings. As they traveled further and further from the house, the open fields gave way to towering trees, and the only sounds they could hear were the rhythmic clop of hooves and the chirping of birds. Chloe relished the tranquility, the silence. She'd lived her whole life in cities. She rarely got the chance to get out into nature.

After they had been riding for around an hour, they reached a crossroads. Gabrielle stopped at the head of the line and turned back to them, a gleam in her eye. "Buttercup here is just dying to stretch her legs. I'll see you at the lake."

Without giving either of them a chance to reply, she wheeled around, urged her horse into a gallop, and disappeared down the left path in a blur of tan.

Dana brought her horse up alongside Chloe, shaking her head. "She does this every time. Rest assured, I won't run off on you. Let's get going. This way is shorter, so we should get to the lake when she does."

They continued down the trail, taking the right-side path. Dana led the way but made sure to stay close. When all three of them were together, the differences between the two women were even more apparent. While Dana was careful, dependable, Gabrielle seemed taken by whims on a regular basis.

A comfortable silence fell over them. There was something relaxing about being out here, in the calm of the woods, not another soul in sight. Time seemed to stretch on and on.

Dana broke the silence. "Gabrielle is missing out, running off like that. There's so much beauty to see out here. I've been coming here with her since my fashion school days, and after all the time I've spent here, the scenery still astounds. I'll never get tired of it."

"It's really something," Chloe said.

"I have to say, you're much better at riding than I thought."

Chloe hadn't even noticed how comfortable she'd gotten in her seat. "It's like riding a bike. I guess those lessons my mom forced me to take paid off in the end."

Dana regarded her curiously. "Forced you?"

Chloe shrugged. "She was a classic stage mom, obsessed with putting me in the spotlight by any means possible. She made me take singing lessons, ballet, tennis, gymnastics, ice skating, piano. She hoped to find some hidden talent of mine that would make me famous."

"Did she find one?"

Chloe shook her head. "Nope." That was only a half-lie. Chloe—Cassidy—had been talented, but she hadn't ever been famous. She'd been close to it, but then she decided she'd had enough. Her mother had been furious. She'd tried to force Chloe to continue with her career, tried to guilt her into changing her mind by telling her how much Chloe owed her for raising her, for providing for her. And when that didn't work, her mother had turned on her entirely, becoming hostile and cold.

"I know what that's like," Dana said. "I sometimes wonder if my parents are still disappointed that I'm not a doctor like my brothers, even though I'm happy and successful. Some parents consider their children extensions of themselves instead of real people with wants, needs, dreams."

That was exactly how Chloe's mom had thought of her. For a moment, she considered telling Dana all about her mother. She'd almost told her everything that night in her studio. She'd been able to relate to Dana's experiences. She'd spent her whole childhood as her mother's doll, a prop for her to live vicariously through. It had been suffocating. But doing what her mother wanted had been the only way she was able to earn her love and affection as a child.

"We're almost there," Dana said. "Why don't we take a cue from Gabrielle and gallop the rest of the way? Do you think you can handle it?"

"Sure." Chloe felt confident enough to go faster now. And she hadn't realized it until then, but she was itching to let loose.

"Go on. Just follow the trail. I'm right behind you."

Chloe tightened her knees around her horse. Silver took a moment to respond, ambling along sluggishly before taking off at a canter. Chloe glanced back at Dana, who was following behind her, then urged Silver on even faster.

This time, Silver didn't hesitate, breaking into an almost terrifying gallop. Chloe's pulse raced, the wind whipping around her.

Recalling her old riding lessons, she loosened her grip on the reins and relaxed her muscles. The adrenaline rushing through her veins, the exhilaration and nerves fluttering in her stomach, were exactly how Dana and Gabrielle made her feel. If she concentrated too hard, thought too much, she felt uncertain, overwhelmed. But if she silenced the doubts in her mind, let her instincts take over, she could soar.

Her heart began to pound. Was it time to finally do that with Gabrielle and Dana? They were all alone out on this secluded ranch, far away from all her troubles and the pressures of her life in the city.

If there was any time to let go, to listen to her desires, it was now.

CHAPTER 18

Dana slowed her horse as the surrounding trees thinned out, giving way to a clearing and the lake beyond it. Chloe had arrived only a moment before her, but Gabrielle looked like she'd been waiting for them for some time. She reclined against a tree in the shade, one leg crossed over the other, a picnic blanket spread out on the ground beneath her. Her jacket and gloves were folded up on top of a saddlebag beside her, and the shirt she wore had half the buttons undone, exposing her flushed chest to the air.

She smiled at them. "You finally caught up."

It was then that Dana noticed Gabrielle was holding a small tumbler filled with something red. "Is that... a Bloody Mary?"

"I thought we might want some refreshments after a hard morning ride."

Dana raised an eyebrow. "You brought Bloody Marys on our ride?"

"Mimosas don't travel as well." Gabrielle cocked her head toward a thermos beside her. "Would you like one? I brought enough to go round."

Dana shook her head. In some ways, Gabrielle hadn't changed at all since college. "Sure, why not?" She turned to Chloe, who seemed far more interested in Gabrielle's unbuttoned shirt than the drinks. "Chloe?"

Chloe blinked. "Sure."

They tied their horses up with Gabrielle's over by the lake, ditching their helmets and gear before joining Gabrielle on the picnic blanket. Gabrielle produced two extra tumblers from the saddlebag and poured them each a drink, complete with a sprig of celery.

Dana sampled hers, murmuring with approval. "This is good."

Gabrielle smiled. "What can I say? I've come a long way since freshman year."

Dana grimaced. "Don't remind me. I've erased that night from my memory."

Gabrielle laughed and turned to Chloe. "After we finally became friends midway through freshman year, I dragged Dana to her first college party. I prepared us a cocktail to take with us, combining every drink I could find. Suffice to say, it tasted terrible, but it got us outrageously drunk. The hangover the next day almost killed me. Dana swore off drinking for months after that."

"It was just *awful*," Dana said. "You were such a bad influence on me back then."

"Only back then? What about now?"

"Now? Now, you're an even worse influence on me."

"Good to know I haven't lost my touch."

Dana shook her head. "Sorry, Chloe. We have a bad habit of reminiscing all the time. When you've known each other as long as we have, it happens."

"It's okay," Chloe said. "You don't have to apologize."

"We don't want you to feel like a third wheel," Gabrielle said.

"I don't feel that way. I like hearing about the two of you, about your history. It makes me feel like..." She glanced down at the picnic blanket beneath her. "Like I'm a part of this. Of your world."

Gabrielle reached out and put her hand on Chloe's. "You already *are* a part of our world. Why do you think we brought you here this weekend? You're the only woman we've ever brought to the ranch."

"Oh." A slight smile crossed Chloe's lips. "I didn't know that."

"Now you do. And if you want to hear even more about the two of us and our history, I have plenty of stories about what Dana and I used to get up to." Gabrielle gave Dana a sideways look. "Don't worry, I won't tell her many of the embarrassing ones."

"Actually," Chloe interrupted. "There is something I've been wondering. How did the two of you end up together? I know you were friends for a while, but when did that change for you? How did it change?"

Dana exchanged a glance with Gabrielle. "I wouldn't say anything really changed between us. The feelings had always been there, but it took something drastic for us to realize that."

"Something drastic?" Chloe asked.

"I got engaged to another woman," Gabrielle said. "It was all very fast. We'd only been dating for a year, but it was true love. At least, that was what I thought at the time. In the end, I learned that our entire relationship was a lie."

Dana resisted the urge to comfort Gabrielle. Although she was speaking casually, Dana could feel the pain in her voice, but she wasn't letting it show.

"When I found out, I called off the wedding and broke up with her," Gabrielle continued. "I was devastated. Afterward, I spent days moping, angry, betrayed, broken. But Dana was there for me through it all, even though I kept trying to push her away out of self-pity."

She gave Dana a soft smile that made her heart melt. There were very few people who had that effect on her.

"Then, the date of my canceled wedding arrived," Gabrielle said. "I barricaded myself in my apartment, refused to speak to anyone. Naturally, it had Dana worried. She came to my door and tried to talk to me. I ignored her, but she refused to leave. I screamed at her to go away, but she didn't. Instead, she sat out there in the hall on the other side of the door for hours, ignoring my pleas for her to leave me alone. I couldn't face the world, or anyone, but I didn't truly want to be alone. Dana knew that. She knew *me*. She always has.

"That was when I realized it. It was Dana, who has always been there for me. Dana, who has always been my everything. She was the one who I'd always loved. I hadn't seen it over the years because I'd been too busy chasing women, having fun. But that night, I finally saw it. So I opened the door, and I kissed her. One thing led to another, and we became a couple."

"One thing led to another?" Dana said. "You make it sound so simple."

"It was simple for me, at that moment."

"It was much less simple for me," Dana said. "Up until then, I'd only ever dated men. I had an inkling that I was interested in women too, but given the woman I was in love with was my closest friend and she was about to walk down the aisle with someone else, I never let myself acknowledge my attraction to women or my feelings for her. But somewhere in my mind, I knew. Because the moment we kissed, everything fell into place."

Gabrielle smiled. "It's a bit of a cliché, isn't it? Falling in love with your best friend? We're just lucky enough that the feeling was mutual."

"That's really sweet," Chloe said. "I'm glad you found each other.

"So are we. Since then, it's been the two of us against the world." Gabrielle turned to Chloe, gazing at her affectionately. "But we've always hoped that one day it would be three."

Dana knew the words Gabrielle really wanted to say, because she herself wanted to say them too.

We've always hoped for someone like you.

Gabrielle leaned toward Chloe, kissing her with a firm tenderness. Dana felt a rush of desire. Jealousy had never factored into their relationship. Seeing Gabrielle and Chloe together only made her want them both even more.

The moment Chloe came up for air, Dana reached for her, drawing her thumb down Chloe's chin, turning Chloe's face toward hers, pressing her lips to Chloe's in a brief, possessive kiss. But as she broke away, Chloe's lips sought hers again, kissing her back hungrily.

The desire inside Dana flickered and pulsed. She glanced at Gabrielle. This was the first time Chloe had kissed either of them in the other's presence. Dana had expected shyness, hesitation from her, but the desperation in her lips said otherwise.

Dana cupped Chloe's cheek in her hand, caressing it firmly. Chloe trembled at her touch, a soft breath falling from her lips.

Dana pushed her down onto the picnic blanket. "You have no idea how long we've wanted this for."

She looked down into Chloe's eyes. They were brimming with lust. Dana turned to Gabrielle. Her eyes matched Chloe's, filled with the same passion.

But Gabrielle made no move to join them. "Don't get too carried away now, Dana." She traced a finger down Chloe's arm. "Chloe made it clear that we can't go any further together until she's explicitly told us she's ready."

Dana pulled away reluctantly. "That's right."

Chloe bit her lip. "I…"

She glanced at each of them. There wasn't a hint of hesitation in her voice, just an unmistakable thirst. Dana wanted nothing more than to quench it. But Chloe had set her boundaries. Dana wasn't going to push them.

So, she waited for Chloe to voice what she so clearly wanted.

But Gabrielle was far less patient. "Is there something you want to tell us, Chloe?"

Chloe nodded.

Gabrielle leaned down toward her, her face barely an inch from Chloe's. "And what would that be?"

Chloe closed her eyes for a moment, taking an audible breath.

Then she looked up at them both. "I'm ready."

CHAPTER 19

C hloe gazed up at Gabrielle and Dana, her heart pounding. She'd wanted this for so long. She'd finally overcome her doubts, her hesitations, had spoken the words that Dana and Gabrielle had been waiting to hear from her since the very beginning. As seconds passed, each painfully slow, she only wanted this—wanted them—even more.

So why hadn't either of them made a move? Why were they just sitting there, gazing down at her?

What were they waiting for?

Gabrielle reached down and traced her thumb along Chloe's bottom lip. "Don't pout at us. We just need to be absolutely certain this is what you want. You say you're ready for us? How ready are you?"

Chloe held back a groan. Were they going to make her beg? And why did the idea only make her hotter?

"Tell us," Dana said. "Tell us what you want."

"I want you," Chloe pleaded. "Both of you."

Gabrielle leaned down, her lips barely an inch from Chloe's. "And what is it that you want from us?"

"Everything. I want to be yours. I want you to make me yours."

Her eyes fixed on Chloe's, Gabrielle ran her hand down the center of Chloe's stomach, stopping just above the apex of her thighs. Chloe exhaled sharply, need sparking deep in her core.

"Are you sure you want this?" Gabrielle asked. "Are you sure you're ready to serve two Mistresses?"

"Yes," Chloe whispered. "I want to serve you. I want to obey you. I want to give myself to you, both of you, together."

Her words lit a fire in Dana's eyes. But it was Gabrielle who pounced, her lips crashing against Chloe's in a fiery, aching kiss that stole all the breath from her lungs. Chloe dissolved beneath her, heat spreading through her body.

Gabrielle drew back, exhaling sharply. "If your words didn't convince me, that did." She turned to Dana. "What do you think? Is she ready?"

Dana nodded. "I think she is."

Chloe's pulse began to race, an exhilarating mix of nerves and desire swirling within her. The way they both looked at her, spoke of her, it was like at this moment, she was the center of the world. All their attention, all their passion, was focused on her alone.

"Your safeword," Dana said. "It's parachute?"

Chloe nodded. If there was any time she needed to keep her wits about her enough to be able to use her safeword, it was now, her very first time with both of them. But she was already losing that battle.

Gabrielle turned to Dana. "There's something I need in

my saddlebags. Will you get our pet here warmed up while I grab it?"

"Gladly." As Gabrielle stood up, Dana straddled Chloe's body, looking down at her hungrily. "Although, you look very warmed up already."

Her eyes drifted down to Chloe's chest, where her pebbled nipples were showing through her bra and thin polo shirt. Dana traced her leather-gloved fingers over them, causing them to harden even further. Chloe inhaled slowly, the ache between her legs growing.

Dana reached down and pulled Chloe's shirt out of her waistband, drawing it up over her head. She dropped it to the blanket next to them before doing the same with Chloe's bra. Chloe's skin prickled from a combination of arousal and the cool, crisp country air on her bare skin.

Dana trailed her hands down Chloe's breasts, circling and sweeping them over her nipples. A tremor went through her, the soft leather of Dana's gloves smooth and cool against her sensitive buds. Dana took one between her fingers and pinched it gently. A moan flew from Chloe's lips, echoing through the surrounding trees.

She clamped her mouth shut and glanced around, her whole body growing hot. They were alone, but she was lying powerless under the weight of Dana's body, half-naked in the open, where anyone could come by and see them.

"Don't worry," Dana said, teasing Chloe's nipple with a finger. "We're miles from the house. We're all alone out here."

"Of course, there's always a chance someone might come wandering by," Gabrielle interjected.

Chloe looked up to find Gabrielle standing over her, a length of rope in her hands. She'd been so enraptured by Dana's touch that she'd forgotten all about Gabrielle.

But now, Gabrielle had her full attention.

"It's always a good idea to bring extra rope along on a ride," she said. "You never know when you'll need to tie something up." A wicked smile spread across her lips. "Or someone."

Chloe drew in a hard breath. It was taking all her willpower to keep herself together.

Gabrielle crouched down beside her. "Sit up for me."

Chloe scrambled to obey. That night on the boat, she'd hesitated before allowing Gabrielle to tie her up, but this time, she didn't hesitate at all. Was she coming to trust Gabrielle, to trust them both?

Gabrielle took Chloe's hands and brought them together behind her back, binding them with practiced ease. "There," she said. "Much better."

She pushed Chloe back down to the blanket. Chloe shifted her weight, positioning herself so that her hands sat comfortably in the small of her back underneath her.

Dana murmured with approval. "I have to admit, I can see why you like tying people up so much. She looks so appetizing, bound like that." Dana's words were directed at Gabrielle, but her eyes never left Chloe's. "There's nothing more appealing than a captive submissive, desperate and eager."

She slid her hand down between Chloe's legs, stroking her through her jodhpurs. Chloe arched against her, desperate to quell the throbbing between her thighs. She didn't need to be bound to be their captive. She would do whatever they commanded of her, would give them whatever they wanted of her own free will, just so she could please them.

Gabrielle rose to her feet. "She certainly is eager. But why don't we make her wait a little longer? After all, we've been waiting for this for so long now. I want to make it last."

Dana nodded. "While I don't like to play games, a little delayed gratification never hurt anyone. I want to savor this too."

Gabrielle smiled. "You're starting to see things my way."

She drew Dana to her, pulling her into a hot, hard kiss. Dana pressed her body against Gabrielle's firmly, her hands sliding down to grab the other woman's hips. Gabrielle grasped onto the back of Dana's neck, a ravenous murmur rising from her chest.

Chloe stared shamelessly. Watching her two Mistresses together, witnessing their passion, was enthralling. Their bodies reacted to one another instantaneously, feeding off each other's desire.

Her lips parted, a soft breath escaping her. She was torn between wanting to watch them and wanting them to return their attention to her.

Not that she had a choice in the matter. With her hands bound, all she could do was lie there, helpless, need pulsing through her.

Their lips still locked, Dana tore open the buttons of Gabrielle's shirt and pushed it down her shoulders. She snaked her hand down Gabrielle's chest, coaxing a purr from Gabrielle's mouth. Gabrielle's hands traveled down Dana's body, skating lightly over her curves with intimate familiarity.

Chloe whimpered. She didn't just want to watch anymore. This was agonizing!

As Dana reached down to unbutton Gabrielle's jodhpurs, Gabrielle grabbed hold of her wrist, stopping her.

"I promised our pet here that next time, she'd get to taste me." She turned to look at Chloe. "And I always keep my promises."

Chloe's heart skipped. She hadn't forgotten Gabrielle's words on her boat that night. She'd been dreaming of this. And Gabrielle knew it.

Dana drew back. "All right. I want to see this."

Gabrielle beckoned Chloe to her. "Come here. I want you on your knees."

Chloe obeyed, somehow managing to lever herself up with her bound hands to kneel before her.

Gabrielle looked down at her feet. "I'd have you take my boots off for me, but it seems your hands are tied. I'll have to do it myself."

Leaning against the tree beside them, she bent down and removed her leather boots one by one, then unbuttoned her jodhpurs, shimmying out of them with swaying hips. Underneath, she wore a pair of crimson silk panties.

She slid her panties down an inch, then stopped. "You can take these off for me."

Chloe's cheeks began to burn. She glanced at Dana, who watched them intently, a combination of amusement and lust in her eyes. Turning back to Gabrielle, Chloe leaned in and tried to nudge the panties down with her chin. When that didn't work, she bit down on the waistband at one side of Gabrielle's hips and drew it downward, then moved around to the other side and did the same. She continued, going back and forth, until the crimson panties fell to the ground.

She sat back on her heels and gazed up at Gabrielle, awaiting her permission. It was taking all her strength to remain in place. Gabrielle looked so inviting, standing over her with her open shirt half hanging from her shoulders, her smooth thighs bared and her nether lips glistening.

She leaned back against the tree and spread her feet wide, parting her legs. "Go ahead," she said. "Now's your chance to return that favor."

Without hesitation, Chloe buried herself in the peak of Gabrielle's thighs, gliding her tongue up her warm, silken folds. Gabrielle's reaction was instant. Her legs quivered, a moan erupting from her that reverberated through her whole body. Chloe lapped and sucked, reveling in her Mistress's pleasure, and in her taste and scent, all sweeter than any champagne and twice as dizzying.

Chloe was so immersed in her that she forgot all about Dana until she felt a hand trail up the back of her thigh.

"I love watching the two of you together," Dana said. "*Hearing* the two of you together."

Chloe felt a sharp swat on the back of her thigh. Her thick jodhpurs absorbed most of the impact, but still, she squealed with surprise, pulling her bound hands up reflexively.

Whether it was Dana's intention or not, this left Chloe's rear exposed. Dana spanked her again, this time across her ass cheeks. Chloe gasped, the throbbing between her legs deepening.

Gabrielle's hands fell to Chloe's head. "Don't stop. Keep going."

Chloe bit back a protest. She hadn't meant to stop, but Dana had distracted her. She refocused her attention on Gabrielle, licking and sucking and darting her tongue urgently.

Dana only seemed to take that as a challenge, spanking her even harder. Chloe let out a muffled cry, getting hotter and hotter with each strike of Dana's hand. All the while, she tried desperately to push Gabrielle over the brink.

Soon, Gabrielle began to shudder. She was close. She pushed back against Chloe, rolling her hips, moving in time with her until finally, she reached a climax. She drew in a sharp breath, her body stiffening as an orgasm overtook her. Her thighs clenched and released, over and over, her fingers curling through Chloe's hair as Chloe worked her tongue and lips.

Finally, Gabrielle's hands slipped from Chloe's head. She slumped back against the tree, chest heaving. "Well," she said between breaths. "You certainly give as good as you take. For someone so sweet, you have a naughty mouth on you."

Chloe's face grew warm. She remained on her knees, flexing her bound hands as she awaited her next command. She glanced at Dana, who was off to the side, pulling off her leather gloves finger by finger.

"Now that you two have had your fun, it's my turn," she said.

She finished removing her gloves and dropped them to the ground, then reached out and drew Chloe down to the blanket again, kissing her firmly. The fire in Chloe's core flared and raged.

Dana let out a satisfied murmur, breaking the kiss and turning to Gabrielle. "I can taste you on her lips."

She grabbed Gabrielle's hand, pulling her down to join them. Gabrielle stretched out beside Chloe, stroking Chloe's cheek with the back of her hand. At the same time, Dana reached down and pulled Chloe's jodhpurs from her legs, taking her panties off with them.

She tossed them aside and looked down at Chloe, her eyes filled with hunger. "I believe you said you want us to make you ours?"

Chloe nodded slowly, unable to speak or move, her head spinning from the heady scent of sweat, leather, and perfume radiating from both women. On her back, her wrists bound under her, she was utterly powerless before them.

Dana pushed her hand down the center of Chloe's stomach, down to where her thighs met. She was already dripping wet at the mere promise of what was to come. She craved this. She craved *them*.

Dana ran her fingers down to Chloe's entrance, slipping them inside. Chloe let out a pleasured groan, the fullness of Dana's fingers inside sending ripples through her.

She closed her eyes, her breaths deepening. As Dana drove her fingers back and forth, Gabrielle explored Chloe's body with her hands, tracing them over her hips and stomach, caressing her breasts, grazing her nipples with her fingertips. Chloe trembled, her skin sizzling in the wake of Gabrielle's touch.

And when Gabrielle replaced her fingers with her lips, Chloe came undone completely. With Dana inside her, Gabrielle kissing and touching her, the pleasure was overpowering. She was drunk on their kisses, intoxicated by their touch.

Why had she been so hesitant about this, about them? Why had she resisted? *How* had she resisted? She wanted them with every fiber of her being, wanted to surrender every part of herself to them. She wanted to be wholly and utterly theirs.

Deep within her, heat rose and rose, until she was moments from climax. "Can I come?" she pleaded.

"Oh?" Gabrielle purred. "Does Dana have you asking for her permission to come? And I thought I was the twisted one." She slid her hand up Chloe's breast, pinching her nipple between the insides of her fingers. "Well? Should we let her come?"

Chloe clenched her fists underneath her back. She couldn't hold on for much longer.

"I think so," Dana said. "She's earned it."

"You heard her." Gabrielle dipped down, her lips brushing Chloe's ear. "Come for us. We want to hear you."

Gabrielle's words were all it took to unravel her. Chloe cried out, her body racked with tremors, pleasure exploding deep in her center, quaking through her unrelentingly. Gabrielle smothered Chloe with her lips, her suffocating kiss and Dana's heavenly touch sending her to heights of pleasure she'd never reached before.

When she crashed back down to earth, both of them were there to catch her.

~

Afterward, Chloe lay snuggled between Dana and Gabrielle on the blanket. It was midday now, the sun high enough in the sky to penetrate the canopy of the trees, the dappled sunlight warming her skin.

She sighed contentedly. She had never felt so utterly satisfied in every possible way. Why had she ever objected to this, being with these two incredible, commanding women who wanted nothing more than to lavish her with pleasure, and all for the price of her submission, something she was desperate to give them? Submission had always felt right to her, but with Dana and Gabrielle, it was different. It was more natural, more effortless.

"You have that look on your face again," Gabrielle said.

Chloe blinked. "What look?"

"Like you're lost in your head."

Chloe shook the thoughts out of her mind. "Believe me, I'm right here with you. There's nowhere else I'd rather be."

Gabrielle smiled. "I told you that we'd give you a weekend you'd never forget, didn't I?"

"I definitely won't forget this."

Gabrielle reached over and grabbed the silver thermos, offering Chloe a drink. When Chloe declined, Gabrielle poured herself a glass, sipping it nonchalantly. Chloe glanced at Dana. She lay still with her eyes closed, and she hadn't said a word since all three of them had collapsed on the blanket.

"Don't worry about her," Gabrielle said. "She always passes out after sex."

Dana frowned, but she didn't open her eyes. "I can hear you."

"She gets grumpy too. It's adorable, really."

Dana's brows drew together. "I'm not grumpy. And I'm *not* adorable."

"Whatever you say, *Mistress*," Gabrielle fired back.

"Don't make me spank you in front of Chloe," Dana said.

Gabrielle scoffed. "You wouldn't dare."

Dana sat up and leaned across Chloe, fixing her eyes on Gabrielle. "You're right, I wouldn't. Because I know how much you'd enjoy it."

The slightest flush crept up Gabrielle's chest. "I doubt that. You never do it hard enough."

Chloe's mouth dropped open. She'd never heard either of them talk to each other like this. What was going on?

"Of course I don't. I'm not going to reward you for your bad behavior." Dana took Gabrielle's chin between her thumb and forefinger, just like she'd done with Chloe many times. "The point is to make you beg for it."

Dana's words sent a shiver along Chloe's skin. What was happening? Was this all just a weird dream? Had she fallen asleep? Everything seemed upside down.

And why did she suddenly feel so hot?

Gabrielle glanced in her direction, her eyes sparkling with amusement. "Dana, honey? I think we broke her."

Dana released Gabrielle's chin. "Well, it was only a matter of time before Gabrielle's little secret came out."

"It isn't a secret," Gabrielle said. "But it's something I don't share with just anyone. It requires a certain amount of trust. But I'm sure you of all people understand that, don't you, Chloe?"

Chloe frowned. "I don't follow."

"It's simple," Gabrielle said. "I'm a switch. In other words, I like to be at both ends of the whip. Although for me, it's more of a need. I'm not content with playing the same role all the time. I need to play another now and then."

Chloe gaped at her. She knew what a switch was, but she still couldn't comprehend the idea that Gabrielle harbored the very same submissive desires that she herself did. Chloe couldn't imagine Gabrielle being subservient to anyone.

"You'd never be able to tell, given what a terrible sub she is," Dana said. "Always pushing boundaries, always breaking the rules. If it weren't for the fact that she gets soaking wet every time I have her on her knees, I'd think she didn't even enjoy it."

Gabrielle, on her knees before Dana? The image alone was enough to make *Chloe* soaking wet.

Gabrielle rolled her eyes. "Don't listen to her. Dana considers the slightest pushback from her submissive to be a personal insult. I just consider that a good time."

Dana let out an exasperated sigh. "And this is where the problem lies. If Gabrielle spends too long playing one role, she turns into an insolent brat. Which is exactly what's happening right now."

Chloe looked from one woman to the other. Despite their words, their body language was relaxed and affectionate, as if this was a friendly, casual conversation. She also got the sense that it was a conversation they'd had many times before.

"Oh please," Gabrielle said. "Just because you can't handle a sub who doesn't bend to your will at the wave of a hand."

Dana raised an eyebrow. "That sounds like a challenge."

"Perhaps it is."

As Gabrielle's gaze locked with Dana's, something

flashed behind her eyes. Chloe knew exactly what it was because she'd experienced it too. It was an intense desire to have Dana do just that, to bend her to her will and take her.

And the idea of sharing that with Gabrielle made Chloe hot all over.

"You've been behaving like this for weeks now," Dana said. "I think it's time I did something about it."

Gabrielle smiled. "I'm dying to see you try."

"Then perhaps it's time we have Chloe here show you how a good submissive behaves." Dana turned to her. "What do you say, Chloe?"

Chloe blinked. "What do you mean?"

"One night," Dana said. "When we get back home, for just one night, both of you will be mine, to do with as I please. Both of you will kneel at my feet. Both of you will call me Mistress."

Gabrielle gave Chloe a wicked look. "So? Do you think she can handle both of us?"

Chloe swallowed. Both women were looking intently at her, waiting for an answer.

She nodded.

"Then it's settled." Dana crossed her arms. "Let's hope Chloe can teach you a thing or two about how a submissive ought to behave."

"You're welcome to try," Gabrielle told Chloe. "But until then, I'm still your Mistress. And right now, I want you back in my arms. Come here."

Chloe lay back down as Gabrielle and Dana both wrapped their arms around her. She let out a slow sigh. She loved the way they could make her feel like she was all theirs with nothing more than their touch.

But what would it be like to be with Gabrielle, not as her submissive, but alongside her, submitting to Dana with her?

Chloe's stomach fluttered. This secret, hidden side of them intrigued her. She wanted more of this, more of them. She'd already fallen head over heels for each of them separately, and now she was head over heels for them together. She was starting to feel something real for them, something that went beyond simple lust.

If they continued down that path, she would have to let them in, to tell them the truth about her, about everything. She wasn't ready for that yet.

But it was only a matter of time before she'd need to.

CHAPTER 20

Chloe climbed out of the heated pool and grabbed a nearby towel, drying herself off before wrapping it around her shoulders to stave off the chill air. It was early on Sunday evening and the sun had almost set. Gabrielle, who was lounging on a pool float in a stylish one-piece that was somehow both modest and revealing, didn't seem to mind the cold at all.

Dana looked up at Chloe from where she sat on the deck, reading a book. "Are you hungry? We can call for dinner."

Chloe nodded. "Sure." Just the suggestion made her stomach rumble. The previous night's dinner had been a sumptuous banquet, one that had left Chloe so stuffed, she'd passed out in her bed immediately afterward. She'd woken feeling fresh and rested, ready for another day in paradise with Dana and Gabrielle. They'd mostly spent it lazing around the mansion, enjoying the fresh country air, luxuriating in the sunshine.

Out of nowhere, one of the housekeepers appeared and

handed Chloe a warm, fluffy robe. Chloe took it gratefully, bundling up in it and taking a seat on the lounge next to Dana. Without looking up from her book, Dana draped an arm around Chloe's shoulders, pulling her close.

Chloe let out a blissful sigh. She'd long let go of any resistance she'd felt toward letting Dana and Gabrielle treat her like their treasured pet. She couldn't remember the last time she'd felt so content. She had everything she could ever want.

And she couldn't deny that it felt good to belong to someone.

Her phone buzzed once on the table beside them. She hadn't checked it since the afternoon. She untangled herself from Dana's arms, stretching out to grab it. It was probably her neighbor with his daily update on Mango. Did Mango miss her? He barely even acknowledged her existence when she was home, so that was unlikely. But inexplicably, she missed him.

She picked up her phone. Sure enough, there was a message from her neighbor. But that wasn't the only message she'd received. There was another, from an unknown number.

A chill rolled down Chloe's spine. She opened up the text message. She only had to read it to know that it was from Tracy.

The end of the month. I want my money, all of it. If I don't get it, I'll tell everyone who you really are.

There was a second message, time-stamped a few minutes later.

Including this new girlfriend of yours.

Dread washed over her. She'd been enjoying herself so

much this weekend that she'd forgotten all about Tracy. This was the first time Tracy had spelled out her threat to reveal Chloe's secret. The idea of being exposed to the world chilled her. Everyone would know who she really was. Everyone would know that she'd lied about everything. Including Dana and Gabrielle.

Her heart sped up. Tracy had written 'girlfriend,' singular, so she probably didn't know anything about Chloe's life. But that didn't mean she was bluffing.

And what if the truth got back to her mother somehow? Chloe had no idea if her mother was looking for her, or if she'd accepted that Chloe never wanted to see her again, which was what Chloe had told her the night she'd left home. She'd done her best to cut all ties with her past self, to make herself hard to find. Although she'd never changed her name officially, because that would have left a paper trail, she'd simply stopped using her old name unless she had to.

For all intents and purposes, she was Chloe Campbell. Cassidy Denning no longer existed.

That was what worried her the most. She didn't want to be stripped of her identity. It had taken her so long to move on from her past, to find herself, to become her own person.

The idea of being forced to revert to her past self terrified her.

"Hey." Gabrielle stood before her, concern written all over her face. "Is everything all right?"

Chloe blinked. She'd been so lost in her head that she hadn't even noticed Gabrielle's presence. "I'm fine. Everything's fine."

She placed her phone down casually, forcing herself to

maintain her composure. It wasn't working. She took a deep breath, trying to calm herself down.

Gabrielle frowned. "You don't look fine."

"It's nothing."

Chloe glanced at Dana. Her expression made it clear that she didn't believe Chloe either. How was it that they could see through her? After all, she was good at pretending. That had been her job once, a lifetime ago.

"Look," Dana said. "It's obvious something is wrong. You don't have to tell us what it is, but if you want to, we'll listen."

Gabrielle nodded in agreement, taking a seat on the other side of Chloe. "You can trust us."

Chloe hesitated. It couldn't hurt to tell them what was going on, could it?

"It's... my ex-girlfriend." As soon as she started to speak, she knew she couldn't stop. "I owe her some money, and she's been hounding me about it ever since we broke up. I've been paying it off, but things have slowed down at the florist shop recently, so I haven't been able to make the payments, and I don't know what's going to happen if I don't pay her soon..."

Chloe trailed off. She didn't want to talk about Tracy's threats because then she would have to explain everything, and she couldn't do that now, not with how unsettled she was.

"What is it?" Dana asked. "Are you worried she'll do something to you? That she'll hurt you somehow?"

Chloe hesitated. Tracy wouldn't go that far, would she?

She shook her head. "I don't think so. But she's never

going to leave me alone if I don't give her what she wants. And I just hate that this money is keeping me tied to her."

She folded her arms across her chest, hugging herself. "Even though we aren't together anymore, she's still trying to control me. She was always like that. I was only eighteen when we got together, and I was all by myself. I was going through a lot, and I couldn't do it alone. Then Tracy came along, and she kind of took me in. I was just happy that this incredible woman who was so together, so experienced, was interested in me. But looking back, she took advantage of my naivety. She liked that I was lost. She liked that I needed her."

From the very beginning, their relationship had been one of power and control. Sure, their sex life had been vanilla, but in every other sense, she had been Tracy's possession, her pet. Chloe hadn't minded at first. She'd thought it was what she wanted.

But she hadn't understood, back then, what it was she'd been seeking. Someone she could depend upon, someone she could give the reins to when she felt the need to let go of all her pain and heartache. It wasn't until she left Tracy that she'd discovered a healthier way to fulfill that need through submission.

But because of Tracy, she'd never been able to bring herself to be vulnerable outside of the bedroom, to let someone take care of her in the way she really wanted, to entrust them with her emotional needs as a partner.

"She became my everything. My girlfriend, my family, my therapist. The only thing I wasn't reliant on her for was money. At least, not at first. I had my own money from a trust set up when I was a kid, so I used that to support myself." It was what was left of the money she'd earned as a child, the part her money-grubbing mother hadn't been able to spend because she'd been legally forced to set it aside for Chloe. That money was how she'd been able to survive when she first left Los Angeles, when she struck out on her own, too lost and wounded to figure out what to do with herself. It had taken her a few years to get her life together, to find her direction.

"But by the time I finished floristry school and was ready to set up my shop, I was a little short of what I needed to cover all the costs. When Tracy offered to pay the rest, I accepted. Opening my own shop was my dream. Achieving it made me happier than I'd ever been.

"And that was when the problems started. Finally getting to live the life I'd been working hard to build did wonders for my confidence. I didn't feel lost anymore. I stopped needing Tracy so much. And that changed things between us." A lump formed in her throat. "Or maybe it was just that I started noticing the way she treated me."

Gabrielle put her hand on Chloe's arm reassuringly. Dana just listened silently. Chloe was grateful for that. Anything more and she would have fallen apart. She just needed to get everything out.

"She didn't like that I was my own person," Chloe said. "She didn't like that I wasn't her needy, wounded girlfriend anymore. She didn't like it when I stood up for myself. She would remind me of everything she'd done for me over the years we were together. I owed her, she'd say. Everything I had was because of her. She made me feel guilty for wanting to live a life of my own."

Her mother had done the same thing, made her feel

exactly the same way when, at sixteen, Chloe had stood up to her for the first time and refused to continue to be her doll. Had it been stupid of her to flee from her manipulative mother only to end up in the arms of a manipulative girl-friend? Chloe knew she shouldn't blame herself. People like Tracy preyed on people like her, who had never learned what real love was supposed to look like. But that didn't stop her from feeling like it was her own fault.

"Eventually, I realized our relationship was toxic, and I needed to get out," she said. "And when I finally broke up with her, it was a huge weight off my shoulders. The only problem was, she said I'd have to pay back the money she'd given me for the florist shop. I didn't have it, so I agreed to pay her back over time. It's been a couple of years since, and I've made a serious dent in what I owe her, but now I've fallen behind. That text message was her reminding me of that. She just keeps hounding me." Chloe felt a tightening in her chest. "I'm just so tired of this. Of being tied to her, after all this time."

"I'm so sorry that all that happened to you, that Tracy treated you that way," Dana said. "And I'm sorry you're in this situation."

Gabrielle nodded, scowling. "This ex-girlfriend of yours sounds like a real piece of work."

Silence fell over them. Chloe glanced from Dana to Gabrielle. They were sharing a look that told Chloe exactly what they were going to say.

She braced herself.

"I know you don't want to hear this," Dana began. "But we need to say it. If you want our help clearing your debts with Tracy, or with your shop, we can take care of it for you. Whether it's just a payment or two, or everything you owe."

"It's no inconvenience to us at all," Gabrielle added. "And we *want* to help. We'd never hold this over your head or expect anything in return."

Chloe shook her head. "I can't. You've already lent me your truck. That's more than enough." Besides, taking money from someone was how she got into this mess. The last thing she wanted was to be free of her debts from Tracy only to be indebted to someone else. "It's not as bad as it seems. This is just a rough patch."

Dana pursed her lips, her displeasure clear on her face. "It's your decision. But if you change your mind, just say the word."

Chloe nodded.

"And if there's anything else you need, let us know," Gabrielle said. "Anything at all."

Chloe looked down into her lap, fidgeting with her fingers. "Well, there is one thing."

"Sure," Gabrielle said. "Anything."

"Can I sleep in your room tonight?" Chloe asked. "It would be nice to have someone there."

Gabrielle took Chloe's hand in hers, holding it tightly. "Of course you can."

Chloe felt a flood of relief. It warmed her heart to know that Gabrielle and Dana had her back.

But there were some things even they couldn't fix.

CHAPTER 21

That night, Gabrielle awoke in darkness, the air in the room still and silent. She turned her head, peering at the alarm clock. It was past 1 a.m. What had disturbed her?

As she rolled over groggily, the answer dawned on her. She and Dana had gone to sleep with Chloe in between them.

Now, only Dana was in the bed with her.

Gabrielle sat up and got out of bed. She crept to the door and stepped out into the hallway. Dimly, she could see a light on in the parlor down the hall. She headed toward it, stopping in the doorway to find Chloe sitting at the window seat, her feet tucked under her, gazing absently out at the ranch grounds.

Gabrielle entered the room. "Having trouble sleeping?"

Chloe turned to her, her face lined with tiredness. "Yeah."

Gabrielle took a seat beside her. "Thinking about your ex?"

Chloe shrugged. "A little. I've always had a hard time sleeping, especially when I have a lot on my mind."

"Is there something I can do to help?"

"I'm okay. Really."

"How about a drink? I can grab you something from the kitchen. Something warm?"

Chloe shook her head vehemently. "It's fine. *I'm* fine."

"Are you sure?"

Chloe scowled. "I said no! I don't need anything."

Gabrielle flinched. She was only trying to help, but perhaps she was being too overbearing.

But before she had a chance to react, Chloe's shoulders slumped, her whole body deflating.

"I'm sorry," she said. "I didn't mean to yell at you. It's just that everything is all jumbled up right now, and I feel so guilty about letting you two help me in the first place, and I'm scared that getting you involved in this is just going to make everything worse." Her lower lip quivered. "I don't want to ruin everything between us."

Gabrielle gave her a sympathetic look. "This ex-girlfriend of yours really did a number on you, didn't she?" No small part of her wanted to track Tracy down and give her a piece of her mind, but that would be crossing a line. Dana had already taken her aside to warn her of that fact without Gabrielle even speaking her thoughts out loud.

Chloe nodded. "I guess she did."

"Come here." Gabrielle held her arms out to Chloe. "Come on. This isn't a request."

Chloe shifted closer, closing the space between them, and leaned back against her chest as Gabrielle pulled her into an embrace. Several moments passed before she felt Chloe's body relax against hers.

"I know it's silly," Chloe murmured. "But after everything that happened with her, I have a hard time accepting help from anyone. Why would anyone help me unless they want something from me, unless they have some other motive, unless they want to use me?" She hugged her knees to her chest. "Even though we broke up long ago, she still has her claws in me. She's still making me doubt everything, making me scared to trust anyone."

"Oh, honey." Gabrielle pulled Chloe in closer, wrapping her arms tighter around her. "I understand why you feel like this. I know what that's like, in a way."

Chloe glanced up at her. "You do?"

Gabrielle nodded. "I told you about my ex-fiancée, but I didn't tell you why I ended our engagement." She paused. It was always difficult, speaking about her ex. "It was because I discovered she was using me for my money. She didn't love me at all. Our entire relationship was a lie."

Chloe blanched. "That must have been horrible."

"I'm just glad I found out before the wedding. And I only found out by coincidence. I came home from work in the middle of the day and overheard her speaking to her sister on the phone about how she was planning to divorce me just as soon we'd been married long enough for her to take half my money with her. After that, I did some digging, and I discovered she'd been married twice before, both times to rich men she'd quickly divorced, taking off with their fortunes."

Gabrielle shook her head. "It was so obvious in hindsight, but at the time, I didn't see it coming. I trusted her, *loved* her. The idea of her being anything other than sincere never occurred to me."

"I can't imagine what that would feel like," Chloe said.

"It was devastating. My whole life was shattered. I'd planned to spend the rest of my days with her. We'd even talked about starting a family. But her words, they were all lies. And ever since then, I've had the hardest time trusting anyone. The only reason I was able to trust Dana is because I've known her for so long, and she has enough money of her own that I know she's not after mine. I know she loves me for me. But I've never been able to let anyone else in, even when I've wanted to."

She looked down at Chloe's face. "But I'm beginning to realize something. Trusting someone, letting them in, is always a risk. But that risk is worth it if it means there's even the smallest chance of finding something wonderful. Happiness. Maybe even love."

Chloe gazed back up at her. "You're right. I know you're right. But it's so hard to see things that way sometimes."

"I know. But remember, you don't have to do this on your own. You have us to help you through hard times. We care about you more than you know."

Chloe looked up and gave her a soft smile. "And I'm grateful for that."

Gabrielle kissed her on the forehead. Chloe settled back against her, resting her head on Gabrielle's shoulder. For the first time, it felt like Chloe actually believed Gabrielle's words. That was progress, at least. She was finally opening up to them instead of shutting them out.

But Gabrielle still got the sense that Chloe was keeping everything close to her chest. When she told them about

Tracy, it had seemed like she was holding something back. Gabrielle longed to know what that something was, for no reason other than to help her fix it. What would it take for Chloe to trust her, trust *them*?

Suddenly, Gabrielle was struck by a bolt of guilt. How could she expect Chloe to trust her when she'd already broken Chloe's trust?

The private investigator. Gabrielle hadn't heard back from him since he started his investigation, so she'd forgotten all about what she'd asked him to do. But she needed to put a stop to it. It was a massive betrayal of Chloe's trust.

Gabrielle had known that from the beginning, but at the time, she'd been too wrapped up in her own fears to consider Chloe's feelings. And perhaps there was a part of her that had wanted to find something, wanted an excuse to push Chloe away before she got too close. She'd been so afraid of how intense her feelings for Chloe were that she'd tried to find a reason not to trust her, to protect herself from getting hurt.

But it was too late now. Gabrielle had fallen for her. She had to trust Chloe.

She had to call the investigation off before it was too late.

CHAPTER 22

D ana headed to the kitchen in search of another cup of coffee. It was morning, and she'd been awake for a few hours, but Gabrielle and Chloe were still sound asleep. While Gabrielle slept in whenever she had the chance, Dana was an early riser, so she was used to spending mornings alone. She liked that it gave her a chance to get her thoughts in order.

She reached the kitchen, fending off one of the older kitchen staff who tried to insist on making coffee for her. Unlike Gabrielle, who had grown up with housekeepers and nannies, Dana had never gotten used to having people serve her. Because of her parents' jobs, her family had been more than well-off, but her mother and father had always emphasized the value of hard work, teaching Dana and her siblings to be self-sufficient. It was that very drive her parents had instilled in her that had led Dana to succeed in her career, even though it wasn't the career they had wanted for her.

Coffee in hand, she returned to the garden courtyard off

the side of the house, taking a seat on an old wooden bench hanging from a large oak tree. She'd spent the morning here, thinking up a solution to Chloe's ex-girlfriend problem. She'd come up with a way to help her that didn't involve money at all. But would Chloe accept it?

All this trouble over a problem that Dana and Gabrielle could make go away in a heartbeat. But she understood why Chloe didn't want them to swoop in and fix everything. And given that Dana herself had just fought off an old woman who had only wanted to make her coffee, Chloe's stubborn, independent streak was something she could relate to.

She took a sip of her coffee, gazing out at the ranch lands that stretched out beyond the garden, relishing the familiarity of them. She'd always thought of this place as a haven of sorts. Although her history with the ranch wasn't as long as Gabrielle's, she'd spent plenty of time here during a difficult, defining period in her life. The ranch served as a reminder that even when her parents had turned their backs on her, she hadn't been alone.

Dana wasn't estranged from her family anymore. They'd apologized, they'd welcomed her back with open arms. They'd accepted her choice of career, and they'd even embraced Gabrielle as her partner without question, which Dana hadn't expected her extremely traditional parents to do.

So why wasn't that enough for her? Why was she still wary of truly letting them back into her life?

And why had meeting Chloe, being with her all weekend, brought those feelings back up to the surface?

Something had changed on this trip. Between herself and Chloe, between Chloe and Gabrielle, between all three of them. How easily Chloe had slipped into that space Dana and Gabrielle had made for her, into the role of being theirs. And how quickly Dana had begun to feel a desperate desire to make sure every one of Chloe's needs was met, every one of her hurts mended. Gabrielle was different with Chloe, too. It was so rare that she took off the mask she wore and let her kind, affectionate side show.

Dana and Gabrielle were sailing into uncharted territory. They rarely got this close to the women they dated. Whenever they had in the past, those relationships had ended before they could begin. Women always got tired of them. The novelty of their relationship—and the money, and the kink—always wore off. Those women always left.

Dana had no reason to believe that Chloe would be any different.

Prompted by nothing conscious, Dana turned toward the door that led into the house to find Chloe standing there. She was still wearing her pajamas, and her unbrushed hair formed a crown of curls around her head. Somehow, she looked even more radiant than ever.

"You're awake," Dana said. "How long have you been standing there?"

Chloe gave her a sheepish smile. "A while. Sorry. I didn't want to disturb you."

"It's all right." Dana patted the bench next to her. "Join me."

Chloe took a seat. "Have you been awake long?"

"A few hours."

"You should have woken me up."

"You looked too peaceful. And you seemed like you needed the sleep." Dana could vaguely recall waking briefly an hour or two past midnight to find Chloe and Gabrielle sneaking back into bed, but she didn't bring it up.

Chloe curled her bare legs underneath her. "What are you doing out here?"

"Just enjoying the scenery. It's magnificent, isn't it?"

Chloe nodded. "It's like a work of art. There really is beauty everywhere."

"You seem to be doing better this morning. How are you feeling?"

"Good, after sleeping on things." Chloe hesitated. "How are you feeling?"

"Why do you ask?"

"Because I've been watching you stare into space, looking like the sky was falling, for the last five minutes and you didn't even notice me standing there."

Dana cursed to herself. She'd let her guard down, out here all alone. "I was just thinking."

"About what?"

"Nothing you need to worry about."

Chloe crossed her arms. "You don't have to tell me if you don't want to. But you and Gabrielle have made this entire weekend about me. You spent half of last night dealing with my mess, my problems. You're always trying to help me, despite my best efforts. The only reason we even met was because Gabrielle was trying to help me out by hiring me for her gala." Her voice grew softer. "I'm not like the two of you. I can't just fix everything, make problems go away with the wave of a hand. But one thing I can do is listen."

Silence fell over them. Chloe waited patiently, not saying another word. And once again, Dana found herself with an urge to open up to her. Not even Gabrielle made her feel that way.

She sighed. "The first time I came here was at the end of freshman year. I'd just dropped out of college and enrolled in fashion school. My parents had told me that if I did that, I wasn't welcome at home anymore, so I came here with Gabrielle for the summer instead. She and her family tried their best to make me feel like one of them, but it didn't stop me from feeling abandoned by my parents. And almost a decade and a half later, I'm starting to wonder if that feeling ever went away."

Chloe gave her a sympathetic look. "It wouldn't be surprising if you still felt that way. It isn't easy moving on from something like that."

"I thought I'd moved on. I've forgiven them, and we're on speaking terms again, but I'm still keeping them at arm's length. I want to let them back in, but it's difficult to trust them again."

"Forgiveness isn't the same thing as trust. It takes time to build trust, especially after it has already been broken. What your parents did would make it really hard to trust them." Chloe paused. "Or to trust anyone."

Was Dana that transparent? Was it so obvious to Chloe that her parents were only half of what was on her mind?

"Perhaps, over time, I've gotten used to the idea that everyone will always abandon me in the end," Dana said. "Everyone except for Gabrielle. She's the only constant in my life. That's how it's always been for me. That's how it's always been for us, with the other women we've dated."

But wasn't Chloe different? Didn't she seem like she was in it for the long haul?

"I've been living with that fear for so long without acknowledging it," Dana said. "And I'm starting to feel like it's getting in the way of rebuilding my relationship with my parents. Among other things."

"I get that," Chloe said quietly. "I really do. It's a risk, letting people in when you've been hurt before. But maybe taking a risk is worth it if it means there's a possibility of finding happiness. Or even love."

Dana studied Chloe's face. "Those are wise words."

"I wish I could take credit for them. I stole them from Gabrielle, actually."

That did sound like something Gabrielle would say. While she could be flippant at times, she always knew the right thing to say when it really mattered.

"To be honest, they were words I needed to hear," Chloe said. "I've been doing the same thing, letting everything I went through with my ex make me mistrust everyone and everything. I'm trying to fix that."

Dana gave her a small smile. "It seems we both have work to do on that front. And while there are some things we have to figure out by ourselves, it doesn't hurt to have some extra help."

Chloe raised an eyebrow. "Why do I get the feeling you're going somewhere specific with this?"

"Because I am. I've been doing some thinking this morning, about how you can get out of this mess with your ex-girlfriend."

Before she could explain further, they were interrupted by the sound of footsteps. They turned to find Gabrielle stepping through the door out into the garden.

Gabrielle joined them on the bench, taking a seat on the

other side of Chloe with a yawn. "I hope I didn't interrupt anything."

"You didn't," Dana said. "I was just telling Chloe I've thought of a way for her to get some help with this problem with her ex." She turned to Chloe. "And it doesn't involve us giving you anything."

"What is it?" Chloe asked hesitantly.

"Well, I don't know the details of this agreement you and Tracy have, but it sounds like it isn't completely above board. And that's not even taking into account the way she keeps harassing you. Have you thought about approaching the problem from a legal perspective?"

Chloe shook her head. "Not really."

"Gabrielle and I have a lawyer friend. I designed the dresses for her upcoming wedding, so she owes me a favor. I emailed her earlier, and she's happy to have you see her for a free consultation. I didn't tell her anything about your situation. I just told her a friend might need some legal help, and she said to send you her way."

Chloe chewed her bottom lip. "I guess that couldn't hurt."

"If anyone can help you, it's her," Gabrielle said. "She's very good at this kind of thing. I think you'll like her."

"You're under no obligation to see her," Dana said. "And you don't even need to tell us if you see her or not. I'll give you her details and you can set up an appointment."

"All right," Chloe said. "But I'll have to think about it."

"Take all the time you need. I'll give you her number when we get back home. And remember, we're here if you need us, for anything."

Chloe nodded.

"Then it's settled." Dana had to admit she'd been expecting more resistance, but she wasn't complaining. "Now that that's out of the way, let's enjoy the morning. We only have half a day left here."

Chloe groaned. "This weekend has gone by far too quickly. I wish we could stay for longer."

"We can always come back," Gabrielle said.

Chloe beamed. "Really? I'd love that."

"Sure," Gabrielle said. "We can come here whenever you'd like."

"But for now, we should decide what to do with the rest of the day," Dana said. "What do you feel like doing, Chloe?"

Chloe thought for a moment. "Honestly? I just want to sit here with you."

Gabrielle smiled. "That's a big ask, but I'm sure it can be arranged."

As she drew Chloe into her arms, Gabrielle's smile disappeared, and Dana caught a flash of something in her eyes. It was almost imperceptible, but Dana knew her well enough to spot all her tells. Gabrielle was worried about something, something big.

What was it?

CHAPTER 23

Amber tapped her fingers on the table impatiently as she sipped on her martini. "Where are the others? I haven't got all day."

"I'm sorry," Gabrielle said. "Are we keeping you from your busy life of leisure?"

"I'll have you know I have important business to attend to today. I'm having dinner with the mayor later on, and I have several phone calls to make this afternoon."

"We're so grateful you were able to find time in your schedule to have lunch with us." Gabrielle placed her hand on Dana's leg. "Aren't we, honey?"

Unsurprisingly, Dana didn't reply. She usually avoided getting involved in Gabrielle and Amber's playful bickering.

But there was truth in Gabrielle's words. It had been a long time since she'd had the chance to see her friends outside of work. They all ran Mistress Media together, so they saw each other almost daily, but it wasn't the same. And lately, everyone had been preoccupied with the opening of the new Mistress offices in Paris. This was the first time in months that they all had a couple of hours to spare at the same time.

"How was your weekend away?" Amber asked. "Gabrielle said the two of you were heading off to the ranch."

Gabrielle nodded. "We had a wonderful time. And it wasn't just the two of us. We took someone."

"Oh?" Amber leaned forward. "And who is she?"

"Her name is Chloe," Dana said.

"Why does that name sound familiar?"

"She's the florist from the gala," Gabrielle said.

"Her?" Amber chuckled. "I knew there was a reason you asked me for that favor. You were trying to impress a new plaything."

"She isn't a plaything," Dana said firmly.

Amber raised an eyebrow. "Really? How interesting."

Gabrielle crossed her arms. "What's that supposed to mean?"

"All I'm saying is the two of you never get particularly attached to these women you date," Amber said. "It's unexpected, that's all."

"You're right about that," Gabrielle said. "But Chloe is different. She's a perfect match for us."

"She's much more than just a good match," Dana interjected. "She's someone truly special. And she's come to mean so much to us." Dana turned to Gabrielle. "I can't speak for Gabi, but I believe our lives are so much richer with her in it."

Gabrielle gaped at her. She knew Dana felt that way, but she'd never heard her speak about her feelings so openly to anyone other than her.

Chloe was changing her. Changing *them*. And Dana was right. It was for the better.

"Good for you," Amber said. "I suspected something was going on when Gabrielle was so determined to have Chloe work the gala. No need to thank me, by the way. I'm sure my favor had nothing to do with facilitating this delightful ménage à trois of yours."

"If anything, the gala almost led to us scaring her off," Dana said. "But it worked out in the end."

Amber leaned back, a smug expression on her face. "Look at you two. I haven't seen you like this since you first got together, and god knows that took long enough. You have no idea how infuriating it was to watch the two of you dance around each other for years."

"We weren't dancing around each other," Gabrielle said. "I was engaged to someone else."

Amber waved her hand dismissively. "A minor obstacle. I hope you're not planning to wait ten years before you tell Chloe how you feel too."

Gabrielle glanced sideways at Dana. "We haven't talked about that yet." She turned back to Amber. "Since when do you care about our love life? Or anyone's? You're not exactly the romantic type."

"What can I say? Perhaps being surrounded by all these happy couples is finally starting to get to me. Besides, I'm not 21 anymore. Settling down doesn't seem like the worst idea. And my mother won't stop nagging me about doing just that, while she's still around. She isn't in the best of health these days."

Although Amber appeared composed as always,

Gabrielle knew her old school friend well enough to see through her façade. Was she worried about her mother?

But she didn't get a chance to ask.

"Speaking of happy couples," Amber said, nodding toward the door.

Gabrielle turned to look. The others had arrived: Madison and Yvonne, Mistress Media's CEO and COO respectively, along with Madison's wife Blair, who worked at Mistress as a journalist. The only people missing were Lydia and her girlfriend, who were away at the new Paris office.

After greeting everyone, they took their seats.

"No Ruby today?" Dana asked, referring to Yvonne's wife.

Yvonne shook her head. "She has culinary school."

"How's that going?" Dana asked.

"It's going well. But I've gained several pounds since she started. I'm going to need a whole new wardrobe soon."

"The sacrifices we make for love," Gabrielle said dryly.

"Well, I'm just happy that Ruby is happy," Yvonne said.

A server came by and took their orders. As they waited for their meals, they sipped on drinks and chatted, filling each other in on their lives. Gabrielle and Dana didn't get a chance to mention Chloe again until they were midway through lunch and Amber decided she couldn't keep that piece of gossip to herself.

She cocked her head toward Gabrielle and Dana. "These two have some news. They have a new girlfriend."

Across the table, Blair sat up straight. "Really? Who is she?"

Madison leaned in expectantly. "Do tell."

Gabrielle barely had a chance to speak Chloe's name before Blair began assailing her and Dana with questions. Blair's reaction was entirely predictable. The red-haired journalist was a hopeless romantic, and far too persistent, which was exactly why she was the perfect match for their CEO.

Just when Blair finally seemed to be satisfied, she crossed her arms and spoke again. "So, when are you going to introduce her to us?"

Gabrielle exchanged a look with Dana. Their friends were an intense crowd. She wasn't going to subject Chloe to them any time soon.

But a part of her couldn't help but wonder what it would look like to have Chloe meet her friends. The women she ran Mistress with, this circle of her nearest and dearest, they were family to her. And she found herself wanting Chloe to be a part of that.

Madison put her hand on Blair's shoulder. "I'm sure they'll introduce Chloe to us when they're ready."

Madison changed the subject and the conversation moved on, but Gabrielle's mind didn't. She thought back to Amber's earlier words. Amber was right. If they were serious about Chloe, they had to talk about how they felt. They had to be honest and get everything out in the open.

Gabrielle felt a pang of guilt. She hadn't yet had a chance to call off the private investigator. She'd intended to, but she'd been busy with work, and—

No, she was lying to herself. She was deliberately putting it off because she simply couldn't bring herself to let go of her doubts. But she had to, for Chloe's sake.

They finished off their lunch. Soon, Amber announced

she needed to leave for her afternoon engagement. After saying their goodbyes, the rest of them headed in the direction of their offices together. It was only a short walk, and Dana's studio was on the way.

When they reached Dana's building, she pulled Gabrielle aside. "We need to talk."

Gabrielle told the others to continue without her. As soon as they were out of earshot, Dana crossed her arms.

"All right," she said. "What's going on?"

"What do you mean?" Gabrielle asked.

"You've been acting strangely ever since we got back from the ranch."

"I don't know what you're talking about." But she knew she couldn't hide anything from Dana.

Dana put her hand on Gabrielle's shoulder. "I've known you since we were eighteen. I can tell when something is wrong."

"It's nothing. I'm taking care of it."

"Talk to me, Gabi. Please."

Gabrielle let out a heavy sigh. There was no point trying to keep this from her. "What you said about Chloe in there. Did you mean it?"

"Of course I did. Honestly, I didn't think I'd ever feel that way about any other woman, but after last weekend, I realized that I really care for her. All this time, I've expected her to disappear like all the others. But she's different. She's special. And I can't stop thinking about how wonderful it would be if she were ours. Not just for a night, not just for a weekend. For good."

Gabrielle's stomach flipped. Dana had fallen for Chloe just as hard as she herself had.

Dana frowned. "But you don't feel the same way?"

Gabrielle shook her head. "No, I do. I really do."

"Then what's the matter? This is *me* you're talking to. You can trust me."

"I know that, but I don't want to pull you into this."

"Into what?"

Gabrielle hesitated. "Do you remember when we were talking about Chloe, about how her background doesn't quite add up?"

"Yes?"

"And do you remember that private investigator I hired after I found out my ex-fiancée was lying about everything?"

Dana's jaw tightened. "*Yes?*"

"I hired him to look into Chloe."

Dana flinched. "You did what?"

"It's just a background check. Nothing as extensive as what he did with my ex. I wanted to be sure Chloe was who she said she was. But that's no excuse. I shouldn't have done it. And he hasn't found anything yet, so I'm just going to call the whole thing off."

"Good, because this is a serious breach of Chloe's trust."

"I know that. And as soon as I get back to the office, I'm going to email the PI and tell him to drop the investigation. And I should tell Chloe, but..." How could she tell her? Chloe would be so betrayed to hear what she had done.

"Hold on," Dana said. "The investigator hasn't found anything yet, correct?"

Gabrielle shook her head.

"Then perhaps it's best if we leave it for now. Especially

considering our plans for tonight. I don't want to do this with anything hanging over us."

"You're right," Gabrielle said.

"And speaking of tonight, how are you feeling about it?"

"I'm feeling fine. How about you?" Gabrielle smiled. "Two submissives at once? That's your ultimate power fantasy. Are you sure you can handle it?"

Dana gave her a firm look. "I'm serious. We've never done this before, not with anyone else. Are you ready for it? To let someone else see that side of us? Of you?"

"Your concern is sweet, but I'm sure. I feel perfectly comfortable doing this with Chloe. If anyone understands that side of me, it's her. I want this. I want to share it with her." Gabrielle traced her hand down Dana's shoulder and leaned in close to her, speaking into her ear. "But what I want even more is to watch you attempt to put me in my place."

Dana's eyes darkened. "Darling, you're very lucky we're in public, otherwise I'd do just that, right now."

"We could always go up to your office."

"No, let's go to yours. Those glass walls would give your employees the perfect view while I show them who their boss really answers to."

"Kinky. I like it. See, aren't you glad you have me to keep you on your toes?"

"You are just…" Dana shook her head. "Just call off that background check. We'll deal with the issue of telling Chloe about it later. We can't afford to have this come between us."

Gabrielle nodded. Amber's quip at lunch about it taking ten years for her and Dana to figure out their feelings for each other had hit its mark. They couldn't make that mistake again or Chloe might just slip through their fingers.

And Gabrielle refused to let that happen.

When Gabrielle returned to the Mistress Media offices, she was almost bowled over by her assistant. Her lunch had been a long one, so she'd missed several important calls and emails.

But they would have to wait.

She waved away her assistant, instructing him that she wasn't to be disturbed before shutting herself in her office and taking a seat in the leather chair behind her desk. She needed to do this. Now.

She took out her laptop and opened up her email inbox. She had dozens of new emails, half of which were marked urgent. No wonder her assistant was so frazzled.

As she skimmed through her inbox, one of the emails stopped her in her tracks.

It was from the private investigator.

Had he finished looking into Chloe already? Did the email contain the answers to all those little discrepancies in her story, all her secrets?

Gabrielle knew what she needed to do. She needed to delete the email, then tell the investigator she no longer needed his services.

Instead, she clicked on the email, opening it up.

She scanned it with narrowed eyes. It wasn't at all what she'd expected. It posed more questions than answers. As she read over the email again, more thoroughly this time, snippets of it jumped out at her.

No records of Chloe Campbell anywhere... false name... ownership of the florist shop is obscured... gone through great lengths to hide her identity...

She frowned. What did this mean? Gabrielle had been searching for skeletons in Chloe's closet, but instead, the closet was empty. Was Chloe lying about who she was? That was far worse than anything Gabrielle had anticipated.

First her ex-fiancée, and now Chloe. How was this happening to her again?

She took a deep breath. She needed to get a grip. She forced herself to read on, finally reaching the last line of the email.

I still have a few leads. The ownership of the florist shop is one of them. I'll get back to you with answers soon.

She leaned back in her chair and closed her eyes, rubbing her temples with her fingertips. There had to be some kind of explanation for it all. Perhaps Chloe had simply changed her name. People changed their names all the time or went by different names day-to-day. Perhaps it was for privacy, for safety. Perhaps it wasn't anything malicious at all.

There just had to be a good reason that Chloe would lie to them. Gabrielle needed there to be one. Because she still felt the same way about Chloe. She still felt, in her heart, that she could trust her. She didn't believe that Chloe would ever mislead them.

But she'd been wrong before.

As if on cue, her phone vibrated. She picked it up from

her desk. It was a message from Chloe, to both Gabrielle and Dana.

I might be a little late tonight, I have a ton of evening deliveries. But I'll definitely be there.

Another message came through a few seconds later.

I can't wait.

Unease prodded at the back of Gabrielle's mind. *Tonight.* Tonight, she was going to show Chloe a part of herself she kept hidden from everyone else, was going to reveal the desires she kept buried deep inside. It was a side of herself she'd never shared with anyone other than Dana. She certainly hadn't shared it with any of the other women they'd dated. She'd never felt comfortable enough with them for that.

Chloe was different. Gabrielle had grown to feel at ease with her, to trust her.

But now that she knew Chloe was lying to them, could she still trust her?

She put her phone down and typed a reply to the PI. *Let me know as soon as you find anything.*

She closed her laptop. This was just a precaution. Until the investigator got back to her, she would continue with the way things were. What choice did she have? She couldn't tell Dana about this, couldn't implicate her in this.

She would go through with tonight. She would trust Chloe, for now.

And she would wait for confirmation that she was right to trust her.

CHAPTER 24

That night, Chloe followed Dana and Gabrielle to their bedroom, her heart thundering in her chest. Her deliveries had taken even longer than she'd planned. She'd barely had a chance to grab something to eat before coming over. After discussing ground rules over a glass of wine, Dana and Gabrielle had led Chloe to the bedroom.

And here they were.

Dana ushered her inside. Gabrielle shut the door behind them.

"Welcome to our sanctuary," she said.

Chloe gazed around the room, wide-eyed. It was as lush and luxurious as she'd expected a bedroom belonging to Dana and Gabrielle would be, but that wasn't what had her enraptured. All this time, she'd been wondering if Dana and Gabrielle had some kind of secret playroom in their house, filled to the brim with erotic delights. After all, that was what Chloe would want if she had all the money in the world.

But from the looks of everything around them, for Dana

and Gabrielle, their bedroom and their playroom were one and the same.

"Like what you see?" Gabrielle said. "Why don't you take a look around?"

Chloe glanced at Dana, who gave her a nod of permission. Chloe stepped deeper into the room, examining everything closely. There were two walk-in closets, one full of clothes, the other full of kinky outfits, accessories, and tools. In place of pictures on the walls, there were cuffs, blindfolds, leather harnesses, ropes, all displayed like works of art. Hanging above the bed in a glass case was an assortment of whips, riding crops, and paddles.

And the centerpiece of it all was a vast four-poster bed adorned in sheets of pure white silk, with half a dozen matching pillows set aside on a nearby chair. The lights on the ceiling were pointed toward the bed, giving the white sheets a golden glow. Restraints hung from each bedpost, keeping them within easy reach.

Chloe reached for the cuff hanging from the bottom corner of the bed. It was leather, soft and pliable. Immediately, she imagined herself bound on the bed, the restraints around her ankles...

She turned back to her Mistresses, self-conscious, her face growing hot.

"Don't do that," Dana chided. "Don't suppress your desires, not in here. This room exists for exactly this reason, so we can explore our passions freely, together." She took Chloe's cheek in her hand. "When you're in here, you're ours. You belong to us. Whatever you want, whatever you desire, we'll take care of it. We'll take care of you."

Chloe's stomach fluttered. How much of Dana and

Gabrielle's lives had been built around this? Around having someone to serve them, to worship them, someone to belong to them, body, mind, and heart? How long had they spent waiting, searching for someone to fill this space they had prepared for that one special woman?

Could Chloe be that woman? Could she truly give herself to them in the way they wanted, in the way that she herself wanted deep down, more than anything?

She drew in a breath. That wasn't a question that she could answer yet. But just for tonight, she could be that woman.

Chloe gave a small nod. Her hand still on Chloe's cheek, Dana turned to Gabrielle, cupping her cheek in her other hand.

"And for tonight, you're mine too," Dana said. "I expect nothing less than your unwavering submission."

Chloe looked at Gabrielle out of the corner of her eye. There was a firmness in Dana's voice that she hadn't used when speaking with Chloe.

"What's your safeword?" Dana asked Gabrielle.

"Umbrella," the woman replied.

Dana turned to Chloe. "And yours?"

"Parachute." Dana already knew what Chloe's safeword was. She wasn't careless enough to forget something that important. But it seemed she wasn't taking chances tonight.

"Use them if you need to. Both of you." She looked pointedly at Gabrielle. "Don't push yourselves."

They nodded.

Dana pointed to the rug at the end of the bed. "Get undressed and stand there. Leave your underwear on."

Without waiting for them to obey, Dana strode over to a

padlocked chest of drawers on the side of the room, her stiletto heels clicking on the floorboards. Producing a key out of thin air, she unlocked one of the drawers and withdrew a long, thin riding crop from it.

Stroking it lovingly, she turned back to Chloe and Gabrielle, the firm expression on her face a wordless reminder of the command she had issued. Chloe stripped off her clothes and folded them neatly on a chair before taking her place on the rug in nothing but her bra and panties.

She glanced at Gabrielle, who was undressing slowly, slipping out of her fitted black dress to reveal a set of lingerie in an alluring shade of red. Tossing the dress aside, she pushed her long, wavy locks behind her shoulders and joined Chloe on the rug.

"That's better," Dana said. "Now you're appropriately attired to stand before your Mistress. Or, better yet, to kneel." She pointed the riding crop at the ground beneath her feet. "On your knees."

Chloe dropped to her knees, her body moving to obey before her mind could process the command. Gabrielle, on the other hand, took her time, getting down on one knee, then the other.

Chloe bowed her head, waiting silently, but inside, she was bursting with anticipation. What did Dana have in store for them tonight? They'd had a thorough discussion beforehand about their limits, their boundaries. They all knew where each other stood. They knew exactly how far they could push.

And as Chloe peered up at Dana, she had no doubt her Mistress was going to push them both.

Dana took a step back, inspecting Chloe's and Gabrielle's kneeling forms. She put her hands on her hips, letting her long black robe fall open just enough to give them a glimpse of the lingerie underneath. The matching bra and panties were ivory with black lace edging, an enticing contrast to her deep brown skin. On anyone else, it would have looked innocent, virginal even, but not on Dana. Only she could manage to look utterly predatory in lacy white panties.

"Tonight," she said, "both of you are mine." She began pacing before them, her robe billowing behind her, tapping the riding crop against her hand. "Mine to command. Mine to possess. And if you're lucky, mine to pleasure. Because as your Mistress, your bodies belong to me. Your minds belong to me. Your pleasure is mine, to give and take as I see fit."

She stretched her arm toward Chloe, reaching down with the riding crop, sliding it up the center of Chloe's throat and tipping her chin upward. Chloe gazed up at her, a frisson of desire running through her. Behind her Mistress's dark eyes, a fire raged, burning hot and bright.

"Chloe," she said. "How I've longed to have you at my feet like this. You're the picture of submission, of unhesitating obedience."

She turned to Gabrielle. "And you. You're no stranger to being at my feet either. It's been so long, but I can see you still remember your place." She traced the riding crop up Gabrielle's shoulder. "You've been waiting for this. Waiting, hoping, wishing for your Mistress to bring you to your knees again."

She drew the riding crop up to the base of Gabrielle's

chin, just as she'd done to Chloe. But Gabrielle didn't look up. She didn't meet her Mistress's eyes. Although Dana didn't react to the obvious insult, it set Chloe's pulse racing.

"You can pretend all you want," Dana said. "But I know how much you crave this. You spend your days holding all that power in your hands, all that responsibility, at work, in every area of your life. But your Mistress knows what you secretly long for. To be brought to your knees, to be made to submit, so you have no choice but to let go and let me take control, all for one sweet moment of carefree surrender."

Gabrielle's breaths deepened, her chest rising and falling rapidly. Was what Dana was saying true? Was that what Gabrielle wanted? Chloe tried to peer at Gabrielle's face without moving her head, but she couldn't make out the expression on it.

"How does it feel to kneel before your Mistress after so long?" Dana asked.

Silence fell over the room. Gabrielle didn't speak. She didn't move. A second passed, then another.

Dana tapped Gabrielle's shoulder with the riding crop. "I asked you a question. How does it feel?"

Chloe held her breath, willing Gabrielle to answer. She couldn't take this. Gabrielle defying her Mistress, the tension simmering between her two women—it was too much for her to handle.

Finally, Gabrielle looked up at Dana, a challenge in her eyes. "If you want to know so badly, let's swap places and you can find out."

Chloe's heart stopped. She looked up at Dana. Her face remained stone, but the fire in her eye blazed even brighter.

"Why do you insist on doing this, every single time?" She snapped the riding crop against her palm, punctuating each word. "It seems you need to be taught a lesson about which of us is in charge here."

Chloe glanced sideways at Gabrielle. Despite her resolute expression, there was a hint of a smile on her lips. Was this some kind of game to her? Was she enjoying this? Was Dana?

"You." Dana gave Chloe a sharp look. "Eyes down."

Chloe lowered her head.

"It's clear you could also benefit from a reminder of who is in charge, Chloe," Dana said. "Consider this a demonstration of what happens when one of my submissives disobeys me."

Dana's words sent a thrill rolling through Chloe. Perhaps she could understand the appeal of this, of challenging her Mistress in the way that Gabrielle had done. But Chloe could never bring herself to do the same. Even if she wanted to, the part of her that needed to obey wouldn't let her.

"Now, about that lesson." Dana held up the riding crop, drawing it slowly through her hand. "I borrowed this from the stables at the ranch. I suspected I'd need it tonight. While I'd never use one of these on a horse, I have no such reservations when it comes to disobedient submissives."

Chloe's mouth fell open. Surely Dana was joking about bringing the riding crop back from the stables. Wasn't she?

"Get down on your hands and knees," she commanded. "And face each other."

Chloe did as she was told. As Gabrielle did the same beside her, she shot Chloe a wicked look.

"Heads down," Dana said. "Both of you."

Chloe bowed her head, her body burning all over. Why did she find this so arousing, sharing this punishment with Gabrielle, her Mistress?

Her heels clicking, Dana moved to stand behind Chloe. Then her hands were at Chloe's hips, pulling her panties down, letting them fall to the floor around her knees. Chloe shivered, both from the cool air and from having her ass bare and exposed, waiting for Dana's riding crop.

Dana gave Chloe's rear a firm slap with her hand before moving to stand by Gabrielle. Although Chloe didn't dare lift her head, she could see Dana's stilettoed feet behind the other woman as she drew Gabrielle's panties down, the riding crop dangling from her wrist.

"Let me test this out," she said.

Holding the crop by the handle, she raised it above Gabrielle's ass and swung it down, snapping it against Gabrielle's skin. Then she raised her arm higher, swinging the crop with more force, once, twice, three times. Gabrielle jolted forward, but she remained silent, her resolute expression unchanged.

"That seems to be in order," Dana said. "Now it's your turn."

She returned to Chloe's side and repeated what she'd done to Gabrielle, tapping the riding crop against Chloe's ass with ever-increasing force. Chloe screwed her eyes shut, letting out soft gasps as Dana's strikes grew harder, each one sending a bolt of electricity deep into Chloe's core.

She shuddered, a fevered whimper falling from her lips. But Dana didn't strike her again. Instead, she kneaded

Chloe's ass cheeks with her hands, drawing a blissful sigh from her.

"Chloe," Dana crooned. "You're just the perfect submissive, aren't you?"

She dragged the riding crop along the center of Chloe's back, over the nape of her neck and the side of her face, caressing her cheek with it. Chloe purred, her body sensitized from the stinging kisses of the riding crop.

"You submit to your Mistresses willingly," Dana continued. "You serve with enthusiasm, and you're always grateful for your Mistresses' affections."

She lifted the riding crop and drew it down Gabrielle's back as she moved to stand next to her.

"But you, my darling," she said to Gabrielle. "You're too conflicted about your desires."

Dana brought the riding crop down on Gabrielle's ass with a loud crack. Chloe jumped. From the sound it made, Dana had struck Gabrielle much harder than Chloe. And still, Gabrielle barely reacted.

"You pretend you don't want this. You resist me at every step. But your Mistress knows better. Your Mistress knows exactly what you need."

The crack of the riding crop against Gabrielle's skin echoed through the room, over and over again. Chloe peered up through her lashes, watching them, captivated. Even though Gabrielle was unmoved by Dana's strikes, it was like Chloe could feel every one of them on her own body.

Her pulse pounded, the throbbing between her legs intensifying. She wanted to feel her Mistress's riding crop against her skin again, wanted the sweet, heady rush of her Mistress's 'lesson.'

But for the moment, Dana was focused on Gabrielle with single-minded determination. And soon, Gabrielle began to pant, her face contorting in an expression that had nothing to do with pain. It was the look of someone trying not to give in.

A hint of a smile crossed Dana's lips. "I know how much you're enjoying this. I know how much you want to surrender." She brushed her fingers up the inside of Gabrielle's thigh. "Don't fight it."

This time, when she brought the crop down on Gabrielle's skin, Gabrielle let out a sharp, trembling cry that sounded almost euphoric. The sight, the sound of Gabrielle coming apart at Dana's hand sent heat flooding into Chloe's center, filled her with a longing to be in Gabrielle's place.

And with each stroke of the riding crop, Gabrielle unraveled further. Her body loosened until she could barely keep herself upright, her eyes glazing over like she was trapped in a fog of lust and bliss.

Chloe knew what that look was. She knew what it felt like to fall into that space where the whole world crumbled away and her awareness shrunk down to nothing but her own body and the overwhelming presence that was her Mistress. That state, uninhibited and primal, was a vulnerable one to be in. It required a deep level of trust.

She felt a stirring inside her. She understood it now, this dynamic between Dana and Gabrielle. She understood why Gabrielle resisted when what she really wanted was to surrender. While for Chloe, submission was an innate, almost automatic thing, for Gabrielle, it was different. She needed her submission to be won from her by a woman that was strong enough to take it. And more than that, she needed a woman who had proven she could be trusted with that power. A woman like Dana.

Dana brought the riding crop down one final time before crouching down beside Gabrielle. "That's it," she whispered. "Just let go."

She gave Gabrielle's shoulder a reassuring touch, then returned to stand by Chloe, trailing her fingertips down Chloe's back in a long, lazy line. She let her hand wander back between Chloe's thighs, stroking up and down her slit.

Pleasure lanced through her. Chloe tried to part her legs further, but her panties were tangled around her knees, keeping her from spreading them any wider.

She whimpered helplessly.

"So wet already," Dana said, teasing Chloe's clit with her fingertip. "Who knew you would take such perverse pleasure in Gabi's punishment?"

Chloe's face grew hot. She bit her lower lip, trying to keep her desire at bay.

"Or is it your own punishment you enjoy? Is that what you crave?"

Withdrawing her hand, Dana brought the riding crop down over Chloe's ass, much harder than before. Chloe's fingers and toes curled, her body stiffening from the unexpected shock. But as the shock passed, it gave way to a burning, aching pleasure.

As Dana brought the crop down on her, over and over, she squeezed her eyes shut, letting it all wash over her. Delicious anticipation. Exhilarating pain. Exquisite pleasure. She relished the kiss of the crop on her skin, relished her

Mistress's intermittent caresses on her ass and the backs of her thighs, relished the feel of Gabrielle's lust-filled eyes on her.

And soon, she was sinking into that same blissful space as Gabrielle, the two of them existing in it together, with their Mistress. As Dana stilled the riding crop, replacing it with her hands on Chloe's cheeks, she found herself sinking even deeper.

"That's enough," Dana said. "Now it's time for the real lesson."

Chloe held back a whine. Her whole body sizzled with need, her mind too clouded by desire to handle Dana's mind games. Chloe wanted her so badly. Every moment without her Mistress's touch was torturous.

"Don't worry, Chloe, you're going to enjoy this." Dana crouched down before Gabrielle, brushing her hair aside to cradle her cheek in her hand. "You, on the other hand, will not. I know how much you enjoyed that, darling. Did you really think I'd reward you for your bad behavior?"

Dana straightened up, gazing down at both of them, a fire in her eyes. "If you haven't figured it out yet, this lesson isn't about punishment, or discipline. The lesson here is that you are *mine*, to do with as I please. Your pleasure is mine, to give and to take.

"And both of you are about to find out just what that means."

CHAPTER 25

"On the bed, Chloe," Dana said. She turned to Gabrielle and pointed to a chair off to the side. "You, sit there."

Chloe rose to her feet, her knees aching, and pulled her panties up around her waist before getting onto the bed. Gabrielle followed in suit, taking a seat in the chair nearby. It was pointed toward the bed, giving her an unobstructed view.

Dana walked over to the padlocked chest of drawers again, returning the riding crop to its place, then opened another drawer and withdrew a pair of handcuffs. Chloe's heart sped up. Were the cuffs for her?

But Dana strode over to the chair Gabrielle sat in instead, brandishing the cuffs. "This lesson is far from over. And this isn't just about tonight. After the way you've been behaving, challenging me, and in front of Chloe? How did you think this was going to go? Did you think I'd play into your hands, just give you what you wanted?"

She traced her fingers up the side of Gabrielle's neck.

"No, you're not going to get any pleasure. You're going to sit in this chair while I pleasure Chloe. You're going to watch and listen, unable to do anything at all."

Chloe's entire body began to smolder. Why was she getting so worked up over the prospect of being the center of Dana and Gabrielle's delectably twisted games?

Dana dangled the handcuffs from a finger. "These are to make sure you don't try anything. Hands behind your back."

For a moment, Gabrielle didn't react. Had Dana gone too far?

Then, Gabrielle put her hands behind her back.

Dana fastened the handcuffs around Gabrielle's wrists, looping the chain around a rung of the chair's backrest. The cuffs now secure, she rounded the chair, moving to stand in front of Gabrielle, and crossed her arms.

"I know how much you love to tease, regardless of which end of the whip you're on," she said. "You're always playing games, always toying with us both. How does it feel to get a taste of that?"

Gabrielle gazed back up at her. "Like I said before, let's swap places and you can find out."

"You never learn, do you?" Dana shook her head, turning to Chloe. "Don't move."

She gave Gabrielle's shoulder a brief touch before disappearing into one of the walk-in closets. As Chloe waited for her to return, she studied Gabrielle silently. What was going on in the woman's head? Her expression was inscrutable, her face half-hidden by her hair, but her eyes still smoldered with the same intense desire as always. She was enjoying Dana's sweet torture as much as Chloe was.

And Chloe hadn't missed all the little ways that Dana

had made sure that this was the case, with a questioning look or a reassuring touch. Dana treated Gabrielle differently than Chloe. With Chloe, she was gentle and caring, while with Gabrielle, she was stricter, firmer.

But at the same time, she was stricter in the way she looked after Gabrielle, more attentive in the way she made sure that Gabrielle was still within the bounds of her limits.

As Dana emerged from the closet, Chloe's eyes were drawn to her. She gaped at her Mistress, unable to decide where to look. Dana had removed her bra, but she still wore her black robe and stilettos, along with the ivory-colored panties. But now, the panties had a clear glass dildo sticking out from them.

"I designed this lingerie myself," Dana said. "I made sure the panties could accommodate a little something extra."

Need welled up inside Chloe. Of course Dana would design her own custom lingerie for the express purpose of looking sophisticated while wielding a strap-on. The dildo itself was striking, glittering like crystal in the light.

Dana sauntered over to Gabrielle and stood before her, hands on hips. Gabrielle stared at her, just as entranced as Chloe was.

"You will watch us," Dana said. "You will not look away. And when we're done, you will beg me to bring you your release."

Gabrielle didn't respond, but the hunger in her eyes said enough.

Dana wheeled around to face Chloe on the bed. "Strip," she ordered.

Chloe took off her bra and panties as quickly as she

could, then lay back down, serving herself up for her Mistress to claim.

She didn't have to wait long. Dana climbed onto the bed and stalked across it toward her on her hands and knees. She straddled Chloe's body.

Then, she slid her silk robe from her shoulders.

Chloe stared up at her, hypnotized. It was the first time she'd seen Dana naked. Her rich brown skin had a gold glow, and her curves were slender but defined, her breasts small but full.

Chloe's admiration must have shown in her eyes.

"From now on, you're allowed to touch me," Dana said. "Above the waist only. Consider it a reward for being a good pet."

Chloe's stomach flipped. Dana was finally letting her touch her.

She took a deep breath and reached for her Mistress tentatively, tracing her hand up the side of her waist. Dana's skin was supple and soft, even softer than it looked.

At first, she didn't react to Chloe's touch, but as her fingertips brushed the base of Dana's breast, she trembled slightly, a barely audible sigh escaping her.

Feeling bolder now, Chloe swept her hands up Dana's stomach, her chest, her shoulders, running her fingers all over Dana's breasts, savoring their softness. As she skated her fingertip over a tiny, stiff nipple, she found herself wanting to kiss it.

But she didn't want to push Dana's boundaries. And the more Chloe touched her, the more she craved her Mistress and that diamond-hard prize strapped between her legs.

"That's enough." Dana took Chloe's wrist and pinned her hand to the pillow beside her head. "I want you, *now*."

She leaned down and pressed her lips to Chloe's in a demanding, unyielding kiss. Chloe arched up into her, her body seeking Dana's, but Dana pried herself away, moving down to part Chloe's legs, positioning herself between them. Chloe's pulse surged, blood rushing to her skin and deep in her core.

Dana took the glass toy jutting out from her panties in one delicate hand. "You don't need to ask for permission before you come. Just be sure to voice your gratitude toward your Mistress when you do."

Chloe nodded. "Yes, Mistress."

Dana dragged the tip of the strap-on down between Chloe's lips, skating it past her aching clit and down to her entrance. She guided it inside carefully. Chloe sucked in a sharp breath and closed her eyes. The heft and hardness of the glass made her feel impossibly full.

She ground her hips, desperate for more. After Dana's "punishment," Chloe's body was primed and ready for release.

But Dana wasn't going to let that happen. Bracing her forearms on the bed beside Chloe's head, she began thrusting between Chloe's hips, slowly, rhythmically, sending jolts of pleasure through her. But it wasn't enough to take her to the edge.

A whine fell from Chloe's lips. This was why Dana had told Chloe she didn't need to ask permission to come. Chloe wasn't going to reach the point of release until Dana permitted it. She had that much control—over herself, over the strap-on she wielded, over Chloe's body—and she was determined to exert it. All Chloe could do was wrap her arms around Dana's waist, clinging to her, rocking in time with her.

As they moved together, skin against skin, Chloe found herself slipping into that state of pure bliss where the world around her vanished and all that was left was herself and her Mistress. And Gabrielle, too. Chloe was aware of the other woman's presence beyond the bed, bound, just out of reach.

Chloe stretched an arm out toward her, her fingers grasping at the slippery silk sheets covering the bed. She turned her head to the side, her eyes meeting Gabrielle's, silently calling out to her.

Dana chose that moment to grant Chloe her release. A cry flew from her as pleasure erupted deep inside. Wave after wave battered her body, drowning her. All the while Dana rocked inside her, keeping her submerged in a state of such ecstasy that Chloe felt like she'd left her body altogether.

When she fell back down to it, she was breathing hard, her muscles slack and weak and her skin shiny with sweat. Dana was holding her tenderly, stroking her hair. It had fallen loose from its ponytail.

Dana pushed a strand of it behind Chloe's ear. "Are you still with us?"

Chloe nodded. "Thank you, Mistress."

"You're welcome, my darling. But we're not done yet. There's something else I need from you."

Dana got up from the bed and walked over to where Gabrielle was bound to the chair, beckoning her to follow. Chloe did as she was told, joining Dana by the chair.

Gabrielle looked up at them. That earlier defiance was still in her eyes, but now the desire in them was greater. And Chloe didn't miss the ravenous way Gabrielle probed Chloe's body with her eyes. Even bound to a chair, she still managed to make Chloe weak with nothing more than a look.

Dana rounded the chair to stand behind it. She slung her arms around Gabrielle's shoulders, her lips beside Gabrielle's ear. "That must have been agonizing for you, watching us, unable to join in." She slipped her hand down between Gabrielle's thighs, stroking her through her panties. "Have you learned your lesson?"

Gabrielle nodded.

"You will speak to me when I ask you a question."

"Yes," Gabrielle said quietly.

"Yes, who?"

Gabrielle said nothing.

Dana straightened up and crossed her arms. "You know what? I'm going to have Chloe deliver the rest of your lesson."

Chloe looked from one woman to the other. What did Dana want her to do? Gabrielle was still her Mistress. The idea of teaching her any kind of 'lesson' felt wrong. Could she bring herself to do what Dana was asking of her?

For a moment, she considered using her safeword.

"Chloe, darling?" Dana said. "I understand your hesitation. But tonight, I am Mistress not only to you, but to her. I am in control of everything that happens in this room, am I not?"

Chloe glanced at Dana's face. There was a subtle meaning in her words, her eyes.

Trust me.

"Yes, Mistress," Chloe said. Dana knew where her boundaries lay. Dana wouldn't ask her to do anything she felt uncomfortable with.

She gave Chloe a firm look. "Then do as I say." She tipped her head toward Gabrielle. "Sit on her lap. Face her."

Chloe lowered herself onto Gabrielle's lap, straddling her. Gabrielle shifted underneath her. Their bodies pressed together, she could feel how hot Gabrielle's skin was, could feel her racing heartbeat, could feel the heaving of her chest.

"Kiss her," Dana said.

It was then that Chloe realized just what kind of lesson Dana had in mind. She'd been right to trust her Mistress.

She drew her hands up Gabrielle's shoulders, cupping her face in her palms, and leaned in, pressing her lips to Gabrielle's. Gabrielle returned the kiss furiously, devouring Chloe's lips and tongue. It was as if Gabrielle—bound, unable to move or touch—was channeling all her lust through her kiss.

Dana spoke up beside them. "Now, play with those lovely pink nipples of hers. That always gets her worked up."

Chloe glanced down at Gabrielle's chest. She was still wearing her bra. Chloe pulled the cups of the bra down gingerly, exposing Gabrielle's generous breasts. Her rosy nipples had already hardened into peaks.

Chloe's lips parted slightly. The first time she'd seen Gabrielle naked, that night on her boat, she hadn't gotten the chance to touch her, not properly. The same was true of the morning by the lake. With her hands bound, she'd been at Gabrielle's mercy.

Now, their roles were reversed.

But even in submission, Gabrielle was still Chloe's Mistress. And Chloe wanted to worship her.

Chloe drew her hands down Gabrielle's smooth, soft breasts, then traced a finger over one nipple, eliciting a shuddering gasp from her. Excitement rippled through Chloe. Touching her tied-up Mistress like this felt so forbidden. And hearing Gabrielle's gasps, feeling her quivering under her weight, was intoxicating.

Her hands still exploring Gabrielle's breasts, she kissed her way down the woman's neck, then painted a trail of kisses down her chest. She took one of Gabrielle's nipples in her mouth, sucking and rolling her tongue over it. Gabrielle moaned softly, her head falling over the back of her chair. Chloe did the same to the other nipple, working it with her mouth until Gabrielle cried out.

Dana leaned down, speaking into Gabrielle's ear. "Had enough yet?"

Gabrielle pressed her lips together silently, but her whole body trembled.

"I can tell you have," Dana said. "And I can give you what you need. You know what I want to hear."

When Gabrielle finally spoke, her voice was barely a whisper.

"Please," she said.

"What was that?" Dana asked. "I didn't quite hear you."

"Please," Gabrielle repeated, louder.

"Please, who?"

Gabrielle hesitated before speaking again. "Please, Mistress."

"That's right. I am your Mistress. Who do you belong to? Tell me."

"You. I belong to you."

Dana trailed her hand down Gabrielle's arm. "Now that wasn't so hard, was it?" Without waiting for an answer, she gave Chloe a nod. "Get down on your knees, my pet."

Chloe slipped off Gabrielle's lap and knelt in front of her.

"Because I'm a fair Mistress, I'll give you what you want," Dana said. "But I'm going to let Chloe do the honors. And she's not permitted to let you come until I say so." She leaned down and draped her arms around Gabrielle's shoulders from behind, holding her tightly. "Go on, Chloe. But take it slow. We can't have Gabrielle forgetting who's in control."

This time, Chloe didn't hesitate to follow Dana's command. Since that morning at the ranch, she'd been dying for another taste of her Mistress.

She reached up to Gabrielle's hips and tugged at the waistband of her panties, working them down her legs and pulling them from her ankles. She placed the panties aside and ran her hands up the insides of Gabrielle's knees and thighs, parting her legs.

Gabrielle shifted her hips forward, arching out toward Chloe impatiently. She was sure that if Gabrielle's hands weren't tied, they'd be at Chloe's head, guiding her to where she wanted her.

But Chloe didn't need guidance. She knew instinctively how to please her. She closed her eyes and dove between Gabrielle's legs, letting the woman's scent and taste overtake her, parting Gabrielle's glistening wet lips with her tongue, sliding it up her slit. A drunken murmur spilled from Gabrielle's lips, her body vibrating.

She ground her hips against Chloe, urging her on. Every part of her longed to give Gabrielle what she wanted. But Dana had commanded her to hold back, had commanded both of them to hold back.

So Chloe took her time, exploring every inch of Gabrielle's silken folds with her mouth. All the while, Gabrielle moaned and shook, somehow keeping her impending climax at bay. Even Chloe could feel the pressure building and building within Gabrielle's body.

After what felt like an eternity, Dana spoke.

"This has gone on for long enough. You can let it all go now, both of you."

Chloe had underestimated just how much Gabrielle had been holding back. All it took were a few sweeps of her tongue before Gabrielle came apart. She threw her head back, bucking in her seat as pleasure racked her body. Her climax seemed to stretch on and on into infinity. But Chloe didn't stop until Gabrielle stilled completely.

Not a heartbeat passed before Dana swooped in and took Gabrielle's face in her hands, planting a brief, firm kiss on her lips. "Are you all right, darling?"

Gabrielle nodded. She was still shaking from her orgasm. As Dana caressed Gabrielle's cheek, Chloe felt warmth stirring inside her. Dana was always gentle with her, but she'd never seen her be so gentle with Gabrielle.

After freeing Gabrielle from the handcuffs, Dana took her and Chloe by the hand, drawing them to the bed. She ushered them onto it before climbing in too, wedging herself between them. Enveloping them with her arms,

Dana pulled them in close, whispering sweet, tender things to them both.

Chloe nestled against her, sinking into her warmth and softness, her arm stretched across Dana to interlace her fingers with Gabrielle's. As she began to come down from her subspace high, the gravity of what was passing between the three of them hit her. This was a side of Dana and Gabrielle that they didn't show to anyone else, but they'd shown it to her. They were giving her parts of themselves, hidden, vulnerable parts, just as she was giving parts of herself to them.

This was what she'd feared when she met the two of them all that time ago, that she would become so irrevocably intertwined with them that she'd lose herself, drown in them. She didn't fear that anymore. She wanted this. She wanted to give them all of her.

Did that include her heart?

CHAPTER 26

Chloe stared at her phone, her brows drawn together. The personal phone number of Dana and Gabrielle's lawyer friend was displayed on the screen. All she had to do was press call.

So why was she hesitating? Things with Tracy hadn't improved. They were getting worse. The month had just ended, and Chloe's deadline to pay the money she owed her had passed. Tracy hadn't acted on her threat yet, but she was bombarding Chloe with increasingly disturbing calls and text messages.

Where's my money?

You owe me.

Does your new girlfriend know who you really are, Cassidy?

The last message was the reason Chloe was finally considering calling this lawyer. The fact that Tracy referred to Chloe's 'girlfriend,' singular, was a sign that she didn't know a single thing about Chloe's love life, but it still made her uneasy. The last thing she wanted was for Dana and

Gabrielle to get dragged into her problems. And she didn't want them to learn the truth about her this way.

In fact, she was having second thoughts about telling them the truth at all. Gabrielle's revelation about her ex-fiancée, the way she'd lied to her, made Chloe hesitant to tell her that she'd lied to her too. Would she be hurt to learn of Chloe's dishonesty?

Maybe that was even more of a reason for Chloe to tell her, tell them, sooner rather than later. If they learned the truth from Tracy, Chloe wouldn't even have a chance to explain herself, to explain why she hid who she really was.

She took a few deep breaths. She needed more time to figure this out, but who knew how long it would be before Tracy acted on her threats? She needed to do something. She needed help. And Dana and Gabrielle were offering it.

Perhaps believing that their help didn't come with strings was a step she needed to take if she wanted to truly trust them, to truly be theirs.

And Chloe wanted that more than anything.

She pressed call, dialing the number Dana had given her. The phone rang and rang.

Just when Chloe was about to give up, a woman answered.

"Melanie Greene speaking." The lawyer had a firm, no-nonsense tone. Was she some high-flying corporate type? If she was a friend of Dana and Gabrielle's, that was likely.

"Uh, hi. My name's Chloe Campbell."

Before she had a chance to say anything more, Melanie interrupted her.

"You're Dana's friend. She told me to expect your call. How can I help you?"

"I was hoping we could set up an appointment," Chloe said.

"How about this evening? I'm holding free clinic hours right now, but you can come by afterward. Around 6:30?"

Chloe blinked. She wasn't expecting to get in to see the lawyer so quickly. "Sure. That would be great."

"Then it's settled. I'll see you in a few hours."

When Chloe arrived at the office where Melanie worked, it was empty, save for a receptionist who looked to be on her way out. The building was surprisingly modest. Perhaps Chloe had misjudged the lawyer when she'd pegged her for a corporate type.

Chloe approached the desk and told the receptionist she was there to see Melanie.

"Go right on through," she said. "Third door on the left."

She gestured down a hall. Chloe headed down it until she reached Melanie's office.

The door was open. She peered into the room. A woman sat behind a desk with her phone to her ear, dressed in a serious-looking pantsuit with her dark hair tied back neatly. Chloe didn't miss how well-tailored the suit was. And while the woman looked around the same age as Chloe, she had the confidence of someone twice her age.

Noticing Chloe, Melanie waved her inside. Chloe entered the room and took a seat.

Melanie gave her a brief nod as she continued her conversation. "No, I haven't had a chance to look at them yet. Just pick whatever color you like." She paused. "Yes, I'll be home for dinner. I need to go, I have a client. I love you."

Melanie hung up the phone. "My fiancée," she explained. "The wedding is coming up, and between you and me, I think she's a little nervous about it." She stretched her hand across the table. "Melanie Greene. You must be Chloe."

Chloe shook Melanie's hand. The woman was much warmer in person than on the phone. "Thank you for seeing me so quickly."

"No problem. I owe Dana a lifetime of favors for making our wedding dresses. Anything for a friend of hers."

A 'friend'? It seemed Dana had been honest when she'd said she wouldn't tell the lawyer anything about Chloe's situation.

Melanie clasped her hands on the table before her. "What can I do for you?"

"It's kind of a long story," Chloe said.

"Start from the beginning. Take your time."

Chloe took a deep breath and told Melanie everything. At least, she told her everything to do with Tracy and the money she'd given her.

"She agreed to let me pay her back a little each month, but I've fallen behind." Chloe looked down in her lap. "And now she won't stop bothering me about it. She's getting more and more persistent, and I don't know what to do anymore."

She glanced up at Melanie. To her surprise, the woman's eyes were filled with sympathy.

"I'm so sorry you're dealing with this," she said. "And I'm sure I can help you out. There are two issues here—the money, and the harassment. Let's start with the money. How much do you owe her?"

"I'd have to check, but it's down to four figures now."

"And you say she gave it to you as a gift, not a loan?"

Chloe nodded. "But that was when we were together."

"That doesn't matter. Gifts aren't conditional. If she gave you that money, then legally she can't make you pay her back. Do you have any evidence that she gifted it to you? Text messages, emails, where she explicitly says that the money was a gift?"

Chloe nodded. "I have some old texts saying that." Tracy had liked to remind Chloe of her generosity at any chance she'd gotten.

"Then you're in the clear. You don't owe her a cent, and you have proof of that. If you'd like, I can send her a strongly worded cease and desist letter informing her of this fact and telling her if the harassment continues, you'll take legal action against her. Are you concerned about your safety in any way?"

Chloe thought for a moment. "I don't think so." She doubted that Tracy was capable of harming her, but she hadn't thought Tracy would ever threaten her the way she was either.

"If you have any concerns at all, I'd recommend you take out a restraining order against her. Do you know anything about restraining orders?"

Chloe nodded. "I've had a little experience with them." She'd almost taken one out on her own mother.

"Is that something you'd consider?"

"I'm not sure." Even if it stopped Tracy from bothering her, it wouldn't stop her from exposing Chloe to the world.

Melanie studied Chloe's face. "Is there something else you need to tell me? I can't help you if I don't have all the relevant information."

Chloe hesitated. "If I tell you, you have to keep everything confidential, right? You won't tell anyone? Not even Dana or Gabrielle?"

"Of course not. I take client confidentiality seriously. This stays between us. You have my word."

"Well, there's more. She's threatening that if I don't pay her, she'll... I don't really know how to explain this."

"Just start from the beginning."

Chloe told Melanie the rest, told her about her past, her mother, her fake identity. It wasn't hard. In fact, there was something cathartic about it. And when she was finished spilling it all out, she found herself wondering if she was ready to tell Gabrielle and Dana after all.

"Once again, I'm sorry you're dealing with this," Melanie said. "I've had plenty of experience with exes getting obsessive, both personally and professionally. These kinds of problems aren't easy to deal with."

Chloe nodded. Nothing about this was easy.

"But there are steps you can take. In legal terms, what Tracy is doing is blackmail. It's a crime, which means you have the option to go to the police and get her charged. With all the texts she's sent you, you have plenty of evidence."

"I don't know." That sounded a little extreme. Chloe wasn't sure if she could do that to Tracy.

But maybe it was time she stopped being so nice and civil when it came to her ex.

"Of course, going through the justice system can be a

long and messy process," Melanie continued. "Another option is, if you want me to send Tracy that cease and desist letter, I'll include the fact that her threats constitute blackmail, and if she doesn't stop, you'll take the matter to the police."

That could actually work. Tracy wasn't scared of Chloe, but a letter from a lawyer might be enough to make her reconsider her threats.

"So, what do you think? Should we start with the letter?"

Chloe nodded. "That would be great."

"All right. I'll have it done by tomorrow."

Relief washed over her. Could it really be this simple?

"Is there anything else?" Melanie asked.

Chloe shook her head. "That's all. And thank you."

"I'm happy to help. Dana seemed very concerned about your situation. She and Gabrielle must really care about you."

Did Melanie know about their relationship? Had Dana told her about it after all, or had she simply figured it out herself? Chloe tried to read the woman's face, but she couldn't see any signs on it.

"I'll keep you posted on that letter," Melanie said. "And don't hesitate to call me if you need anything else."

"You've been a big help already," Chloe said.

She left the office, a spring in her step. Was this it? Were all her problems solved thanks to Dana and Gabrielle?

But she was getting ahead of herself. Only time would tell if this was enough to get Tracy out of her life for good.

CHAPTER 27

When Dana arrived home that night, the house was silent. "Gabrielle? Are you home?"

She headed down the hall, but there was no sign of Gabrielle in any of her usual evening spots. It wasn't until she reached the kitchen that she found Gabrielle looking absently into the fridge. Dana stood there for a few moments, but Gabrielle didn't notice her.

"Gabi?" she said.

Gabrielle turned, her hand jumping to her chest. "I didn't hear you come home." She shut the fridge. "How was work?"

"It was fine." Dana examined Gabrielle's face. She seemed preoccupied. "Is everything all right?"

Gabrielle nodded. "My mind is still on work, that's all. We're officially opening the Paris offices next month, so I have a lot on my plate."

That was odd. Gabrielle wasn't the type to get stressed or overwhelmed by work. If anything, she thrived in busy, high-pressure situations. It was why she was so good at her job. And her recent behavior—the way she kept avoiding Dana's eyes, evading her questions—it didn't point to stress.

No, this was something else.

"Did you get Chloe's message?" Gabrielle said. "She wanted us to give her a call when we got home."

Dana fished her phone out of her purse. Sure enough, there was a message from Chloe. "Give me a few minutes."

After putting away her things and slipping into a more comfortable outfit, she headed to the living room, phone in hand. Taking a seat next to Gabrielle, she dialed Chloe's number and started a video call. They'd gotten into the habit since it was simpler for three people.

Chloe answered the call, greeting them both energetically. She had a towel wrapped around her hair and her face looked freshly washed, as if she'd just gotten out of the shower.

"I just wanted to thank you," she said. "I met with Melanie after work today, and we talked about my problems with Tracy. I think she can really help."

"That's wonderful," Dana said.

"Thanks for sending me her way. I appreciate it, really. I wish there was a way I could make it up to you both."

Dana shook her head. "There's no need to. No strings, no obligations, remember?"

"I know," Chloe said. "But this isn't about obligations. I just want to show my gratitude."

"You don't need to," Gabrielle said. "Your presence in our lives is more than enough."

Chloe smiled. "I just wish it wasn't so late. I'd love to see you tonight."

"It isn't that late," Gabrielle said. "Sure, it's a school night, but why not be a little naughty? You could sneak out, come over?"

"Believe me, any other night, I'd be there. But I have a ton of early morning deliveries to make tomorrow."

"Oh?" Dana said. "So business is going well?"

"It is," Chloe replied. "Everything is looking up."

"I'm happy for you." Dana turned to Gabrielle. "Isn't that great?"

But Gabrielle hadn't heard her. She was looking down at her own phone, holding it just out of view, her brows drawn together, her eyes narrowed.

"Gabrielle?" Dana said.

Gabrielle's head snapped up at the sound of her name. She put her phone away hurriedly. "That was just work."

Dana frowned. Something was off. Was Gabrielle lying to her? She never lied to Dana. They told each other everything. They shared everything.

What could Gabrielle possibly be keeping from her, and why?

"Now, where were we?" Gabrielle said to Chloe. "You want to see us? How about this weekend?"

Chloe beamed. "Sure. I'd love that."

"Good, because I've been dying for a repeat of the other night, but this time with me holding the riding crop. I've had my fill of being at the other end of it for now. And I've missed having you at my feet."

It was hard to make out on the small phone screen, but Dana thought she saw Chloe blush.

As they discussed their weekend plans, Dana watched Gabrielle out of the corner of her eye. She was acting perfectly normal again now. What was going on with her?

After a brief interruption from Chloe's cat, they settled on a plan for Chloe to come over on Saturday night. Beside Dana, Gabrielle stretched out and yawned.

"You'll have to excuse me," she said. "It's getting late. I'm going to get ready for bed. Don't you two stop on my account." Gabrielle rose from the couch, addressing Chloe one last time. "It was good to see you."

"You too," Chloe said. "And thanks for everything."

As Gabrielle disappeared down the hall, Dana and Chloe continued to talk, but she couldn't shake that nagging feeling she had about Gabrielle. Something was wrong. Dana knew it.

But she wouldn't push Gabrielle to tell her what it was. Gabrielle would tell her herself, with time. She never, ever kept anything from Dana.

At least, she never had until now.

Gabrielle shut the door to the bathroom and pulled her phone out of her pocket. An email from the private investigator was waiting for her. Now that she was alone, she could finally read it.

She'd spent the past week agonizing over her decision to continue with the investigation. She'd almost called it off several times, especially after that night in their bedroom. It had made her realize just how strong her feelings for Chloe were.

But that was all the more reason she needed to know she could trust Chloe. She couldn't get her heart broken again. She needed answers.

And those answers were right at her fingertips.

Gabrielle opened the email. It contained a dozen attachments, pages and pages of information dug up by the investigator. One of them, the email said, was a report, a summary of everything he had found.

Gabrielle opened the report. It began with some background on Chloe, starting with her real name. *Cassidy Denning*, not Chloe Campbell. Chloe Campbell was entirely fictional, just like the PI had suspected. Next was her birthday, and a list of everywhere she'd ever lived. She was born in a small California town and she'd moved to Los Angeles as a child, which was where she'd lived until age eighteen. Her family consisted of her mother and a few relatives scattered in Minnesota. She had no siblings, and her father had passed when she was a baby.

Gabrielle recalled what Dana had told her about the night she'd taken Chloe to the ballet. Could it be that the person they'd run into hadn't mistaken Chloe for someone else? Chloe *was* Cassidy from LA. She'd spent her entire childhood in California, and she'd never lived in Minnesota like she'd told Gabrielle. And what she'd said to Gabrielle about her parents was half true. The report showed that her mother was very much still alive in Los Angeles.

So Gabrielle's suspicions had been justified. Chloe had been lying to them from the beginning.

But why had she lied?

Gabrielle read on, putting all the pieces together as she did. As a child, *Cassidy* had had a minor modeling and beauty pageant career, which had led to her mother moving them to Los Angeles. She'd continued to model and enter pageants, moving on to acting before she even hit her teens.

At first, she'd only gotten minor gigs—commercials, the occasional background role in a movie or an episode of a TV show. But she'd finally gotten her big break at sixteen when she was cast in a main role in a blockbuster film. However, before production began, she'd dropped out abruptly without explanation. From then on, Cassidy hadn't had any further acting or modeling jobs.

The report included several photos of Cassidy from her childhood and teenage years, headshots of a waifish girl with pale skin and soft, strawberry blonde curls. She was almost unrecognizable, save for the wide, sparkling green eyes that Cassidy and Chloe shared.

From there, the report contained no further references to her acting career, or anything of note, save for a series of police reports. The reports told of domestic disturbances involving Chloe's mother and an unnamed sixteen-year-old child who had to be Chloe, all called in by neighbors. Since the altercations had never been physically violent, the police hadn't taken action.

But the last report was different. The date put it at less than a month after Chloe had turned eighteen. From what Gabrielle could gather, the police had been called to the house by Chloe herself. She had tried to leave, her mother had tried to stop her, and things had gotten physical.

But Chloe had declined to press charges against her mother, for whatever reason. And after that incident, she left Los Angeles and started going by her current name. Cassidy Denning had disappeared, existing only on legal documents. Even her florist shop was registered under the trust that had been opened for her when she was a child. Presumably, the trust had been for the money Cassidy had made from acting and modeling. It was the only thing that connected Cassidy and Chloe.

As Gabrielle finished the report, everything fell into place. Cassidy—Chloe—had been thrust into the spotlight at a young age, too young to have made such a decision herself. Had she ever been a willing participant, or had she been the puppet of an overbearing stage mom all along? Regardless, at some point, her relationship with her mother had turned. The records of verbal altercations bad enough to attract police attention suggested that. Was that why Chloe had fled when she'd turned eighteen? Had she been so desperate to escape from that life that she'd created a whole new identity for herself?

Guilt tugged inside Gabrielle's chest. Chloe had good reasons for keeping her name, her past, secret. Any lies she'd told them were justified by the wounds she harbored from that time.

But none of that mattered. Gabrielle shouldn't have gone digging through Chloe's life. She shouldn't have betrayed Chloe's trust. She needed to come clean to her. But if she did, Chloe would be crushed.

And everything between all three of them would fall apart.

Gabrielle cursed under her breath. If Chloe couldn't forgive her for this, Gabrielle could live with that, as painful as it would be. But the thought of ruining what Chloe and Dana shared was too much to bear. Although Dana had nothing to do with the investigation, that wouldn't matter to Chloe. She wouldn't be able to separate Gabrielle and Dana.

Just when they'd found someone who they both felt

strongly about, who they saw a future with, Gabrielle had ruined everything.

A knock on the bathroom door interrupted her thoughts.

"Gabi?" Dana's voice was muffled by the door, but Gabrielle could make out the concern in it. "Is everything all right in there?"

Gabrielle cleared her throat. "Yes, I'll be out in a minute."

She drew in a breath, steeling herself. Then, she deleted the email. She couldn't risk hurting the two people she cared about the most.

But could she take a secret so big to the grave?

CHAPTER 28

C hloe turned off the tap and dried her face, inspecting herself in the bathroom mirror. She hadn't straightened her hair in days, and it was starting to curl, but she liked the way it looked. And now that she'd dyed her roots to hide her blonde hair, she felt enough like 'Chloe' that the curls didn't bother her.

She smiled to herself. It was Friday night. The weekend was finally here. She had plans to see Gabrielle and Dana again tomorrow, and she was practically giddy about it.

But right now, she was ready to crash. After the busy week she'd had at the florist shop, she was exhausted in the best way.

She returned to her bedroom, almost tripping over Mango in the hallway outside her door. As she got into bed, he leaped up to join her. But instead of settling at his usual spot at the foot of the bed, he padded up to the pillow and curled up by Chloe's head.

Tentatively, she reached up and petted him, trying her best not to disturb him. This was the first time he'd behaved this way. Was he finally warming up to her, after all this time?

She let out a contented sigh. Her life couldn't be more perfect right now. Sales were up at her florist shop and she hadn't heard a peep from Tracy in days. She must have received the letter Melanie had sent.

Did this mean Tracy was out of her life, once and for all?

It was a huge weight off her shoulders, that was for sure. Plus, not having to pay Tracy back would mean that she could focus on her other debts. While she had plenty of those, if business at her florist shop continued as it was, it wouldn't be long before she got on top of them. Things were finally looking up.

But there was still the matter of Gabrielle and Dana.

Not that they were a problem. Everything between them was going so well. Maybe it was time to finally be honest with them.

But a part of her was still afraid of opening up to them, telling them about her past, the life she'd run from. What if they didn't understand it? What if they judged her for it? What if they were upset that she'd lied to them?

She shook her head. Here she was, looking for problems, excuses, reasons to keep herself from opening up her heart to them. Because anything as perfect as what the three of them shared could never be real, could it? Good things never lasted. Love, happiness, all those things she'd searched for her whole life—they always turned sour in the end. Those beautiful flowers she spent her days arranging, they always died.

"Is it crazy to believe that this time things will be different?" she said.

She turned to Mango, who was kneading the pillow next to her head. Apparently, he didn't have the answer either.

Chloe reached across to her nightstand and turned off the lamp. As she settled into sleep, her phone began to ring.

Who was calling this late?

Groaning, she rolled over and grabbed her phone from the nightstand. She didn't recognize the number. She hesitated, then picked it up.

"Hello?" she said.

A deep male voice responded. "This is Officer Andrews with the Midtown Police Department. Am I speaking to Chloe Campbell?"

Chloe's heart skipped a beat. "Yes."

"You're the owner of Blossom Flowers?"

"Yes, that's right."

"I'm sorry to inform you of this, but there's been a break-in."

Chloe's stomach turned to stone. Someone had broken into her shop?

From there, she only heard snippets of the officer's words. *Vandalized... serious damage... no witnesses...*

Her pulse began pounding furiously. This wasn't happening. Had she been robbed? What had been taken?

What if there was nothing left?

"Ma'am, are you there?" the officer asked.

Chloe swallowed. "Yes. I'll be right there."

She hung up the phone and got out of bed, her heart in her throat. She needed to get dressed and get to the florist shop as quickly as possible.

But she couldn't do this alone.

Her hands shaking, she called the two people she wanted the most right now.

~

As soon as the stoplight turned green, Dana sped off from it. There wasn't much traffic at this hour, but the drive to Chloe's shop was taking forever.

She glanced sideways at Gabrielle in the passenger seat. Gabrielle had a hard, blank expression on her face, one that most people found inscrutable. But Dana knew that face. It was the mask Gabrielle wore whenever something was bothering her.

It made sense that she was rattled, given the circumstances. Chloe's panicked late-night phone call was enough to unsettle anyone. However, Gabrielle's strange, evasive behavior had started long before Chloe's phone call.

They stopped at another stoplight. Dana reached across and placed her hand on Gabrielle's leg.

"Darling?" Dana said.

Gabrielle turned to her. "Hm?"

"Is everything okay?"

Gabrielle nodded. "I'm just worried about Chloe."

"I'm worried about her too. But that's not the only thing on your mind. You've been behaving strangely lately, like you're preoccupied."

"It's nothing. I have a lot going on right now, that's all."

The light turned green. Dana floored the accelerator. They were almost at the florist shop, but Dana couldn't keep her mouth shut any longer.

"I know that's not true. Gabi, we've known each other

for almost fifteen years. I can tell when something is wrong." Dana's voice cracked slightly. "I'm worried about you. And it's not like you to shut me out like this." Gabrielle was the one person in her life that she'd always been able to trust unconditionally. But for the first time ever, she felt like their relationship was fraying at the edges, threatening to unravel entirely.

And that scared her.

Gabrielle closed her eyes, cursing softly. "God, you're right. I'm so sorry, I didn't mean to shut you out. I've been so wrapped up in this mess I've caused that it didn't occur to me that keeping it from you would hurt you."

"What mess? What's going on? Please, just tell me."

"I will. I'll tell you everything, I promise, but..." Gabrielle looked out the window. "It's a long story, and we're almost there. Chloe needs us right now."

Dana clenched her jaw. "You're right. But as soon as we sort this out with Chloe, I need you to tell me what's going on."

Gabrielle nodded. "I meant what I said. I'll tell you everything."

Dana pulled the car up to the curb across the street from Chloe's florist shop, right behind a police car. The lights were on inside the shop, illuminating Chloe's silhouette as she talked to the two officers, her arms wrapped around herself dejectedly.

They got out of the car and rushed inside. The scene they were faced with was far worse than anything Dana had expected. All around them, shelves were overturned and vases and pots were in pieces, trampled flowers strewn all over the shop. All of Chloe's carefully crafted displays had been destroyed, and the floor was covered in broken glass. The entire store had been trashed.

Chloe turned toward them, relief washing over her face. "Thank god you're here."

She rushed over to meet them. Dana pulled her into an embrace at the same time that Gabrielle did. As they held her, she clung to them tightly, as if she couldn't hold herself upright without them.

Beside them, a police officer cleared his throat impatiently. Dana and Gabrielle both gave him a sharp look. He didn't make a sound again.

After a moment, Dana broke away, holding Chloe by the shoulders. "What happened?"

"I think..." Chloe swallowed. "I think Tracy did this."

Anger rose in Dana's gut. "Did you see her?"

Chloe shook her head. "But it had to be her. Whoever did this, they didn't even take anything, they just destroyed everything. The change I left in the register is still there. And they didn't break in. They used a key. I gave Tracy a key when I first opened the shop, back when we were together." She shook her head, her voice trembling. "I didn't think to get it back from her when we broke up. I never thought she'd do anything like this. I never thought she'd go this far."

Gabrielle put her arm around her. "Oh, honey."

"We're going to get this sorted out," Dana said. "Have you told the police about Tracy?"

Chloe nodded. "But they said they can't do anything."

Gabrielle turned to the nearby officer, her face clouding over with anger. "And why not?"

"Well, you see, ma'am," the officer said. "There's no

evidence that this Tracy person is responsible. There are no cameras nearby, and no one saw the vandalism happen. We'll speak to her, but without any proof that she did this, there's nothing we can do."

Gabrielle threw her hands up. "Nothing you can do? Can't you dust for fingerprints? Look for witnesses? You have to investigate this!"

"With all due respect, we don't have the resources to waste on minor crimes like this."

"Waste?" Gabrielle's eyes clouded over. "Someone has come in here and destroyed Chloe's store, her livelihood. She's spent years pouring her heart and soul into this place! And you think it's a waste? You-"

Chloe put her hand on Gabrielle's arm. "Just forget about it."

"I will *not* let this go."

"Gabrielle, please," Chloe said.

"Look, ma'am," the officer said. "I promise you, we'll do all we can for your friend here."

"Girlfriend," Gabrielle corrected him.

"All right. We'll do what we can for your girlfriend. But our resources are stretched thin, so I wouldn't get your hopes up. I'm sorry, but that's just the way it is."

"It's okay," Chloe said to the officer. "Thank you."

Dana dragged Gabrielle away as the police officers took more details from Chloe. It wasn't until the officers were wrapping everything up that Gabrielle finally cooled down.

As the police officers left the shop, Dana took Chloe's hand. "I'm so sorry all this has happened. Are you all right?"

"I'm fine," Chloe said. But even as she spoke, her hands were trembling.

"What can we do to help?" Dana asked.

Chloe shook her head. "I don't know. I can't even think straight right now. I can't believe this is happening. My shop, it's ruined. Everything is ruined."

"No, it isn't," Gabrielle said. "We can fix this. We can help you."

"How?" Chloe snapped. "Let me guess, with money?"

"Just enough to get you back on your feet again," Dana said. "I'm sure you have insurance, but we can give you the funds you need to tide you over until you can get everything sorted."

"Unbelievable," Chloe muttered.

"I know you don't like accepting our help," Dana said. "But these are exceptional circumstances. If we're going to fix this-"

"Don't you get it?" Chloe yelled. "Money can't fix this. *You* can't fix this. My shop, it's been hanging by a thread for months. Even if I fix the damage, with all the problems I've been having, my reputation is as good as ruined. I'm going to lose all my customers. I can't come back from this." Her voice quivered, tears brimming in her eyes. "Nothing can fix this."

"I'm so sorry," Gabrielle said. "Come here."

As they pulled her in close, Chloe buried herself in their arms, her shoulders trembling.

Dana squeezed her tighter. They held her there for what felt like hours, silence stretching out between them.

Finally, Chloe spoke, her voice muffled. "I'm sorry. I didn't mean to yell at you. I know you were just trying to help. I just feel like I've lost everything."

"You haven't lost everything," Gabrielle said. "You still have us."

"That's right," Dana said. "And while we might not be able to fix this, or make everything better, we're going to take care of you, okay?"

Chloe pulled away and nodded, her eyes brimming with tears that she wouldn't let fall.

"Let's get you home," Gabrielle said. "We'll stay with you if you'd like."

Chloe nodded. "Can we go somewhere else? I don't want to go home."

"Are you worried Tracy will come after you?" Dana asked.

Chloe shook her head. "I don't think so. She did this because she knows she can't come near me anymore. I'd just feel more comfortable somewhere else."

"We'll take you back to our place," Dana said. "You'll feel better in our bed."

CHAPTER 29

Dana fluffed up the pillow behind Chloe's back. "Are you comfortable? Do you need anything else? More blankets? Something to eat?"

Chloe shook her head. "I'm fine, really."

It was past midnight now, and Chloe was sitting in Dana and Gabrielle's bed, a warm cup of cocoa in her hands, courtesy of Gabrielle. She was dressed in a nightshirt she'd borrowed from Dana, who was also responsible for the pile of blankets she was cocooned in.

Both of them were treating her like she was incapacitated. At any other time, she would have found it irritating. But right now, it was exactly what she wanted. She hadn't known that until this moment.

How did Dana and Gabrielle know what she needed better than she herself did?

"Are you sure?" Gabrielle asked. "We can get you anything you want. Anything at all."

Chloe thought for a moment. "Well, there *is* something I want."

"What is it?" Dana asked.

Chloe reached across the bed and set her half-empty mug down on the nightstand. "I want the two of you to stop fussing over me and get into bed."

Gabrielle smiled. "I don't know about the first part, but we can definitely make the latter happen."

Still in their clothes, she and Dana got into the bed, one on either side of Chloe, slipping under the covers with her. As they wrapped their arms around her, Chloe closed her eyes and sighed.

"Thanks," she said quietly. "I really needed this. And I'm sorry again for yelling at you earlier."

"And again, it's fine," Dana said firmly. "Stop apologizing."

Gabrielle kissed Chloe on the forehead. "I'd listen to her if I were you. You saw what happens if you don't last time we were in here."

A smile pulled at Chloe's lips, but it wasn't enough to settle the sea of emotions inside her. "All right. But I just want you to know I wasn't angry at you. I know you were trying to help. I was just so upset. Seeing everything I've worked for destroyed..."

Her lower lip began to tremble, hot, thick tears gathering at the corners of her eyes. She'd spent the last hour holding everything back, trying to keep herself together.

But it was late and she was exhausted, and she just couldn't do it any longer. Her flower shop was everything to her. It was proof of the life she had built for herself, the person she had become, her own person.

But now it was gone, and everything was falling apart.

A tear trickled down her cheek. She couldn't pretend she was okay. She wasn't okay, not anymore.

"Hey," Dana said, hugging her tighter. "Everything is going to be all right. You'll get through this. *We'll* get through this."

Chloe nodded. "It's just hard to see it that way right now."

Gabrielle put her hand on Chloe's cheek, turning her face to hers. "I know it's hard. But we're here for you." She wiped Chloe's tears away with her thumb. "It's just like we told you last time you were here, in this room. You're ours. We'll take care of you. And not just while we're in here. Whenever you need us, we'll be there, always."

Chloe's heart began to flutter, emotions swirling inside her. She was hurt, and angry, and lost. But there was one bright spot in all this, one thing that gave her hope, and that was the two women beside her.

Maybe, with Dana and Gabrielle by her side, she could get through this.

"I know," she said. "I know I can count on you both."

Wiping away the last of her tears, Chloe closed her eyes and kissed Gabrielle gently, letting the warmth and softness of her lips wash over her. She wanted to get lost in those lips forever. Was there any reason why she couldn't, why she couldn't let herself drown in her, in them?

She reached behind herself for Dana, a murmur of longing rising from her. Why was it impossible to kiss them both at once? Breaking away, she turned to Dana and kissed her desperately. As always, Dana's kisses were just like she was—firm, possessive, reassuring, getting more passionate the longer the kiss drew on.

Again, she found herself reaching back blindly, for Gabrielle this time, trying to urge her close. Somehow, Gabrielle understood what she wanted. She wrapped her arm around Chloe's waist, cradling her with her body. Her lips tickled the back of Chloe's neck, sending warm shivers trickling down her back.

Chloe grasped at Gabrielle's hip, relishing the feel of Gabrielle against her, of Dana's lips against hers. She felt raw, all her emotions exposed. She just wanted to be close to them, to become one with them both.

Breaking the kiss, Chloe pulled back slightly, then drew her borrowed nightshirt up and over her head, leaving her naked save for her panties. She needed to feel them, skin against skin.

But she didn't need words to tell Dana and Gabrielle that. Without hesitation, Dana stripped out of her dress, then unclipped her bra and took it off too. Chloe's gaze was drawn to her body like a magnet. She could have spent hours just looking at Dana's smooth, flawless skin, the subtle swells of her breasts, the perfect roundness of her dark, pebbled nipples.

But there was another woman Chloe wanted to immerse herself in. And Gabrielle was already undressing, pulling her skirt from her legs. As she did, Chloe reached out and unbuttoned Gabrielle's blouse, button by painstaking button.

Once she finally had it open, she pushed it from Gabrielle's shoulders, then did the same with her bra, freeing her porcelain breasts. How was it that Gabrielle's body was so different from Dana's, but Chloe adored them both equally? She adored every part of them equally. Their bodies, their presence, the way their words, their touches, could turn her into a puddle of lust.

The way they both made her feel like she was the center of their world.

She couldn't imagine ever having to choose. And she felt so lucky that she didn't have to.

"I want you," she whispered. "Both of you."

Dana moved in close, her bare breasts pressing against Chloe's back, kissing her down her neck and the backs of her shoulders. Her hands drifted up Chloe's side, along the curves of her hips and breasts, her fingertips skimming over Chloe's nipples. At the same time, Gabrielle pressed her lips to Chloe's, her hand wandering down to where Chloe's legs met. She ran her fingers over Chloe's panties, sliding them up and down her slit through the now damp fabric, setting off sparks inside her.

Chloe drew in a trembling breath, arching into Gabrielle. Then, Dana's hands were at the waistband of Chloe's panties, pushing them down carefully past her hips, down her thighs, past her knees and ankles, stripping them from her feet. Dana pressed herself against Chloe again, reaching around Chloe's hip and down between her thighs. Her fingers sought out Chloe's clit, tracing slow, tight spirals around it.

A moan fell from Chloe's mouth. Gabrielle smothered it with a kiss, her lips achingly tender. Chloe let herself be swept away in them both—in their touches, their kisses, their scents, all mingling together in an intoxicating cocktail that was both of them. She couldn't separate them from each other, couldn't separate herself out from the tangle of limbs and lips and passion.

Dana withdrew her hand, only to slide it between Chloe's legs from behind, teasing Chloe's entrance with a finger. Chloe pushed her hips back against Dana, urging her on. She wanted Dana inside her, to fill her up, to soothe the ache within the way only she could.

Dana dipped a finger into her, then added another, then slipped them inside her all the way. Chloe let out a shuddering gasp, pleasure lancing through her.

As Dana began thrusting inside her, Chloe wrapped her arm around Gabrielle's neck, holding on to her tightly. Her lips still on Chloe's, Gabrielle drew her hands down her shoulders, down her breasts, to circle and graze her nipples. She and Dana worked in tandem, showering Chloe with exquisite pleasures. No part of her was left untouched, no inch of her skin uncaressed, no sensitive places unteased. Time stretched on until finally, she reached that sweet oblivion.

A cry flew from her as she came apart. Her head lolled back against Dana's shoulder as she bucked against Gabrielle, her body seizing at the orgasm ripping through her. Neither of them relented, continuing to pump and kiss and caress, stretching her climax on and on until, at last, she succumbed to exhaustion.

After taking a moment to recover, Chloe turned to Dana and planted a grateful kiss on her lips. She ran her palms up Dana's bare stomach languidly, all the way up to her chest. Now that Dana had permitted her to touch, Chloe wanted to do so every chance she got, to savor this privilege that Dana had granted her.

As Chloe let her hands linger on Dana's smooth, round breasts, Dana arched toward her, welcoming her touch. At the same time, Gabrielle spooned Chloe's body with her own, her hands stroking Chloe's arm, her head resting against the back of her neck.

Chloe continued, drawing her hand down Dana's side, along the valley of her waist, and over the mound of her hip. It was only when her fingers brushed Dana's thigh, causing her breath to hitch, that Chloe realized her mistake.

She pulled her hand back sharply. "I'm sorry! I got carried away."

Dana had only given her permission to touch her above the waist, no lower. It was unlike Chloe to forget something like that. And now that her lust-addled head was clearing, she realized she'd been uncharacteristically demanding of Dana and Gabrielle the entire time they'd been in bed together. Usually, all she wanted was to give and give and give, and she wanted them to take and take.

But tonight, Chloe yearned for something different. She didn't want her Mistresses. She wanted Dana and Gabrielle. She wanted to rip down any walls between them, to tear away the masks that were their roles. Just for tonight, she wanted to simply be with them.

"It's all right," Dana said softly. "Keep going."

Chloe searched Dana's eyes. "Are you sure?"

Dana nodded.

Chloe glanced behind her at Gabrielle. Gabrielle gave Chloe's arm a reassuring touch before pulling away slightly, as if giving them space. Was this a big moment for Dana?

Then Chloe had to make it perfect.

She reached for Dana tentatively, running her hand up the side of Dana's neck, kissing her, soft and slow. She shifted downward, letting her hands wander Dana's body, feathering her lips down Dana's neck, all the way to her chest. She kissed the swell of Dana's breasts, pursed her lips around Dana's nipple, sucking and swirling with her tongue.

A murmur rose from Dana's chest. Chloe pulled back, looking up at her.

"Is this okay?" she ventured.

Dana nodded. "Keep going."

Chloe continued, painting kisses over Dana's breasts. At the same time, she slipped her hand down past Dana's panties, gliding her palms along Dana's thighs, her fingers drifting inward to touch the supple skin between them. She traced her fingertips up to the apex of Dana's thighs, stroking them over Dana's panty-covered nether lips.

Chloe looked up at her again. "Is this okay?"

Dana nodded.

Chloe took the waistband of Dana's panties and slid them down slightly, exposing the top of a triangle of soft, dark, neatly trimmed hair. "Is this-"

"Yes," Dana said, her voice quivering with need. "Yes. Everything you do is okay. Everything you do feels divine." She lifted her hips and slipped her fingers into the waistband of her panties, pulling them down the rest of the way, then placed them aside carefully before lying down on her back. "I trust you. Don't you dare stop now."

Chloe bit her lip. Here Dana was, naked and laid out before her, offering herself to her. Chloe wanted to make the moment last, to treasure it. But she didn't want to make Dana feel self-conscious, to draw attention to the vulnerable position Dana had put herself in.

Moving in close to her, Chloe ran her hand up Dana's

thigh. Dana inhaled slowly. Chloe let her fingers brush over Dana's nether lips, eliciting a shudder from her. She was wetter than Chloe thought possible.

How did Dana always focus so much on Chloe and Gabrielle's pleasure without having her own desires satisfied? Was it sheer willpower? Did she find gratification in self-control? Or was it something different? Was it a deep intimacy, like that of tonight, that Dana required to truly let go?

Chloe withdrew her hand. She wanted more than just to touch Dana. She shifted down Dana's body further, letting her lips graze the inside of Dana's thigh, kissing higher and higher until she reached the peak where Dana's thighs met.

She drew back and looked up into Dana's eyes. "May I?"

Dana nodded.

As Dana opened her legs up to her, Chloe positioned herself between them, the scent of Dana's arousal filling her head. She dipped down and parted Dana's lips with her tongue, sliding it down her slit, tasting her sweet nectar. A soft hum spread from Dana's chest, reverberating through her whole body.

Chloe ran her tongue up to Dana's clit. She barely nudged it, but Dana began writhing and groaning as if struck by electricity.

Chloe peered up at her. Who knew that her hard, reserved Mistress was so sensitive?

"Keep going," Dana whispered.

Chloe continued, burying her head between Dana's thighs once again, this time taking more care around Dana's swollen bud. She lapped at Dana's entrance, flicking her tongue against it, making Dana gasp. She pursed her lips around Dana's nub, sucking it as lightly as she could, causing Dana's whole body to vibrate.

Gradually, Chloe increased the pressure, sucking and licking harder. Dana let out a long, slow moan, shifting her hips, grinding back against Chloe's mouth.

It barely took seconds for Dana to come. Her hips rose from the bed, her thighs clenching around Chloe's ears. Although Dana was silent, Chloe could feel the pleasure rocking Dana's body, could feel her tremors, until finally, she fell back down to the bed.

Chloe crawled back up to her pillow, collapsing on the bed between Dana and Gabrielle. Her exhaustion had finally overtaken her completely. Dana planted a tender kiss on her lips before settling beside her, her arms slung protectively around Chloe's waist. On the other side of her, Gabrielle did the same, nestling close to her as the call of sleep pulled at them all.

And as Chloe drifted off in their arms, weak and spent, she could feel all her problems looming, shadows at the edges of the dark room. Her florist shop. Tracy. The elaborate web of lies that was her life and her past.

They weren't going to go away. She would have to deal with them, and sooner rather than later.

CHAPTER 30

Dana lay on the bed on her side, watching Chloe get dressed, the morning sun streaming through the window.

Beside her, Gabrielle yawned and stretched. "We can't tempt you to stay any longer?"

Chloe shook her head. "I need to feed Mango. He gets upset if he doesn't get his meals on time. And I want to go take another look at the shop."

"We can help, if you'd like," Dana said. "Help you clean up, sort everything out."

Chloe gave her a soft smile. "I don't think I'm ready to tackle that yet. I just want to survey the damage and see if anything is salvageable. And really, I just need time to process everything. I wasn't in any condition to do that last night, but I'm feeling a lot better this morning, all thanks to you two."

"Glad we could help," Gabrielle said.

"You really did. Last night felt..." Chloe's cheeks began to glow a radiant shade of pink. "Special."

Dana felt a stirring in her chest. What had passed between them the night before hadn't been planned. She hadn't made the conscious decision to give Chloe free rein over her body. She'd simply been so in the moment that she'd just let her desires take her, let her feelings take her. She trusted Chloe now, enough to give her that part of herself she'd never given to anyone other than Gabrielle.

Gabrielle smiled. "It *was* special. You have no idea how long it took before Dana let me do that with her. I'd be jealous if I didn't find watching the two of you together so hot."

Dana glanced at Gabrielle. She was acting like her usual self now, but to Dana, her behavior seemed forced. Was she trying to hide whatever this thing that was bothering her was?

Chloe retrieved her hair tie from the nightstand and pulled her dark locks up into a ponytail. They had curled into soft ringlets. While she looked striking with straight hair, Dana liked Chloe's curls better.

She grabbed her purse from a nearby chair. "I should get going."

Dana got up from the bed. "Let me drive you."

Chloe held up her hands. "I assure you, I'm capable of making my way home by myself."

"At least let us call you a car."

"It's fine. You've done enough. Seriously." Chloe climbed onto the side of the bed on her knees and leaned over, planting a kiss on Dana's cheek, then Gabrielle's. "Thank you. For being there."

They said their goodbyes, and Chloe left the room. Dana

waited until she heard the distant creak of the front door opening, then turned to Gabrielle.

"I hope you haven't forgotten about our conversation last night," Dana said. "You promised you'd tell me what's going on."

Gabrielle nodded. "I remember."

Dana crossed her arms. "Well? And please, don't try to blow me off again."

"I'll tell you, but you're not going to like this." Gabrielle sighed. "Remember when I told you I hired a private investigator to look into Chloe?"

"Yes, but you called it off."

"Well…"

Dana's jaw tightened. "Gabrielle? Did you call it off or not?"

"I was going to, but then the PI sent me some information about Chloe. He said that her name, her identity, it's entirely fake. I just couldn't let it go, so I told him to keep looking. And I was right all along. Chloe *does* have skeletons in her closet. But I can't blame her for keeping them in there."

Chloe was lying about her identity? Dana knew she shouldn't pry, but it was too late now. They were in too deep. And she needed to know more. She needed to understand what could possess Chloe to hide who she was from them.

"What did he find?" she asked.

Gabrielle told Dana everything the investigator had discovered about Chloe. Her real name, her acting career, her conflicts with her mother. Slowly, everything clicked into place. All the little things Chloe had told Dana about her past, her relationship with her mother, made sense. *She had this idea in her head of what she wanted me to be... her perfect little doll.*

Her obsession with turning me into what she wanted consumed our entire lives.

"That explains everything," Dana said.

"It does. She was never trying to deceive us. She was only trying to protect herself." Gabrielle shook her head. "I realize how bad this is. I should never have contacted the PI in the first place. But I was afraid. I wanted reassurance that I could trust her…"

Dana put a comforting hand on Gabrielle's arm. They both understood how deep Gabrielle's trust issues ran. But that didn't justify this invasion of Chloe's privacy.

"We have to tell her that we know," Dana said.

Gabrielle nodded. "We do. We need to be honest. But there's no way to tell her without hurting her. She kept this from us for a reason. She went to the effort of creating a whole new identity. No one would go to such extremes unless they had some serious wounds."

"And that's exactly why we need to tell her. The longer we wait, the worse it's going to be when she finds out that we know. I don't want to lose her."

"Neither do I. Last night made me realize something important. It made me realize what I really feel about her."

"What are you saying?" But Dana already knew the answer.

Because she felt it too.

As Gabrielle opened her mouth to speak, a chill went down Dana's spine, the hairs on her skin standing up. Something was wrong. She could sense it.

She looked at the door, then back at Gabrielle. Gabrielle's expression told her that she sensed the same thing.

Before Dana could react, she got up from the bed, strode over to the door, and opened it.

Standing in the doorway, her face frozen with pain, was Chloe.

"Chloe," Gabrielle said. "We were just-"

"You knew." Chloe's voice was devoid of all emotion.

Dana cursed to herself. "Chloe, we-"

"You knew," Chloe repeated. "Both of you. You knew."

Gabrielle held up her hands. "Dana didn't know. I-"

"I heard you. I heard what you said. How could you?"

"Just let us explain," Dana said calmly.

Chloe's hands tightened into fists at her sides. "What is there to explain? You went digging around in my past. You knew everything about who I was, and you kept it from me. You pretended you didn't know a thing, you just played along. I can't believe this."

"That's not how it is," Gabrielle said. "Please, let's just talk about this."

Chloe shook her head. "I don't want to hear your excuses." She looked at the chair at the side of the room. Her coat was slung over it. She marched over to it and snatched the coat up. "I forgot this."

As she turned to leave, Gabrielle put her hand on Chloe's arm. "Wait."

Chloe shook her off. "Leave me alone!" Her eyes were dark and furious, but they were brimming with tears. "I trusted you. I believed you when you said you wanted me to be a real part of your relationship. I actually started to think that I meant something to you, that I wasn't just some temporary plaything like all those other women. But you never thought of me that way, you never trusted me, otherwise you wouldn't have done something like this."

"Chloe," Gabrielle begged. "We—"

"No wonder women always leave you."

Dana's heart lurched. She saw Gabrielle's face fall.

For just a moment, Chloe hesitated, a flash of regret in her eyes. And Dana wanted to seize that. *Please*, she wanted to say. *Don't go. We can work this out.*

But Chloe's words were seared into Dana's mind.

So instead, she did nothing. And Chloe turned and marched out of the room.

A moment later, they heard the front door creak open, then slam shut.

CHAPTER 31

C hloe unlocked the front door to her apartment and stepped inside, closing the door behind her. She took a few deep breaths, then sank to the floor. She couldn't take another step.

She leaned back against the door, hugging her knees to her chest. After spending several days moping around her apartment, she'd forced herself to finally go back to her florist shop to survey the damage.

But the verdict was clear—there was no salvaging it. Too much was ruined. She'd need to start from scratch if she was going to rebuild, but that would take far too long. She'd lose all her customers.

This was it. Her florist shop was done for.

That alone was enough to send her spiraling into misery. But there was something else that was making her feel even worse.

Chloe felt a sharp stabbing in her gut, a mix of pain and humiliation. How long had Gabrielle and Dana known the truth about her, about her past, about who she was? All this time, they'd never said a word. She'd never felt so humiliated.

She'd trusted them, and they went digging deep into her past. This was the first time she'd trusted anyone since Tracy. The first time she'd opened her heart. She'd even started to think that she'd found something special with them.

That maybe, she could even come to love them.

As she buried her face in her knees, she heard the patter of tiny paws. She looked up to find Mango in front of her, his usual expression of displeasure on his face. What did he want? Was it his dinner time?

"Stop looking at me like that," she muttered. "I'll feed you in a moment."

Instead, he lay down and continued to stare at her.

Chloe sighed. She closed her eyes. For what had to be the hundredth time that day, the conversation she'd over-heard from outside Dana and Gabrielle's bedroom played in her head. She couldn't stop it. Her mind kept going back to it, over again and again. Was it her subconscious looking for signs that this was a mistake, looking for reasons to forgive them? After all, the entire conversation had been muffled, only half heard through the door.

But there was one part of the conversation that she'd heard clearly. Gabrielle's words, before Chloe had been caught eavesdropping. *Last night made me realize something important... what I really feel about her.*

What had Gabrielle wanted to say? What had Dana's response been?

What if Chloe was wrong about them and she was throwing away her chance at finally finding happiness?

Because she *had* been happy with them. Dana and Gabrielle, they'd become her everything. Her friends, her lovers, her rocks. She'd come to trust them, to rely on them. On Gabrielle, with her ability to make Chloe smile, no matter what. To make her feel warm and loved. And Dana, who was so dependable and strong, who would go to any lengths to solve all Chloe's problems, and always made her feel safe and secure. They were everything she'd been missing her whole life.

But things had changed now. She couldn't go back to feeling that way around them, not after what they'd done. And not after what she'd said to them.

Why had she thrown those words in their faces when she knew how much it would hurt them? Did she even believe the words she'd said herself?

A tremor went through her, the beginnings of a sob. She swallowed it back. She was *not* going to fall apart.

As she stifled another sob, Mango meowed at her loudly. She looked up at him, glaring. "Just leave me alone."

Instead, he padded over to her, climbed onto her lap, and lay down, purring sympathetically.

Her lower lip began to tremble. Was she so obviously, pathetically distraught that even Mango felt sorry for her?

That was all it took for her to fall to pieces. She hugged him close, burying herself in his fur as she sobbed, all her emotions pouring out of her.

And once all her tears had run out, she dried her eyes, steeling herself. She didn't need Dana and Gabrielle. She didn't need anyone.

She was perfectly fine being alone.

Gabrielle was sitting in an armchair in the living room, nursing her usual nightcap of a glass of scotch, when Dana walked into the room.

"Are you coming to bed?" Dana asked.

"Not yet." It was getting late, but Gabrielle was wide awake. "Heard anything from Chloe yet?"

Dana shook her head. "Nothing."

Gabrielle took another sip of her drink, barely tasting it. They hadn't heard from Chloe in days. At first, they'd given her space before reaching out to her, but their calls had gone unanswered, their apologies ignored. To top it off, she'd unceremoniously returned Dana's truck to them, dropping it off while they weren't home and shipping the keys to their address without a word. It was painfully clear that Chloe wanted nothing to do with either of them.

Gabrielle's stomach swirled with guilt. She hadn't known how much losing Chloe would hurt. She couldn't help but feel the irony of it. All this time, she'd feared she couldn't trust Chloe, but in the end, it had been Gabrielle's mistrust that had driven Chloe away.

Dana sat on the arm of the chair and put a hand on Gabrielle's leg.

"Don't," Dana said.

"Don't what?"

"I can see what you're thinking. Stop beating yourself up over this."

"But it's my fault," Gabrielle said.

"No, this is on both of us. You told me about the background check after we came back from the ranch, and I told you not to tell her. I made the choice to keep the truth from her."

Gabrielle shook her head. "That isn't the same thing."

"It doesn't matter. What matters is that we messed up with how we handled this, and now we're paying the price. But we'll get through this. We always do."

It was true that they always got through difficult times together. So why didn't Gabrielle believe Dana's words?

Perhaps it was because she knew Dana well enough to tell when she was lying. And Dana was lying, both to Gabrielle and to herself.

She kissed Gabrielle on the cheek before getting up and disappearing toward the bedroom. It was the most they'd touched in days. There was this distance between them now, this rift that was growing with each passing moment.

Losing Chloe had fractured them. She'd become a part of them, of their relationship. They hadn't realized it until now, but they needed her.

Before they'd met Chloe, they'd never needed anyone else. While they'd yearned for something intangible that they couldn't quite express, they'd never felt like they weren't whole.

And then Chloe had come along, and she'd filled a hole in their hearts that they hadn't even known was there. She had changed them, both individually and together. They could never go back to how they were before.

And every moment Gabrielle and Dana spent in each other's presence was just a reminder of what they were missing.

CHAPTER 32

"You look like hell," Amber said.

Dana crossed her arms. "Hello to you too." Normally, she found Amber's outspokenness refreshing, but she wasn't in the mood for it today. "Come in. Gabrielle said you'd be stopping by."

Amber swept through the front door in her usual regal manner. As Dana closed the door behind her, she saw the large black car Amber had arrived in parked out front, her driver standing next to it.

"I won't be here long," Amber said. "I just need to get some files from Gabrielle."

"She's probably in the sitting room." Dana didn't know for sure. The two of them had been spending their days apart, retreating to opposite ends of the house. Was it intentional? Dana couldn't tell. All she knew was that when they were together, the absence of Chloe, the pain of losing her, was magnified.

Dana directed Amber to the sitting room. Sure enough, Gabrielle was there, perched in an armchair, gazing out the window listlessly. While Gabrielle blamed herself for what had happened, Dana felt even more responsible. She was the one who always fixed things, who held them together. She had failed Gabrielle and Chloe both by letting everything fall apart.

No wonder women always leave you. Just like everyone else did.

Gabrielle turned to the doorway. "Amber?" She blinked. "I completely forgot you were coming. Let me get those files."

Amber frowned. "You look even worse than Dana. What's going on?" She looked from Gabrielle to Dana and back again. When neither of them replied, she crossed her arms. "Well? What happened?"

"It's Chloe," Gabrielle finally said. "And it's a long story."

Amber took a seat in a nearby chair and folded her hands neatly in her lap. "Go on."

Gabrielle let out a heavy sigh and began telling Amber everything. Dana listened silently, all the pain of losing Chloe rising to the surface.

But as Gabrielle continued, her voice wavering, that pain turned to guilt. Why hadn't she and Gabrielle talked about this? Why had they been so distant with each other when they should have been dealing with this together? Dana had been so wrapped up in her own feelings when she should have been supporting Gabrielle.

Dana perched on the arm of the chair next to Gabrielle and took her hand. Gabrielle looked up at her and gave her a weak smile, squeezing her hand gently before turning back to Amber.

"We haven't heard from her since then," Gabrielle said.

"She's made it clear that she doesn't want to speak to us, and I don't blame her."

She fell silent. After a moment, Gabrielle let her head fall against Dana's hip. It felt good to have her close again. Perhaps they'd be all right after all, just the two of them. They'd gotten through rough patches before, hadn't they? They didn't need anyone else.

No, that was a lie, and it always had been. The truth was, they'd built up this wall around themselves, one that had only contained the two of them, feeding off each other's doubts and fears. Chloe's presence in their lives had exposed that, had forced them to tear those walls down, to open their hearts to her.

And now, without Chloe, their relationship felt empty.

Was this the thing that would finally break them after all these years together?

"So that's it?" Amber said.

Dana scowled. "What do you mean?" She hadn't expected hugs and tears from Amber, but she'd expected a little sympathy at least.

"That's it?" Amber repeated. "You're just going to give up?"

Gabrielle spoke up beside her. "It's not like we have a choice. Chloe made her feelings clear."

Amber let out an exasperated sigh. "Will the two of you stop being so pathetic? So you messed things up with your girlfriend. Stop moping about it and fix it."

Dana set her jaw. "We can't fix something like this."

"Why not?" Amber gestured toward Gabrielle "You co-founded and run a multi-billion-dollar company. And Dana, you built an internationally renowned fashion label from nothing after your own family cut you off for daring to follow a dream. In comparison, this is nothing."

"It isn't the same thing," Gabrielle said. "Chloe is a person, not a company. She has feelings, and a heart, and we hurt her."

"So you're just going to sit here feeling sorry for yourselves?"

"We already apologized," Dana said. "What else can we do?"

"Apologizing isn't enough," Amber said. "You need to show her how sorry you are. And you need to show her how you feel. Look, you told me that she's special, that she's come to mean so much to you. Show her that. Show her how much she means to you. Show her the important place that she holds in your lives, your hearts. Show her that what's between you is real and that you're in it for good."

Dana looked down at Gabrielle. Gabrielle had always been the one to show her love and warmth, and Dana had always been Gabrielle's strength, her rock. So why wasn't Dana being that person, the person she needed to be now more than ever? Why was she ignoring everything that had happened instead of confronting it head-on?

Why was she letting Chloe fall through their fingers?

"She's right," Dana said. "We need to show her."

Gabrielle gave her a soft smile, nodding.

Amber huffed. "Of course I'm right. I'm always right. Now, how are you going to fix this?"

Gabrielle shrugged her shoulders. "I don't know yet, but we'll figure it out."

"Whatever you do, it needs to be something grand," Amber said. "The two of you *really* screwed up."

Gabrielle held up her hands. "Trust me, we know. You don't need to remind us."

"I'm just trying to help," Amber said.

Dana examined Amber's face. "I have to admit, your interest in our relationship is... unexpected."

"Well, you're my friends," Amber said. "I just can't stand the two of you being this miserable. You *need* her. With Chloe in the picture, you seem more complete, somehow." She brushed a stray piece of lint from her dress. "Besides, I'm starting to see the appeal of all this. Settling down, having someone who makes you feel the way that you all make each other feel. It seems... nice."

Before either of them could comment on Amber's sudden change in attitude, she rose from her seat.

"I best be off," she said. "I'll leave you to it."

"What about the files?" Gabrielle asked.

"Another time. You have far more important things to do right now." With a brief farewell, Amber swept out of the room.

Dana watched her leave, her mind spinning with Amber's words. *Show her how you feel. Show her how much she means to you.*

Show her you're in it for good.

They were in it for good, weren't they? Wasn't that what they wanted? Chloe by their side, permanently?

Gabrielle broke the silence. "Amber is right. We need to fix this. We need to make things right. We *need* her, Dana."

Dana nodded. "We do."

They both spoke at the same time.

"I know what we have to do."

CHAPTER 33

Chloe swept the broken glass and dead flowers into a pile on her shop floor. Night had fallen, and she'd spent the whole day in her store, working her way through the mess.

She'd long given up on the idea of starting over, but she didn't know what she was going to do now. With her florist shop closed down, she had nothing. She had no purpose in life. She was lost.

And despite everything, she desperately wished for the comfort of the two people who had given her so much already.

She scooped up the last of the glass and debris in her dustpan, staring down at it mournfully. Among the wilted, browned flowers were roses, carnations, orange blossoms, all torn, trampled, and broken. So much for love. She'd been right about one thing. In the end, flowers always died.

She emptied the dustpan into the trashcan and headed into the back room. Although the front of the shop was clear now, she had plenty of work to do, plenty of paperwork to sort out. She still owed money to her suppliers, and while her insurance was covering the property damage, it wasn't much help otherwise.

And as she'd predicted, the police had been no help either. Without evidence of Tracy's involvement, they couldn't charge her. But Chloe knew the truth. Tracy had trashed the florist shop in retaliation for Chloe finally deciding to stop playing nice with her.

Would this be the end of everything with Tracy? Chloe had thought that the lawyer's letter had scared her off, but what if she was wrong? What if Tracy exposed her anyway? She didn't care who found out the truth about her, not anymore. But what if news of her new identity got back to her mother? She wouldn't put it past Tracy to make that happen, just to hurt her. Chloe didn't know what Tracy was capable of anymore. And the uncertainty scared her.

What if Tracy kept finding ways to get to her, to pull her back into her orbit? What if she was stuck dealing with Tracy forever, looking over her shoulder for her for the rest of her life? What if she never escaped her?

In the space of one night, everything she'd built for herself had come crumbling down.

The bell hanging above the door to the florist shop jingled. She hadn't bothered to lock it. Who would come into her visibly trashed shop, especially this late in the day? Was it a lost customer?

Chloe stepped out of the back room. "Sorry, we're clos…"

She trailed off. The woman standing in front of the counter wasn't a customer. She was someone Chloe both longed to see and never wanted to see again.

Gabrielle.

Their eyes locked, just like they had that fateful day in the florist shop. But now, instead of that irresistible mixture of command and playful suggestion, Gabrielle's eyes were filled with an almost painful yearning.

She gave Chloe a weak smile. "It's good to see your face again."

Chloe's stomach churned, joy and heartache warring inside it. She pushed those feelings down. "What are you doing here?"

"I know you don't want to see me, or either of us. But we need to see you, to speak to you one last time. And we want to show you something."

Chloe crossed her arms, saying nothing.

"I'm not asking you to forgive us or to give us another chance. All I'm asking is for a moment of your time. After that, you'll never hear from us again, if that's what you want."

Chloe hesitated. She'd never seen Gabrielle like this, that warm spark of hers gone. It hurt just to hear her speak.

She sighed. "Okay."

"Dana is waiting for us," Gabrielle said. "Come with me."

Chloe followed her outside and into the back seat of a waiting car. The ride passed in silence, Chloe staring out the window the entire time.

After a few minutes, the longest minutes of Chloe's life, the car pulled to a stop. Chloe got out of it. They were out front of the Mistress building, the towering skyscraper where Gabrielle worked.

"Not here," Gabrielle said, joining her on the sidewalk. "Next door. Come, Dana is waiting."

Silently, Chloe followed Gabrielle to the shop next door. It was an old convenience store that had seen better days. There was a 'closed' sign hanging from the door, but that didn't stop Gabrielle from opening it and striding inside.

Chloe stepped into the shop behind her. It looked almost abandoned, the shelves half empty. What were they doing here?

Without warning, Dana stepped out from one of the aisles.

"Chloe," she said. "Hello."

Chloe's heart skipped a beat. Dana was as stone-faced as ever, but her eyes were full of emotion. Hurt. Regret. Affection.

"Wh… why did you bring me here?" Chloe asked.

"We wanted to talk to you, face to face," Dana said. "We've already told you how sorry we are. And we meant it. We betrayed your trust, and we're sorry. But the real reason we brought you here is because we want to show you how much you mean to us."

"I don't understand." Chloe looked around. "Why are we in some run-down convenience store?"

"Oh, this?" Gabrielle said. "It's not going to be a convenience store for much longer. The owner is selling the shop. The timing couldn't be better, not to mention the location. Your old florist shop was so hidden away, hard for people to find organically. But here, you'll have plenty of traffic, along with a large potential customer base right next door in the Mistress building. Lots of busy executives and business-people who work long hours and have money to burn. They need gifts for their neglected spouses and partners when they come home late at night. This is the perfect place for a florist shop."

"A florist shop?"

"Not just any florist shop," Gabrielle said. "*Your* florist shop. But you should know, we're not gifting this shop to you, or loaning it to you, or anything like that. Instead, we've gathered some investors. They've all chipped in to have partial ownership of the business. It will still be yours, but they've provided enough capital to set everything up in exchange for shares in the business. All you have to do is run it."

Chloe frowned. "You found investors. For my florist shop?"

"It sounds like overkill," Dana said. "But we wanted to make sure it was an arrangement you were comfortable with. A business arrangement, not a personal one. The investors all have large portfolios, so your shop will be just a small addition. You can buy everyone out at any time, no questions asked."

"And with the amount of traffic you'll get here, I'm sure it won't be long until you do," Gabrielle said. "But I'm getting ahead of myself."

Chloe shook her head. "I don't know what to say. This is very generous of you, but I can't accept it."

"We knew you'd say that," Dana said. "But please, take the time to think about it. You don't have to give us an answer now. Just know that all this is because we want to help you, help make things better for you."

"We care about you," Gabrielle said, her words ringing with longing. "Yes, we want you back. You complete us. We didn't know that anything was missing from our lives until you came along and made us realize that what was missing was you. But more importantly, we want you to be happy, whether you're with us or not."

Chloe's stomach skittered. It was only then that she noticed a large potted plant with a bow tied around it perched on a table beside Dana.

"Ah, we almost forgot." Dana waved a hand toward the plant. "This is for you."

Chloe took a step toward it, examining the tiny potted bush with narrowed eyes. Among the green leaves were a sprinkling of familiar white flowers, small and sweetly scented.

Her breath caught in her chest. "H… how? How did you know?"

"Know what?" Gabrielle asked.

"Orange blossoms," Chloe whispered. "These are my favorite."

"We didn't," Dana said. "We did some research, and we learned that orange blossoms symbolize everlasting love. We thought you'd appreciate the meaning behind them. We wanted something that would show you how much you mean to us, and that we're in it for good."

Gabrielle patted the pot gently. "It's a little impractical compared to a bouquet, but if we'd gotten you the flowers instead, they'd die in a week. This plant will last for years and years. Forever, even."

She took Chloe's hand. Chloe's heart began hammering inside her chest.

"We know how badly we hurt you," Gabrielle said, her voice wavering. "And we will never, ever hurt you like that again. We understand if you can't forgive us. We understand if you don't want to be with us. But we want you to know that you'll have a place with us, in our lives and in our hearts, always."

Always. Wasn't this what Chloe had been searching for, *longing* for, all this time? Weren't *they* who she'd been searching for?

She had finally found her forever. And she wasn't going to let it get away from her.

Still holding Gabrielle's hand, Chloe took Dana's hand with the other. "I want that," she said. "I want to be with you. The way you make me feel, it's impossible for me to explain or describe. It's like, when I'm with you, everything just feels right." She closed her eyes for a moment, taking a deep breath. "I love you. Both of you." She hadn't known that was what she felt for them until that very moment.

Gabrielle's hand tightened around Chloe's. "And I love you. We both do."

Dana nodded. "It's true. We've fallen for you. I love you too, Chloe."

Chloe drew them into an embrace, then kissed them one by one. When she pulled away, Gabrielle had a soft smile on her face, while Dana, her face still stone, was clearly trying to hold back tears.

Chloe turned to the table next to them where the orange blossom plant sat. She leaned over it, inhaling the sweet scent of the little white blossoms, smiling. "This is perfect. This shop is perfect too." She looked around. "I can't believe this is all mine. I can't wait to get all set up." The space was three times as big as her old florist shop. There were so many possibilities.

"You have Dana to thank for the shop," Gabrielle said. "It was her idea. But the orange blossom was mine."

That didn't surprise Chloe at all. Dana always had to fix everything, to take care of all her problems. But Gabrielle, she just wanted to make Chloe feel happy and loved. The two of them were so different in some ways, but so similar in others. And there was one thing they shared. They both loved Chloe.

Chloe felt so lucky to hold the hearts of them both.

"If you ever need us, I'll be right next door," Gabrielle said. "And Dana's studio is just a block away. We'll always be close."

"That's good to know." It wasn't like Chloe wasn't capable of being apart from them, but it was reassuring all the same. "Thank you. For all this, for everything."

"I'm glad we could help," Dana said. "And if there's anything else you need, let us know."

Chloe thought for a moment. "Actually, there is one thing I could use your help with."

CHAPTER 34

C hloe knocked on Tracy's front door. It had taken less than five minutes of browsing her ex-girlfriend's social media to learn that she still lived in the same old apartment. It had been years since Chloe had left Tracy's apartment for the last time. And here she was, back at her door.

But this time, she had Dana and Gabrielle by her side.

She could see now that having a little help now and then wasn't a bad thing. Especially when that help came in the form of her two strong, confident girlfriends. Dana and Gabrielle were everything Tracy had always wished she was. Successful. Powerful. In control. If there was a way to intimidate Tracy into backing down permanently, this was it. Dana and Gabrielle had Chloe's back.

But that didn't stop her nerves from going into over-drive as she waited for Tracy to come to the door.

She glanced at Dana and Gabrielle behind her. Dana remained silent and steel-faced, while Gabrielle put a reas-suring hand on Chloe's shoulder. She felt a surge of confidence. She could do this. She was going to make sure that Tracy never bothered her again.

If she wanted to move on with her life, with her new relationship, she needed to do this.

The door swung open. Tracy stood before them in a pair of sweats, her blonde hair in disarray.

She blinked. "Chloe." She looked at Dana and Gabrielle standing on either side of her. "Who are you? What the hell is this?"

Chloe gave Tracy the smile she reserved for her most difficult customers. "This is Dana, and this is Gabrielle. They're my girlfriends."

Tracy's brows drew together. "Girlfriends?"

"That's right. I asked them to come here with me, just to make sure you don't pull anything. You already vandalized my shop."

"What makes you think that was me?" Tracy said.

"I'm not an idiot. I know you just couldn't help but get the last word in."

Tracy crossed her arms. "What are you going to do about it? You don't have any proof."

"I don't need it. That shop, everything to do with it, it's all behind me now. I've moved on to something new. Something better. I'm closing the door on that chapter of my life. Speaking of which..." Chloe reached into her purse and pulled out a bundle of crisp $100 bills. "This is for you."

Tracy stared at the wad of cash, wide-eyed. "What is this?"

"It's the money I owe you. Well, technically I don't owe you anything, as you already know from the letter my lawyer sent you, but I want to put this debt behind us."

This was the last tie she had to Tracy. She needed to sever it, once and for all. "And clearly you need this money more than I do since you've been hassling me for it all this time."

Tracy's face turned crimson. She was a proud woman. It was obvious that she was bothered by the implication that she needed the money. Chloe knew that it wasn't really about the money for Tracy. But she needed to show Tracy that she knew that. She needed to show her she wasn't going to stand for her bullying anymore.

Tracy looked at Dana and Gabrielle. "Is this your doing? Did you put her up to this?"

Dana gave Tracy her stony glare. "I don't know why you're addressing us. Chloe is talking. I suggest you listen to her."

Tracy flinched. Her bravado and boldness had always been fake. Next to Dana and Gabrielle, two women who radiated power, that was even more apparent.

"To answer your question," Chloe said. "They didn't put me up to this. This is all me. But I get why you wouldn't believe that. You never saw me as a person of my own. You saw me as nothing more than a thing to be controlled. And that's why you were never able to make me yours."

She thrust the money toward Tracy. "Take the money. It's everything you gave me, and more. Now, you have no reason to ever come near me again. And if you do, I'll call the police."

Tracy looked back at her, a false plea in her eyes. "But Chloe-"

Gabrielle crossed her arms. "I think Chloe has made herself very clear, don't you, Dana?"

Dana nodded. "I agree. Chloe, darling? Do you have anything more you'd like to say?"

Chloe shook her head. "I'm done."

"Good," Gabrielle said. "But before we leave this predator to her money, it's our turn to speak." She gave Tracy an icy smile. "I want you to know that if you ever come near Chloe again, it isn't just her, or the police, that you'll need to worry about. She has us looking out for her. And we were very, very unhappy about what you did to her florist shop."

A shiver went down Chloe's spine. Gabrielle could be utterly terrifying when she wanted to be.

"If you ever pull anything like that again," Dana said. "If you ever do anything to hurt Chloe again, we will come for you, and we will tear your world down."

Tracy cringed. Chloe couldn't tell exactly what Dana meant by her threat, but it was clear that Tracy never wanted to find out.

"Do you understand?" Dana said.

Tracy nodded, barely able to look any of them in the eye. "Yes."

Chloe tossed her the bundle of money, which she fumbled, but managed to catch. Chloe didn't wait around for farewells. She turned on her heel and strode down the hall, Dana and Gabrielle close behind her.

It wasn't until they'd left the building and were down at the street that Chloe let out the breath she'd been holding.

"I can't believe I just did that." A smile spread across her lips. "I'm finally free of her."

In truth, she hadn't needed to give Tracy the money, but she'd wanted to wash her hands of everything to do with her. She needed to be all in on her relationship with Gabrielle and Dana. And given that the money was such an insignificant amount to them, it had been no loss at all, not to Dana and Gabrielle, or to Chloe herself. She no longer felt conflicted about accepting their help. She trusted them when they said the money didn't come with strings. She trusted them with her whole heart.

Besides, she secretly intended to pay them back once she got her new florist shop up and running and was making money again, but she hadn't told them that. Maybe she would buy them a gift with the money instead.

"We're happy for you," Gabrielle said. "And we meant what we said. If Tracy comes after you again, we're going to make sure she regrets it."

"I'm sure it won't come to that," Chloe said. "Thanks for backing me up in there."

Judging by how shaken Tracy had looked, she'd gotten the message loud and clear. Chloe wouldn't be hearing from her again.

With Gabrielle and Dana at either side of her, she wrapped her arms around their waists. "Let's get out of here."

CHAPTER 35

Gabrielle had almost finished tying Chloe's wrist to the bedpost when Chloe woke up.

"Good morning, sleepyhead," Gabrielle said.

Chloe blinked, disoriented. Her curly hair was in disarray, and she'd slept in nothing but her panties. She looked even more irresistible than ever.

She glanced up at her wrist, her eyes growing wide. Gabrielle gave her a moment to acclimatize to her situation. Chloe had confessed a desire to be woken up this way, so Gabrielle had decided to do just that.

She'd waited a few weeks, just to keep Chloe guessing. And judging by her reaction, it had worked. Chloe hadn't expected this at all. It was a sign of how much she trusted her Mistresses that she felt comfortable sharing this particular fantasy with them.

Gabrielle gazed down at her lovingly. Over the past few weeks, she, Chloe, and Dana had only grown closer. They'd spent every spare moment together, exploring with each other, deepening the connection they shared.

If it hadn't been clear before, it was clear now—they were a perfect match, each of them fulfilling a need in the others in their own unique way. Gabrielle had discovered that between Dana and Chloe, she was perfectly able to satisfy her desire to be at both ends of the whip, to experience the thrill of submission and the rush of being in control, sometimes at the same time.

As for the others? Dana now had Chloe, the obedient, devoted submissive she'd always wanted, and she still had Gabrielle to keep her on her toes. And Chloe had not one, but two Mistresses to feed her insatiable need to submit, two girlfriends who wanted her so much that they would do anything to have her.

But these parts they played, they weren't just roles. They pervaded every aspect of their relationship. Chloe was *theirs*. And she was finally comfortable having them show her that, in and outside of the bedroom. They'd already made plans for Chloe to move in with them so that she could be theirs always.

Chloe turned her head to the other side of the bed, apparently looking for her other girlfriend.

"Dana is elsewhere," Gabrielle said. "Which means I have you all to myself. But I expect you to keep it down. We both know she wouldn't approve of me playing with our toy without her, so we'll have to make sure she doesn't find out."

It was a rule Dana had imposed on them, one that had nothing to do with jealousy. No, Dana simply wanted to impose her control over them both, just because she could. Now that she had Chloe, a woman who wanted nothing more than to serve her, the power was going to Dana's head. For someone who claimed she didn't like to play games, she sure seemed to enjoy toying with Chloe and Gabrielle.

And while Chloe clearly loved being the target of Dana's power plays, Gabrielle was starting to feel the need to push the boundaries, to have a little fun of her own.

What Dana didn't know wouldn't hurt her.

Gabrielle gave Chloe a firm look. "You can keep quiet, can't you?"

Chloe nodded.

"Good, because I don't want to have to gag you. I want to be able to kiss those lips of yours."

Gabrielle dipped down, her lips hovering over Chloe's. But as Chloe strained to meet her, she drew back slightly. A whine spilled from Chloe's mouth.

Gabrielle shushed her. "Not yet. Now, hold still."

Chloe did as she was told, her thirst clear in her eyes. She was wide awake now. Gabrielle finished tying Chloe's wrist to the left bedpost before taking hold of the other, stretching Chloe's arm up to the corner of the bed. The large bed was designed with dozens of tie points, giving Gabrielle a wide range of options. While Gabrielle rarely passed up a chance to show off her rope bondage skills, with Dana lurking elsewhere in the house, speed and discretion were vital, so she simply chose to tie Chloe's other wrist to the right bedpost, leaving her restrained with her arms stretched out wide above her.

Gabrielle pulled on the ropes, testing her knots. It was all for effect. Her knots always held. But she wanted to make sure Chloe knew that too.

"There," she said. "Now you can't wriggle your way out of this."

Predictably, Chloe tested her bonds herself, pulling at them and wriggling.

"Oh please," Gabrielle said. "Don't pretend you're not enjoying this as much as I am. Keep moving like that and I'll tie your legs together and spend the whole morning spanking you instead."

Chloe seemed to consider the idea for a moment before acquiescing. Gabrielle made a mental note to try that in the future. It would be delightful, watching Chloe squirm about with her legs tied together, tormenting and touching her everywhere except for where she wanted to be touched.

But this morning, Gabrielle wasn't in the mood for that. She wanted to lavish Chloe with pleasure, to have her wishing she could cry out for more.

She looked down at Chloe, desire stirring within. "Now that I have you all to myself, what should I do with you?"

Chloe trembled with anticipation, the need in her eyes impossible to ignore now. Gabrielle leaned down and let her lips graze Chloe's cheek and chin, then planted a feather-light kiss on her lips. Chloe rose into her, her body seeking Gabrielle's.

Gabrielle purred. "Someone is eager."

She reached down and slipped her hand inside Chloe's panties, sliding her fingers down to the silken heat between her thighs. Chloe parted her legs reflexively, her chest heaving with her breaths. When Gabrielle withdrew her fingers, they were coated with Chloe's wetness.

"How are you this wet already?" Gabrielle asked. "You just woke up. Did you spend last night having all kinds of naughty dreams about us?"

A flush crept up Chloe's chest and face. For someone

who struggled to relinquish control in her everyday life, when she allowed herself to let go, it was so easy to unravel her. Gabrielle would never grow tired of doing so. She loved drawing this side of Chloe out. She loved the way Chloe's body responded to her.

She loved everything about her.

"Oh, Chloe," she said. "Why did it take us so long to find you?"

Chloe blushed even more at that.

But Gabrielle didn't have time for sentiment. Straddling Chloe's body, she leaned down and kissed her again, this time firmer, more possessive, more insistent. Chloe let out a soft moan, her lips and tongue pressing hard against Gabrielle's. Gabrielle trailed her lips down Chloe's chin, kissing her way down her soft, pale neck. Chloe's head fell back, her naked body quivering underneath Gabrielle.

She let her hands wander up Chloe's chest, her fingertips teasing Chloe's nipples. Then, she replaced her fingers with her mouth, coaxing Chloe's nipples into tiny peaks with her lips and tongue. Chloe drew in a stifled gasp, her chest arching up.

Gabrielle smiled. "This is so easy. I barely have to touch you to set you off. It's like your body knows exactly who it belongs to." She slid her hand down to where Chloe's thighs met again, this time over her now damp panties. "But do you know who you belong to? Do you know who your Mistress is?"

Chloe spoke for the first time that morning. "You," she whispered. "I'm yours."

"That's right." Gabrielle peeled off Chloe's panties and tossed them over her shoulder, then leaned down and spoke into Chloe's ear. "You're mine. And I'm never, *ever* going to let you forget that."

Before Chloe could react, Gabrielle pounced, assailing her with ravenous kisses—on her lips, on her body. She kissed her way over Chloe's breasts and stomach. She ran her hands down Chloe's hips and thighs. She swept her lips along the curve of each of Chloe's hip bones, getting ever closer to the sweet prize between her legs.

All the while, Chloe panted and writhed, her skin warm and slightly damp with sweat. Gabrielle reveled in her, in the sounds she made, in the taste of her skin and the softness of her body.

Gabrielle was so immersed in her that she almost didn't notice when the door to the bedroom creaked open behind her.

"I hope this isn't what it looks like. Because it looks like the two of you are having fun without me."

Gabrielle turned. Dana stood in the doorway, her hands on her hips, a hard look in her eyes.

A smile pulled at Gabrielle's lips. "Oops."

CHAPTER 36

Dana shut the door and strode over to the bed, glaring down at Gabrielle and Chloe with disapproval. Disapproval wasn't the only thing she felt, but she wasn't going to let them know that.

"You know the rules," she said. "No playing with our toy without me."

"Can you blame me?" Gabrielle said. "Chloe looked so enticing this morning. I just couldn't help myself."

Dana held back a sigh. This particular rule of hers was aimed solely at Gabrielle. She was, after all, Dana's submissive. Dana needed to keep her in check. Although, there was some flexibility in the role Gabrielle played. She and Dana still enjoyed topping Chloe together, and they did that as often as not. That was the advantage of their relationship. They could mix it up. And allowing Gabrielle to remain as Chloe's Mistress kept the worst of Gabrielle's bratty impulses in check.

Well, it usually did.

"No excuses," Dana said. "You know what happens when you break the rules. You know the drill by now." This was by no means the first time. "On your hands and knees."

Gabrielle gave her an irritated look but did as she was told, getting into position next to Chloe on the bed. Chloe looked on helplessly, still bound to the bedposts. Judging by the red flush covering her skin, Gabrielle had been toying with her for some time now.

But she would have to wait a little longer. Dana had to deal with Gabrielle.

From a nearby chest of drawers, Dana grabbed a leather paddle. It was thin, thinner than the width of her hand. It was the best of both worlds, combining the satisfying weight of a paddle with the sting of something slimmer and more flexible, like a riding crop.

She returned to the bed, instructing Gabrielle to turn around and face the foot of it, giving Chloe a much better view. Positioning herself beside Gabrielle, Dana reached down and pulled the hem of Gabrielle's nightie up around her waist. She wasn't wearing any panties underneath.

Dana dragged the paddle slowly up the side of Gabrielle's thigh. "You should have learned, by now, exactly what your place is."

She didn't give Gabrielle a chance to speak before striking her firmly on the ass with the paddle. Gabrielle jolted, but she didn't make a sound.

However, Dana was just getting started.

She continued bringing the paddle down on Gabrielle's ass over and over, ramping up the force with each impact, the skin on Gabrielle's cheeks slowly turning a tantalizing shade of pink. It didn't take long before Gabrielle began to shudder and pant with every strike. Dana relished it, the cries Gabrielle made, and the sound and feel of the paddle as each impact reverberated up her arm.

It wasn't Gabrielle's pain that she relished, or even the satisfaction that came with wielding power over her. No, what Dana loved the most was pushing Gabrielle to her limits. That was what Gabrielle wanted from her Mistress. She wanted to challenge herself in the way that she challenged Dana.

That was the main difference between Gabrielle and Chloe. Gabrielle liked to be pushed. But for Chloe, these games of power and control and discipline served as a sweetener, something to enhance her pleasure, both by stimulating her body and reminding her of her place as their beloved pet.

In both cases, it took a skilled, attentive Mistress to give each of them exactly what they needed, no more, and no less. It was a delicate balancing act.

As Dana spanked Gabrielle with the paddle, Chloe watched, her arousal visibly growing. It was delicious, the way Chloe's chest hitched with every impact, the way she squirmed while she waited for the paddle to fall. It was almost like the connection between them was so strong that Chloe could feel what Gabrielle felt. Anticipation, pain, pleasure, every other delectable sensation.

Dana couldn't resist it any longer.

She placed the paddle to the side and drew her hands up Gabrielle's thighs and ass cheeks. They were bright red now. "Do you have anything to say to me?"

Gabrielle spoke between heavy breaths. "I'm sorry."

Dana huffed. Gabrielle's apology wasn't at all convincing, but that didn't matter right now. Once again, Gabrielle's real punishment was yet to come.

Leaving Gabrielle on her hands and knees, she rounded the bed and sat down on the other side of it, next to where Chloe lay bound. "Do you think Gabrielle has learned her lesson?"

Chloe glanced at Gabrielle, then nodded, clearly eager for her Mistresses to return their attentions to her.

Dana glided her hand up Chloe's stomach and chest, rolling one of Chloe's nipples between her fingertips. "I really should punish you too, you know."

She pinched Chloe's nipple lightly, just enough to make her jump. Chloe gasped, her toes curling into the bed beneath her.

"But I know this was all Gabi's doing," Dana continued. "You were powerless to resist her, weren't you?"

Chloe lowered her gaze, saying nothing.

"How noble of you, not wanting to implicate Gabrielle. I don't blame you. It must be torturous, having your loyalty split like this, between your two Mistresses. I don't blame you for falling for Gabrielle's seductions either. She can be very persuasive." Dana ran her hand up to cup Chloe's cheek. "I'll let you off with an apology. What do you have to say for yourself?"

"I'm sorry, Mistress," Chloe said.

"Good pet." Dana kissed her tenderly, then got up from the bed, gesturing toward Gabrielle. "You two may continue what you were doing. But only because I want to watch."

That was one command Gabrielle didn't hesitate to

follow. She prowled across the bed to where Chloe lay bound. Permitting this went against Dana's every instinct. However, right now, her desire was greater than her need to maintain control.

"Go on," Dana said. "Kiss her."

Gabrielle leaned down and kissed Chloe greedily, her hands sliding down Chloe's bare shoulders. Chloe murmured blissfully, her hands straining against the ropes around her wrists.

Dana folded her arms across her chest. "When I said kiss her, I didn't mean on the lips."

Gabrielle drew back, smiling wickedly. "I'm so sorry, Mistress. I'll correct that right away."

She crawled down Chloe's body and pushed her knees apart, burying her head between Chloe's thighs. Immediately, Chloe began to whimper and gasp in that telltale way. Was she that close to climax already? How long had Gabrielle been playing with her?

"Slow down," Dana said. "Don't let her come yet."

Gabrielle eased up and slowed her pace, causing Chloe to whimper even more. But Dana needed time to prepare. She didn't intend to just watch the two of them. She intended to join in.

She returned to the chest of drawers, this time opening the bottom drawer. Inside was her collection of strap-on harnesses and toys of various shapes and sizes. This morning she was looking for something specific.

Spotting it, she reached into the drawer and pulled it out. It was a strapless strap-on, angled in the middle with one short end and one long one.

She slipped out of her clothes and underwear, then took

the strap-on over to the bed, watching her girlfriends for a moment. Chloe lay back, her mussed-up hair half covering her face, her eyes screwed shut as Gabrielle devoured her. Her fingers were wrapped tightly around the ropes tying her to the bedposts as if she were holding on against the unrelenting pleasure Gabrielle was inflicting on her.

It was clear that Chloe was losing that battle.

"Stop," Dana said.

Reluctantly, Gabrielle pulled back. Chloe opened her eyes, her lips parting slightly as she saw Dana standing there naked, dildo in hand. For a moment, Dana thought Chloe was going to come at the mere sight of her.

"It's my turn now," Dana said.

Ordering Gabrielle aside, Dana climbed onto the bed, positioning herself between Chloe's legs, the sheets beneath her hips damp from Chloe's perspiration and arousal. Dana pushed the short end of the dildo down between Chloe's lower lips, sliding it inside her wetness with ease, sending a fevered murmur tumbling from Chloe's lips.

Once the dildo was firmly anchored inside her, Dana pushed Chloe's legs together and straddled her hips, positioning herself right above the long end of it.

"Don't come until I say you can," she said. "You're going to come with me."

Chloe nodded weakly. She was nearing the end of her rope. Fortunately, Dana was already turned on enough from watching the two of them together that it wouldn't take her long to come either.

Slowly, she lowered herself down, sinking onto the dildo until its length was sheathed inside her. She began rolling her hips, a moan sliding from her lips completely unbidden. With her every movement, the dildo rocked inside her, hitting that sweet spot that sent electricity arcing through her body. Beneath her, Chloe trembled and bucked her hips, her pleasure mirroring Dana's own.

Dana grabbed onto Chloe's waist and rode her hard, grinding and thrusting her hips. Beside them, Gabrielle toyed with Chloe's bound body, tweaking her nipples and kissing her all over. Chloe panted and groaned, her chest heaving, the sound only spurring Dana on.

It didn't take long until Dana was right at the edge. She held herself there for a moment, holding on to Chloe as she looked down at her.

"Come with me," she commanded.

Chloe closed her eyes, her mouth opening slightly. Together, they rocked their hips in tandem, moving with fervent abandon.

It only took seconds for Dana to reach the brink. She threw her head back as a powerful orgasm ripped through her. At the same time, Chloe shuddered beneath her, a cry rising from her as her body clenched in an unmistakable release. They fed each other's pleasure, moving together as one until neither of them could take any more.

Dana collapsed onto the bed. Summoning the last of her strength, she untied Chloe's wrists from the bedposts, silently cursing Gabrielle for tying such effective knots.

Once Chloe was free, Dana issued her a command. "Make her come." She waved her hand toward Gabrielle. "And make sure she enjoys it because this is the last time Gabrielle is allowed to come until I decide she's learned her lesson. She will not be permitted any pleasure until I say so.

And who knows how long that will be. A week, two? A month, perhaps?"

Gabrielle's mouth gaped open, but Dana didn't give her a chance to protest.

"And don't try to get around this by sneaking behind my back with Chloe," she said. "She isn't permitted to give you any pleasure either. I know that she'll obey this particular command because if she doesn't, she'll face the same punishment."

Chloe pouted, looking just as dismayed as Gabrielle.

"This is what happens when you break the rules, darlings," Dana said. "Go on."

Gabrielle muttered a retort that Dana couldn't quite make out, but she let it go, just this once. She was far too exhausted. Instead, she settled beside them, her arm slung around Chloe's waist as Chloe began working her fingers at the peak of the other woman's thighs, coaxing out moans and quivers that escalated with every stroke.

Dana savored the sight and the sounds they made, savored their pleasure. When Gabrielle finally came, her cry of ecstasy sounded just as sweet as Chloe's had.

And Dana didn't even mind when Gabrielle snuck her hand between Chloe's legs and brought her to climax for the second time that morning, rendering Chloe completely senseless. Dana took pleasure in taking control, in having power over them, but she enjoyed their pleasure even more, so she permitted them this uninhibited moment.

And after Dana was certain that all three of them were satisfied, she kissed them both and drew them into her arms, caressing them tenderly while she crooned to them about how much she loved them both, and how lucky she was that they were hers. She'd always felt lucky to have Gabrielle, that constant presence in her life. But now, they had Chloe too, this sweet, loving woman who wanted nothing more than to be theirs.

Together, with each other, they had everything they could possibly need.

EPILOGUE

"We're here," Gabrielle said.

She knocked on the door. Faintly, Chloe could hear music and chatter coming from inside the apartment.

She shifted from one foot to the other nervously. The past few weeks had been a whirlwind of travel. It was the holiday season, and both Gabrielle and Dana had been using the opportunity to have Chloe meet their families. They'd spent Christmas at the ranch before hopping on a plane to Paris so they could ring in the new year with a family of a different kind.

Their friends.

It had been almost a year since that day in what had since become Chloe's new florist shop. Since then, she'd met most of Dana and Gabrielle's friends several times. However, there was one pair she hadn't met yet—Lydia and Kat. They lived in Paris now, running Mistress Media's international office, so Chloe hadn't had the chance to see them in person until now. This was their apartment. They'd invited everyone here for New Year's Eve.

Chloe was just as excited about it as she was nervous. Gabrielle and Dana's friends were a little intimidating. After all, they were the owners of Mistress Media, all of them wealthy and successful. Then again, Chloe's girlfriends were a world-famous fashion designer and Mistress's CMO. She had grown used to being a part of that world now.

No, what really made Chloe nervous was the fact that Dana and Gabrielle were even closer to their friends than they were to their families. Chloe wanted to make a good impression.

Dana put her hand on Chloe's shoulder. "Stop worrying. Lydia and Kat are going to love you, just like everyone else does."

"I hope so." Chloe smoothed down her dress, a Christmas present Dana had handmade for her, and tucked one of her curls behind her ear. She'd dyed her hair light brown, somewhere between her natural strawberry blonde and the dark brown it had been for most of her adult life. She liked her lighter hair, but she didn't want to go back to her natural color, at least not yet. Maybe one day.

After what felt like an eternity, a woman answered the door. She was older, with auburn hair. She had to be Lydia.

She smiled. "You're here. I'm so glad you could make it."

"We wouldn't miss this for the world," Gabrielle said.

Lydia gave Gabrielle and Dana a warm hug, then turned to Chloe. "And you must be Chloe."

"That's me," Chloe said.

"It's taken us far too long to meet. These two will *not* stop talking about you." Lydia put her arm around Chloe's shoulders, ushering her inside. "Make yourselves at home, but don't go too far. I'll go find Kat so I can introduce you."

As Lydia wandered off in search of her girlfriend, Chloe looked around. The Paris apartment was enormous, not to mention ornate and beautiful. The balcony provided an amazing view of the city.

They headed into the lounge room. Everyone else was already there. Madison and Blair, Yvonne and Ruby. Even Amber Pryce was there, lounging casually in an armchair as if she weren't an heiress and minor celebrity. It had taken Chloe a long time to get used to the idea of having her as a friend.

And these women weren't just their friends. As Chloe had later quickly found out, they were the 'investors' that Dana and Gabrielle had found for her florist shop. Chloe's shop was successful enough now that she could easily buy them all out, but after some discussion with Gabrielle, who had a good mind for business, she'd decided to use her profits to grow her business and open several other florist shops around the city.

Spotting them, Amber waved them over. They all exchanged greetings.

"It's good to see you again," Amber said to Chloe. "Still keeping these two out of trouble?"

Chloe nodded. "I'm trying my best."

As they took a seat on the couch, Kat appeared alongside Lydia. She introduced herself to Chloe before handing them all drinks and perching on a chair beside them.

"How have your holidays been so far?" she said.

"Good," Gabrielle replied. "We spent Christmas at the ranch."

"With your parents?" Lydia asked.

"No, they're off traveling," Gabrielle said. "We visited them a couple of weeks ago in the Caribbean. We invited Dana's family to the ranch for Christmas so they could finally meet Chloe."

"Oh? How did that go?" Lydia asked carefully.

"It went well, actually," Dana replied. "I can't say I was expecting my parents to understand our relationship, but it seems they've realized that if they want to be in my life again, they need to accept me for who I am, and that means accepting the people I love." She took Chloe's hand and squeezed it gently. "And they did seem to love Chloe. It helps that she has this way of charming everyone she meets."

"That's wonderful to hear," Lydia said. "It sounds like things have improved between you and your parents."

Dana nodded. "They have. I'm glad I decided to give them another chance. But while I'm grateful for my renewed relationship with my parents, if I've learned anything, it's that family is who you choose." She looked at Gabrielle and Chloe, then at everyone else. "And I have all the family I need right here."

Across from them, Madison spoke up. "I'll drink to that." She raised her glass of wine, looking around the room with misty eyes. "Look at us, all together again after so long. Who would have thought when we started Mistress all that time ago that we'd end up here? This little family of ours just keeps on growing. And Chloe, we're glad you've joined it."

As Madison brought her glass to her lips, the others did the same, drinking in unison. Chloe felt her face flush, warmth growing in her chest.

Beside her, Gabrielle downed her drink and placed it on the table before murmuring loudly to her, "Now that you're 'part of the family,' you have to listen to our CEO here give emotional speeches every time we get together. She just can't help herself."

Madison waved a dismissive hand at Gabrielle. "All I'm saying is, it's lovely to have you with us, Chloe. And I'm glad these two have found you. You both seem much happier now. More content."

"I can't speak for Gabrielle," Dana said. "But I certainly feel that way."

Gabrielle smiled. "So do I."

The conversation moved on, slowly splitting off into smaller groups around the room. Lydia took the opportunity to speak with Dana about Obi's upcoming fashion line, and Gabrielle and Amber caught each other up on high society gossip, so Chloe found herself chatting with Kat. In a room full of wealthy businesswomen, Kat was refreshingly down to earth.

Several hours passed. As midnight approached, Chloe found herself standing alone by the window, watching over everyone in the room. She couldn't help but smile. Wasn't this what she had always wanted, what she'd dreamed of? Not just a girlfriend, or a partner, or even two. What she'd longed for was a place where she belonged, people she belonged with, who loved her.

Now, she had more love than she could handle.

She was so lost in her thoughts, grinning at nothing at all, that she didn't even notice when Gabrielle and Dana joined her by the window.

Gabrielle raised an eyebrow. "Are you all right? Had a little too much champagne, have you?"

Chloe shook her head. "I'm just happy, that's all."

"We have something for you that will make you even happier," Dana said. "A gift, of sorts. To celebrate the new year."

"You shouldn't have," Chloe said. "You spoiled me too much at Christmas already."

"This was actually supposed to be one of your Christmas gifts," Gabrielle said. "But the paperwork wasn't ready until earlier today."

Chloe frowned. "The paperwork?"

Gabrielle produced a folded sheet of paper and held it out to Chloe. "Here. It's just a copy. The original is safe at home."

Chloe took the paper from her and unfolded it. "What is this?" It looked to be some kind of legal document. It had an address at the top of it, along with Chloe's name, which she'd finally legally changed, plus Dana and Gabrielle's names. "This address. Is it the ranch?"

Dana nodded. "That's right. You now own a third of it, along with the two of us."

Chloe's mouth fell open. "But... the ranch. It's *yours*. It's so special to you."

"It's special to *us*," Gabrielle said. "All three of us. You can't deny that, especially with how much time we spend there these days."

That was true. The ranch had become Chloe's second home. Together, in the courtyard garden, the three of them had planted that orange blossom, the tiny potted shrub Dana and Gabrielle had given her. Although, it wasn't tiny anymore. It had grown and grown. And Chloe tended to that courtyard garden with love and care, like it was her own.

Still, Chloe shook her head. "You can't give this to me. The ranch has been in your family for generations."

Gabrielle let out an exasperated sigh. "You'd think those god-awful Christmas sweaters my mother gave us would have given you the message." She took Chloe's hand. "You *are* family. *Our* family. We love you, and that's never going to change."

Chloe gripped the sheet of paper, holding it tightly to her chest. "I don't know what to say."

"You don't have to say anything," Dana said. "Just as long as you know you're ours."

Chloe smiled. "I do."

She threw her arms around them both, pulling them into a hug. She would have stayed like that forever, with them in her arms, if Lydia hadn't interrupted them.

"It's almost midnight, everyone," she said. "Let's go watch the fireworks."

Beaming, Chloe dragged Dana and Gabrielle out onto the balcony, joining the others.

As the clock struck midnight and fireworks exploded over the Parisian skyline, Chloe shared a kiss with each of the women she loved.

ABOUT THE AUTHOR

Anna Stone is the author of lesbian romance bestsellers Being Hers, Tangled Vows, and more. Her sizzling sapphic romances feature strong, passionate women who love women. In every one of her books, you'll find off-the-charts heat and a guaranteed happily ever after.

Anna lives on the east coast of Australia. When she isn't writing, she can usually be found with a coffee in one hand and a book in the other.

Visit **annastoneauthor.com** to find out more about her books and to sign up for her newsletter.

 facebook.com/AnnaStoneRomance
twitter.com/AnnaStoneAuthor

Printed in Great Britain
by Amazon